The Adventures of

Sherlock

Holmes

and the

Glamorous

Ghost

Volume Four

Harry DeMaio

Hardcover ISBN 978-1-80424-203-2
Paperback ISBN 978-1-80424-204-9
ePub ISBN 978-1-80424-205-6
PDF ISBN 978-1-80424-206-3

Published by MX Publishing
335 Princess Park Manor, Royal Drive,
London, N11 3GX
www.mxpublishing.co.uk

Cover design by Brian Belanger

Dedicated to GTP

A Most Extraordinary Bear

And to the late Ms. WoofAn

Extremely Sweet and

Loving Dog

Acknowledgements

These stories have evolved over a long period of time and under a wide range of influences and circumstances. I am indebted to many people for helping to bring my versions of Holmes, Watson, Mrs. Hudson, Lady Juliet and Pookie to the printed and electronic page. Thanks most especially to my wife, Virginia, for her insights and clever suggestions as well as her unfailing enthusiasm for the project and patience with its author.

To Steve, Sharon and Timi Emecz for their outstanding support of my twenty-one book Octavius Bear series, the four volume plus Glamorous Ghost collection and my other Holmes pastiches. To Derrick and Brian Belanger for publishing The Glamorous Ghost Book One and several of my other Holmes and Solar Pons efforts. To Dan Andriacco, Amy Thomas and David Chamberlain for their enthusiastic encouragement. And to all of my generous Kickstarter backers and reviewers.

To my sons, Mark and Andrew and their spouses, Cindy and Lorraine, for helping to make these stories more readable and audience friendly. To Cathy Hartnett, cheerleader-extraordinaire for her eagerness to see these alternate worlds take form.

Thanks also to Wikipedia for providing facts and specifics of Victorian England and elsewhere. And additional kudos to Brian Belanger for his wonderful illustrations and covers.

Obviously, these stories are tongue in cheek fantasies and require the reader to totally suspend disbelief. I do hope they are entertaining fun. I'm not sure what Heaven is really like but I hope to find out one day.

If, in spite of all this support, some errors or inconsistencies have crept through, the buck stops here. Needless to say, all of the characters, situations, and narratives are fictional. Some locations, devices, historical figures and events are real.

By the way, I am an American and use American English throughout this book. No point in trying to fake it.

5

The Adventures of Sherlock Holmes and the Glamorous Ghost

Book Four

Table of Contents

Note to Reader: Each of these stories are separate and standalone. Their placement does not follow a single timeline or sequence. A few are from Holmes' early days. Several are post the Great Hiatus and a few stretch to Holmes' retirement. All share the celestial presence of Lady Juliet Armstrong, Baroness Crestwell after her untimely demise.

The Adventures of Sherlock Holmes and the Glamorous Ghost

Book Four Prologue

She's back yet again! Welcome Lady Juliet Armstrong, Baroness Crestwell once more to our pages. A former sensation of the London musical stage; a feisty member of the British nobility by marriage but recently, a most definitely *deceased* arrival at the Elysian Fields. The obstreperous noblewoman was not content to don her halo and bland heavenly garb and join the other celestial denizens in eternal bliss. She had been shot and wanted to find the blighter who did it and bring him/her to justice before going to her eternal reward. Who else to solve the mystery than Sherlock Holmes and Doctor Watson? Clad in her scarlet Parisian high fashion evening gown and wearing a chic halo fashionably tilted on her head, she persuaded the powers that be in Heaven to allow her to return to Earth and seek out Holmes' assistance. Thus began the first story in Book One of this collection of tales that takes the Glamorous Ghost, Holmes and Watson on a wild tour of crimes, personalities, situations and locations.

Holmes, no believer in ghosts, reluctantly acknowledged the noblewoman's otherworldly existence and agreed to cooperate with her in what has

7

evolved into a series of semi-supernatural adventures. Watson followed suit.

Another ghostly and no less glamorous character aids and abets throughout. Pookie, a very clever and highly opinionated Bichon Frisé who predeceased her Baronial mistress but waited for her at the Rainbow Bridge. She barks, whines and wags her way into the proceedings at every turn. She's an accomplished aerobatic flier and winner of Top Gun status with the True Angel's Flight Demonstration Team. She performs with the Lipizzaner Stallions and plays multi-dimensional fetch in the Meadows with her canine companions. Unruly as her owner, she is always instrumental in keeping the action going.

In Books Two and Three the Baroness and her dog continued their excursions from Paradise back to Earth with Holmes and the good Doctor. She and Pookie flitted to locations around the world but always returned to their heavenly mansion under the careful scrutiny of Director Raymond and the Committee. Becoming aware of the two winsome wraiths, Mrs. Hudson also linked up with the merry band. Many characters from previous Holmes and Lady Juliet stories also pass through those pages. New entries including Juliet's family and the wonderful Lipizzaner stallions arrived.

Now in Book Four, the madcap mystical mischief and mayhem carries on. Of course, Holmes, Watson and Mrs. Hudson are front and center. But there's also a Pinkerton witch and her snowshoe hare familiar. Appearances by Queen Victoria, Prince Albert, Empress Sisi, King Edward VII, Queen Alexandra, Chief Inspector Lestrade, Confucius, Leonardo DaVinci, Pegasus and more of the Lipizzaner Stallions. And even the Virgin Mary and Mary Magdalen. Join Lady Juliet and Pookie for more fantasy and tongue-in-cheek fun!

The Adventures of Sherlock Holmes and the Glamorous Ghost

Volume Four

Jones' Justice

The Daily Mail

2 July 1903

Countess Faulkner Arrested for Murder

By George Grissom

Inspector Athelney Jones of Scotland Yard's Criminal Investigation Department today announced that Lady Marie Everett, Countess Faulkner, has been arrested and remanded to Holloway prison to await a coroner's jury in the death of the Dowager Countess, Lady Phyllis Everett.

Inspector Jones stated that the Dowager's death was caused by poisoning of her bed time tea. "The

Countess and Dowager had a long-standing dislike for each other and had political and social disagreements that culminated in this heinous murder. I am sure she is guilty. As is well known, poison is a woman's choice of weapon."

He stated further that "Lady Marie was an active member of the Women's Social and Political Union (WSPU), an all-women suffrage advocacy organisation recently formed by Emmeline Pankhurst and her daughters, dedicated to "deeds, not words." The group, identified as independent from – and often in opposition to – political parties is becoming known for physical confrontations: smashing windows and assaulting police officers. The Countess is therefore no stranger to violence and will soon have her comeuppance at the gallows!"

A legal team is actively pursuing bail for the Countess. The Daily Mail will follow these developments closely.

New Scotland Yard–Victoria Embankment– Criminal Investigation Department

Athelney Jones read and re-read the article. A smile wreathed his jowly face as he contemplated an upswing in his career. *Chief* Inspector Athelney Jones. It had a nice ring to it. Perhaps he'd be second in command to the Superintendent. This case was ideal for ensuring advancement. It had all the ingredients. Murder, feuding nobility, those infernal suffragists, the voracious press. And of course, a keen witted investigator in charge of the process. He'd finally surpass those dullards Gregson, Hopkins and Lestrade. What could go wrong? Just as long as the coroner did his job.

*****

221B Baker Street-Residence of Sherlock Holmes, Dr. John Watson and Mrs. Hudson

(Sherlock Holmes was preparing to move from his long time residence at Baker Street to his new retirement home is South Downs, Sussex. The Baroness Juliet Armstrong, Mrs. Hudson and Watson had persuaded him to relax and take up a new occupation - raising bees and harvesting honey and beeswax – and oh, yes, brewing mead. Watson had come by to assist in the logistics.)

Watson threw down his copy of the Daily Mail and looked over at Sherlock Holmes who was working on arranging his file of monographs for shipment to Sussex. He was re-reading his learned effort on foot size to height ratios of men and women in the UK and continent.

"Holmes, Athelney Jones has managed once again to put his oversized foot in his even larger mouth. Here, read this."

The Great Detective took up the paper, quickly scanned the article, snorted and said. "The London legal profession will have a field day. He has managed to prejudice any potential coroner's jury; given a free pass to the real killer; brought the noble Great and Good down on the Home Office and Scotland Yard's composite necks; given fodder to the scandal mongers; sold additional copies of the Daily Mail and stirred up the suffragists in one shot. Not a bad day's work for an imbecile like Jones. Oh well! Soon, he'll be back walking a beat or out of his police job altogether. Can you imagine, Watson? Athelney Jones in private practice as a, God help us, consulting detective. He neither sees nor observes. Totally unconscious and unreceptive. He is probably sitting in his office right now smugly awaiting the plaudits of his fellows and superiors. Thank God. I'll have nothing further to do with him."

Unfortunately and unusually, Holmes was in error.

Watson wondered how long it would take the Great Consulting Detective to get involved.

Not long!

*****

New Scotland Yard–Victoria Embankment– Criminal Investigation Department

Detective Sergeant First Class Montrose popped his head through the half open door of Jones' office and said, "Excuse me, sir. The Superintendent is on the line."

Jones smirked and prepared himself to modestly accept the Super's congratulations. He picked up the phone and in his most authoritative voice said, "Jones here!"

"Jones, this is Superintendent Murchison."

"Yes sir, I recognize your voice."

"Good! Before I get through with you, you'll hear my voice echoing in your worst nightmares."

What was this? Not the adulation he expected.

The Super continued, "I just got off the line with Commissioner Bradford. I probably won't sit for a week. It took all the persuasive power I have to keep

14

him from having you dragged up to his office, fired on the spot and then thrown into the street."

Jones sputtered. "The Commissioner? Commissioner Bradford? Fired on the spot?"

"Do you have trouble hearing, Jones?' Get up off your sorry backside and go to your window. You do have a window, don't you? Tell me what you see."

There was a large gathering of women in white with violet and green sashes, waving placards and pushing and shoving the constables who were trying to keep them from storming the entryway.

"There seems to be some sort of disturbance, sir. Women, I believe.

"Very perceptive Jones! Do you know who they are and why they are there?"

"No sir!"

"Let me enlighten you. They are suffragists and they are there in response to your idiotic remarks to the Daily Mail reporter accusing the ladies of abetting murder. The Commissioner and Home Office have also gotten an avalanche of complaints from MPs, members of the government, the Church and God only knows how many private citizens. Even the Prime Minister's office has been besieged. You're a one man public relations disaster."

"I don't understand, sir."

"That's the problem, Jones. You don't. My first reaction was to agree with the Commissioner and personally haul you up to his office for an official defenestration. But cooler heads have prevailed. The Commissioner does want to see you. But you are going on a damage control expedition, doing repairs, finding the Dowager's real killer and restoring the Yard's reputation. You and your sergeant who is suffering from guilt by association will be in the Commissioner's office in twenty minutes. Is that understood? I'll meet you there and I'll try to keep my hands off you. First I have to eat crow and help calm those suffragists "

*****

New Scotland Yard–Victoria Embankment–Office of the Commissioner

Commissioner Sir Edward Bradford stood looking out the windows of his office at the melee dying out below. The frown slowly disappeared from his distinctive face. Superintendent Murchison and a group of constables had managed to quell the ire of most of the suffragists and only Emmeline Pankhurst, her two daughters and a few of the more militant protestors remained arguing. A full scale riot had been averted. Murchison is a good man. Steady and competent. Handling those women should have been a Chief Inspector's job but that position is currently vacant. He'd have to do something about that before his planned retirement in March. Meanwhile he'd place a merit citation in the CID Superintendent's file.

He turned and looked at the pile of wire flimsies on his desk. All protests and concerns over Athelney Jones' stupid remarks. Concerned members of the Bar. The Home Office weighing in. Even one from the Prime Minister. It didn't take them long to react. Would the King be next? What a way to end the Commissioner's career in law enforcement! His first reaction was to fire the incompetent outright but he also needed a plan for damage control. He needed to talk with Murchison.

He was also about to meet with the errant Inspector Jones and read him the Riot Act. Most appropriate in this case. Reduced to having a single functioning arm courtesy of a tiger's attack while he was serving in India as a colonel in Her Majesty's Army, he was incapable of doing what he wanted to do. Throttling Jones! A verbal tongue-lashing would have to suffice for the nonce.

After that, he and Murchison would seek assistance and pour oil on the turbulent waters. The press would not be silenced, of course. Swift action was necessary. Above all else, the true killer had to be found and quickly. It seemed highly unlikely an exemplary woman such as Countess Faulkner with her gentle devout reputation could be a murderess.

Suffragist or not! Her husband, the Earl, is a major political figure and has already brought pressure on the Home Office. The Countess has been released from Holloway on her own recognizance. There will still be a coroner's enquiry if an unbiased jury can be assembled. "Oh Jones. You have much to answer for."

A knock on the door and a secretary appeared. "Excuse me, Commissioner. Superintendent Murchison, Inspector Jones and Sergeant Montrose are here as ordered."

"Show them in."

The Superintendent and Inspector entered and took seats in front of Sir Edward's imposing desk, covered as it was with outraged wires. The sergeant stayed standing at attention.

"At ease, Sergeant. In fact, you can go. Our business is with the Inspector."

As the sergeant turned to leave, the Commissioner cast a baleful look in Jones' direction and said, "I don't imagine you have anything to say that would mitigate this situation. In fact, you have said far too much already to the press and anyone else who would listen to your half-baked theories and accusations."

Jones, big of mouth and small of diplomatic brain, replied. "I must protest, sir. I have applied all of my extensive knowledge and experience to this case and am convinced that my conclusions are correct."

Murchison interrupted before the Commissioner could respond. 'Let us get one thing very clear, Jones. Your extensive knowledge, experience and lack of sense have created a major public cock-up that has acutely disturbed and humiliated a member of the nobility, embarrassed the Yard and Home Office and left us with an unresolved case of murder and an unpunished villain."

The Commissioner joined in. "You are lucky that for the moment I have not had you thrown out into the street. Right now, your days as an Inspector, indeed as a member of the CID and the Met, are severely numbered. I could simply turn this over to another Inspector but I won't. Not yet! The only thing that will save your skin is solving this mess to my satisfaction and that of the many parties who are so interested in having your scalp. I am ordering you to re-think and re-investigate this situation and bring the true murderer to justice."

He continued, "And don't even think of trying to resign beforehand. If you do, I will personally see to it that you cannot get a job or assignment as a private investigator anywhere in the United Kingdom. Even finding lost cats. I am not finished with you but I have some steps I must take before I call in a final judgement. Meanwhile, you and your sergeant get cracking and go over all your evidence with a fine tooth comb. I'll call you back in due course. Now get out! Murchison, stay on for a few moments."

Stunned, Athelney Jones left the room. All thoughts of ascending to Chief Inspector shattered. Of course, it was all Sergeant Montrose's fault. He mishandled the evidence and caused Jones to go down the wrong path. He would give him a good ear-blistering as soon as he returned to his office.

Commissioner Bradford looked at the Superintendent. "Why is he an Inspector? I had thought by now our standards had improved to the point where we could be proud of our force and their leaders."

Murchison shrugged. "You may not believe this, Sir, but as a constable and then sergeant, he had accumulated quite a positive record of arrests that resulted in successful prosecutions. He may not have been the very top pick of the crop but he showed significant promise. So much so that my predecessor felt he should be promoted to Inspector. I think that's when Jones went off the rails. What the previous Super and I both missed was the man's unbelievable ego. He came to believe he was a member of the leadership team by divine right, was infallible and could do no wrong. You've seen that. I had no specific cause to demote or fire him other than he inspired strong dislike among his fellows and the men reporting to him. I counselled him about it a number of times but it didn't seem to take. Now I regret I didn't act but this incident may be the proverbial straw that breaks the camel's back."

The Commissioner was not an impulsive or vindictive man but he had his limits. He said, "We probably should have fired him on the spot but I'd prefer to have him recant his remarks and solve the case. It would place us all in a better light. What do you think the odds are that he will?"

"Not very high, Sir. But perhaps we can get him some assistance in resolving this issue. Assistance from a proven source."

"Yes, but whom?"

"Sherlock Holmes!"

"Are you serious? Even I know the two of them can't stand each other. How could we possibly get Holmes to work with Jones?"

"His brother. You and Mycroft Holmes have worked together in the past and I'm sure he'll want to accommodate you and get the Home Office and the Yard out of the soup. I'm willing to wager that he has a favor or two he can call in from his younger sibling."

They both smiled for the first time in this unfortunate affair.

221B Baker Street-Residence of Sherlock Holmes, Doctor John Watson and Mrs. Hudson

"Watson, we have received a dinner invitation from Mycroft for this evening in the Stranger's Room at the Diogenes Club. 'Timeo Danaos dona ferentes' "

"Pardon?"

"Oh, Watson. What has happened to your classical education? 'I fear the Greeks even when they bear gifts.' Virgil's Aeneid."

"Oh yes! Of course! What do you suppose your brother wants?"

"I don't know but it can't be good.

"Well, Let's find out. The Diogenes food and drink are always of the highest quality."

"But it always comes at a cost."

"Are you going to refuse?"

"I see no point. Whatever he wants, he'll make sure he gets it one way or another. Might as well get a good feed out of it. Mrs. Hudson, the Doctor and I will be going out to dinner this evening."

*****

Beyond the Pearly Gates - The Mansion of Baroness Juliet Armstrong

Juliet's mother, Lucinda Armstrong, came sailing through the opalescent doors of her daughter's celestial villa, waving a copy of the Celestial Gazette and almost tripping over Pookie in the process. The dog yipped and hid under a table.

"Juliet, Juliet! Terrible news. It says right here. Our good friend Lady Marie Everett, Countess Faulkner has been arrested. and remanded to Holloway prison to await a coroner's jury in the death of the Dowager Countess, Lady Phyllis Everett. You remember! We used to march with Marie in the Suffragists' parades." She handed the newspaper to the Baroness. "The two of them didn't get along but Marie was the last person on earth to commit murder. Poison no less! The Scotland Yard inspector sounds so positive."

The Baroness did remember. It was the only time she wore a white dress, festooned with a green and violet sash. (<u>G</u>reen <u>W</u>hite <u>V</u>iolet- <u>G</u>ive <u>W</u>omen the <u>V</u>ote) She hated white but scarlet was hardly the color for Suffragists. "Oh. no! She's been arrested by that idiot Athelney Jones. He's a first class misogynist and anti-Suffragist in addition to being a consummate fool. I've had run-ins with him before. You're right! Without even knowing the details, I can swear Marie is innocent. I need to talk with Holmes. Let's find Raymond."

The Diogenes Club – The Stranger's Room

"Brother mine, I had to reserve this room for our meal. Several other members wanted to use it but as

23

you know, I am one of the club founders. There are some privileges I insist on maintaining." Thus spake Mycroft Holmes.

Watson smiled. "The roast quail was delightful as is this cognac." (He was astonished to see Mycroft pack away six of the succulent birds.)

Sherlock folded his serviette and pushed back from the table keeping a firm hold on his glass of XXO brandy. "Now, Mycroft, we have been classically wined and dined and you have filled the conversation with reminiscences of our joint adventures - all of which, I may remark, involved you performing something to my advantage. At this stage, I am supposed to be overwhelmed with feelings of guilt, debt and gratitude which I am sure you are about to play upon. Let us advance the ball, as they say. What do you want?"

"Ah, young sibling, subtlety and indirection are wasted on you. I do indeed wish to beg a boon."

Watson chuckled. Holmes snorted. "Out with it. I'm about to retire as you well know."

"It requires your unique expertise but nothing dangerous or exerting. You know how I detest expending physical energy."

"Yes, we are well aware. Will you get to it, Mycroft!"

"I have a request from Commissioner Bradford and given our strong relationship, I am eager to accommodate him. It involves you."

"I suspected as much. I am well acquainted with the Commissioner. Why doesn't he come to me directly?"

"He believes you will turn him down – without my intervention."

"Don't overestimate your influence, brother. What is this non-threatening and physically benign activity that requires my unique expertise?"

"You have no doubt seen the Daily Mail article about Countess Faulkner's arrest."

"Yes, one of Athelney Jones' finer moments. As usual, he has jumped to the wrong conclusions taking the Countess, Scotland Yard and the Home Office over the cliff with him."

He paused. The light dawned. "Oh, no! I refuse to become involved with that idiot. Let the Yard and the Home Office clean up their own mess. "

Mycroft smiled. "In this instance, I am the Home Office. While I pride myself on my rare intellectual abilities, I bow to your talents in detection and bringing the guilty to justice."

"You want me to repair Jones' lopsided version of justice?"

"No! The Commissioner and Superintendent Murchison have decided to have the wretch make amends and bring in the true murderer himself. They are allowing him to stay on the job provided he acts under the supervision of a uniquely skilled and perceptive coach. You! He pursues the solution. You keep him on track. I am not sure I would have been so lenient."

"You do realize the man's stupidity is only exceeded by his ego. He will never agree to such an arrangement. He detests me and I return his feelings. I'm sorry, Mycroft! Please extend my apologies to the Commissioner and Superintendent but their plan is unworkable."

The senior Holmes smiled. "You tell them and tell the Countess. She is free on bail but her session with the coroner's jury is still on the docket. She is in peril until Jones formally withdraws his charges."

"Brother, you are a swine."

He laughed. "I'll take that as an agreement."

*****

New Scotland Yard–Victoria Embankment–Office of the Commissioner

Superintendent Murchison knocked on the Commissioner's door. Sir Edward raised his noble visage. He had been contemplating fox hunting after his upcoming retirement next month.

Among many other things in the thirteen years he had held his position, he had raised the police force to a new level of efficiency and respect, reorganized the Yard and the Met several times, upgraded procedures and recruitment and built more police stations. In return he was awarded a number of honors culminating in being created a baronet. And now, that damn fool Jones was going to spoil all of that with this ridiculous mess he'd created. Well, there was still hope. He had just heard from Mycroft Holmes. His brother Sherlock had, most reluctantly, agreed to act as Jones' mentor of last resort. Now, it remained to shove the prospect down the Inspector's throat. Time for military command treatment.

He waved at the door.

"Come in, Murchison. Our campaign is progressing. Mycroft Holmes persuaded his unenthusiastic brother to oversee our recovery project. Summon Jones and this time have him bring his sergeant. I suspect that if there are any brains in that pair, they belong to the first line supervisor. We'll find out.

New Scotland Yard–Victoria Embankment–Criminal Investigation Department

Athelney Jones had just finished berating Detective Sergeant First Class Montrose for carelessness, inefficiency, lack of judgement and all the other negative characteristics that he himself exhibited. Save one. Montrose did not share his unlimited egotism. The Sergeant was not taking the criticism well and started to push back when a call came down for the two of them to present themselves at the Commissioner's office 'tout suite.' *(Or 'tout de suite' for fastidious Francophones.)*

"All right Montrose. Let us beard the dragon in his den."

The Sergeant was astounded at the Inspector's unbounded and unfounded self-assurance, believing that he could talk the Commissioner and Superintendent out of their 'fits of pique.' Montrose was actually looking forward to Athelney Jones getting his comeuppance. He hated him.

The two detectives arrived at the executive floor and Jones breezily strode past Sir Edward's secretary, rapped on the door and proceeded unacknowledged into the office. He sat down next to the irritated Superintendent and stared at the Commissioner. Sergeant Montrose stayed standing. Jones said, "Here as requested, Sir. Can I assume that you have decided to support my efforts in this case and will allow me to pursue bringing this guilty woman to justice."

The Commissioner exploded. "Which is it, Jones? Are you deaf? Have you no memory of our last session or are you just irretrievably stupid?"

"Sorry, sir. I don't know what you mean."

Murchison intervened before the one-armed Commissioner struck the Inspector. "What the Commissioner means and what we communicated to you at our last meeting is that you are standing on extremely thin ice, Inspector or perhaps it should be ex-Inspector. Against my better judgement, we're about to offer you a proposition you had better accept or your entire career will end up in the dustbin or worse."

"A proposition? What sort of proposition?"

Sir Edward regained his composure and said, "Let me spell it out in simple, careful terms that even you can understand, Jones. We no longer trust you to act on your own on this case but for appearances sake you will be the one eating crow and recanting. Not the Yard or Home Office. Your sergeant has skill and sense but he lacks sufficient authority to rein you in. So while we are ordering you to clean up this debacle and find the killer, it will be under the guidance of a very well respected detective whose abilities are of the highest order."

Jones couldn't envision such a paragon - at least one who was superior to his own talented self. He was about to dig himself further into a hole by saying so when Sir Edward cut him off. "We have secured the services of Sherlock Holmes to act as your monitor and mentor."

It was if the air had been sucked out of the room. Athelney Jones for once was stunned. Finally, he squeaked, "Sherlock Holmes? Oh no, Commissioner! Quite impossible! That charlatan and I could never work together. What are you and the Superintendent thinking?"

Murchison snarled, "We are thinking you will do as you are told and demonstrate full cooperation with the Consulting Detective or spend the rest of your life contemplating the wreckage of your career and life. Is that clear enough? You and Sergeant Montrose will join me as we call on Mr. Holmes and establish the so-called rules of engagement."

The Commissioner frowned at Jones. "This will be cleared up satisfactorily and with dispatch, Jones. No alternative. I'm sure you know I will be retiring next month. I intend to leave knowing true justice has been done. Now, get out!"

221B Baker Street-Residence of Sherlock Holmes, Doctor John Watson and Mrs. Hudson

"Hello Holmes! Doctor Watson! I don't suppose you were expecting me and Pookie." An evanescent Juliet was standing shimmering in the middle of the room. The dog scampered through a pile of paper without disturbing it and sat down on her haunches. They both looked around the room at the crates and packages. *"Getting ready to move, are you?"*

"On the contrary, milady. I was expecting you. I am familiar with your close friendship with Countess Faulkner before you were murdered. I was certain you'd make an appearance, ephemeral though it may be. And yes, Watson and I are getting ready to move my goods and chattels to South Downs. "

"Yes, Marie and I were chums when I was still alive. Couldn't stand that old bat mother-in-law of hers, though. Not really sorry she's gone. By the way, she is not in heaven. I don't know who killed her but I'm sure it wasn't the Countess. Another bit of splendid police work by that clown, Athelney Jones."

"Agreed! This time the Inspector has really outdone himself. Unfortunately, my brother and the Commissioner have conspired to have me act as his tutor and make him repair the damage he has done."

The Baroness collapsed in laughter. *"Oh, no! That is so rich. You supervising Jones. He'll never agree to it."*

"His alternative is to be thrown out on the street and being blackballed from all police forces throughout the Empire. He won't be able to get a private enquiry agent's license either. Even Jones can figure that out. He's on his way over here now"

"Well, I've come to help. I know Marie and her family. Miss Dog and I may be able to track the killer down.

Approaching 221B Baker Street

In the police auto on the way over to the home of the *Great Pretender*, Athelney Jones' mind was awhirl with intense emotions. Anger at his undeserved treatment. Embarrassment and resentment at being subjected to the whims of Sherlock Almighty Holmes. *(When this is over and he has been vindicated, he would retaliate for this humiliation.)* One other emotion - fear. Suppose, unlikely as it might be, that he was truly wrong. No! Impossible! The Countess is guilty. The Dowager was cruelly slain by her daughter-in-law.

They reached 221B Baker Street and Superintendent Murchison told Sergeant Montrose to ring the bell. A woman of middling age answered and after a brief conversation, stepped aside to allow the short procession to enter and follow her up a flight of stairs. As they neared the door to Holmes' and Watson's lair, a sour taste arose in Jones' gorge. He was momentarily moved to turn about, descend the stairs and leave. The urge was brief. He'd play along. He'd outwit this charlatan and prove that he was the true genius and not Holmes.

She knocked. The door to the rooms was opened by the detective's toady, Watson. A medical quack and author of unbelievable and scurrilous tales in which Sherlock Holmes always triumphed and the police always looked foolish. Such twaddle.

The Doctor smiled (or was he laughing). Come in, Gentlemen! Superintendent! Good to see you again. And Sergeant Montrose, is it not? Hello, Inspector!"

They were sitting amid an array of packing cases and baggage. The Baroness and her dog were perched invisibly on a steamer trunk.

Holmes waved diffidently and asked Mrs. Hudson to bring tea. The social niceties, such as they were, having been disposed of, he wasted no time getting to the core of the matter. "It seems Commissioner Bradford, through the good offices of my brother Mycroft, has asked me to concern myself in helping to untangle this conundrum involving Countess Faulkner and the late Dowager Countess. This has been your case, has it not, Inspector Jones."

Athelney Jones, seething, nodded his head.

And yours as well, Sergeant Montrose?"

"Yes sir. I have done much of the spade work, so to speak." *(What he didn't say was 'The Inspector wouldn't dirty his hands. He just pontificates.')*

"And of course, you have managerial responsibility, do you not, Superintendent?"

Watson interjected. "Murchison, I heard you defused a near riot of suffragists protesting the arrest of the Countess. Neatly done. I support their objectives but not always their methods."

Jones sniffed dismissively, "Harpies!"

Holmes plowed on. "Let us review the bidding, shall we? Perhaps we can dispose of this issue in one sitting. Ah, here comes the tea. Thank you, Mrs. Hudson."

The Sergeant, Superintendent and Watson took up the refreshments, especially Mrs. Hudson's ginger biscuits. Pookie stared longingly at the cakes she couldn't eat. Holmes and Jones abstained.

"I have taken the liberty of securing the records of this incident and have reviewed them carefully. I congratulate you, Sergeant on your fastidious and comprehensive observations, data gathering and note taking."

"Thank you, sir."

Jones exploded, "Here, Mr. Holmes who gave you access and permission to scrutinize the crime records of my case?"

Superintendent Murchison looked at him, "I did!"

The Inspector soundlessly pulled in his horns.

"The body was discovered by the Dowager's maid on the morning in question. She has been in the lady's service for fifteen years and is generally agreed to be above suspicion. Yes?"

"Yes."

"Only the Countess and the Dowager ate dinner together that evening. The Earl was at an event at his club."

"Correct!"

"The butler reported that a disagreement broke out once again between the two women over the Countess' support of the suffragists. He said it was a frequent source of tension at dinner. The Dowager was quite upset, near hysterical. The Countess was furious, withdrew prematurely from the table and went to her rooms. She was not seen again all night. The Dowager finished her meal and proceeded to her chambers after ordering her customary cup of tea which she took each evening with a dose of laudanum to help her sleep."

Jones interrupted. "Which the Countess intercepted and altered, creating the overdose that killed the Dowager. We've been over this time and again."

"Did anyone see the Countess tampering with the Dowager's tea?"

Jones said, "No, but their rooms were adjoining. It would have been quite simple for her to wait for the Dowager to go to her lavatory to prepare for bed and put an additional fatal dose in the cup."

"Laudanum has a very distinctive and bitter flavor. The extra dose would have been quite apparent to the Dowager. The tea would have tasted different. "

"Not if she was used to it. The woman was in her dotage."

"She was more than that. She was fatally ill."

"What?"

"You should take more time reviewing your case notes, Inspector. You would have found a report from the family physician confirming a specialist's diagnosis of incurable cancer. She was dying."

"Perhaps the Countess decided to put her out of her misery."

"The doctor's report specifically stated that he was instructed by the Dowager to tell no one of her condition. Not her son, not the staff and certainly not the Countess. They barely spoke except to argue."

"The sergeant looked perplexed. "Then who killed her? The doctor?"

"No! The only person besides the doctor, who was aware of her condition. The Dowager herself. The Lady wasn't suspicious of the enhanced dosage of laudanum because she prepared it. Lady Phyllis Everett, Dowager Countess Faulkner committed suicide."

Athelney Jones was dumbstruck as were the Sergeant and Superintendent.

Murchison looked at the Consulting Detective. "Will you testify to that effect, Mr. Holmes?."

"There is no need, Superintendent. You, the Sergeant and the Inspector can read the record as well as I. In our system, the Countess is innocent until proven guilty. In the absence of any shred of dispositive proof of her involvement, I strongly suggest that Inspector Jones should withdraw his accusation and acknowledge that the Dowager contrived her own demise rather than face an agonizing death by cancer. I am sure the doctor would feel he has been released from his obligation to secrecy with the Dowager's demise and the unfortunate imprisonment of the Countess. The coroner and his jury should be more than willing to accept a verdict of self-inflicted death. I suspect the suffragists may be mollified but one never knows with the Pankhursts."

"Please give my best regards to the Commissioner. You may tell him that I too am entering retirement and would appreciate any thoughts on the process he may care to share."

The Superintendent finished his tea and turned to Athelney Jones. "Well, Jones, unless you're going to persist in pursuing your accusations, you have your work cut out for you. The Commissioner, Mycroft Holmes and I will give you a draft statement that you can take before the coroner's jury absolving Countess Faulkner of all suspicion of murder and explaining the recent discovery of the Dowager's fatal illness. The doctor's testimony of being sworn to secrecy should go far in supporting the argument for her self-inflicted death...suicide. How the Commissioner intends to resolve your own situation is another matter. I know how I would like to see it handled but that is up to him. You may hope that with his upcoming retirement and the settling of this business, he will be lenient about the public uproar you triggered off.. Keep your opinions to yourself and take a lesson from a true professional, Sherlock Holmes."

Only Holmes, Watson and Mrs. Hudson heard the applause from the Baroness.

Epilogue

The Daily Mail   5 July 1903:
Countess Faulkner Exonerated

By George Grissom

Inspector Athelney Jones of Scotland Yard's Criminal Investigation Department today testified to a coroner's jury that in light of new facts that have arisen in the death of the Dowager Countess, Lady Phyllis Everett. the arrest warrant for Lady Marie Everett, Countess Faulkner, is withdrawn.

Inspector Jones stated that the Dowager's death was caused by a self-provided overdose of laudanum in her bed time tea. Doctor Roger Clark. M.D. attested to the fact that the Dowager was afflicted by an incurable case of cancer. It is his opinion and the supportive judgement of Scotland Yard and the Home Office that the noblewoman took her own life rather than suffer through an agonizing death.

39

The jury agreed and her demise has been certified as a self-inflicted injury with the intent to die.

Emmeline Pankhurst chair of the Women's Social and Political Union (WSPU), an all-women suffrage advocacy organisation recently formed by and her daughters, dedicated to "deeds, not words." stated that she and her organization had been confident of their member's innocence and rejoice in her exoneration. She questioned Inspector Jones' competence.

The Adventures of Sherlock Holmes and the Glamorous Ghost
Volume Four
Jones' Justice
The End

The Adventures of Sherlock Holmes and the Glamorous Ghost

Volume Four

Bye, Bye Bees – A Novelette

(**Note to reader:** The final story in Glamorous Ghost Volume 3 - **Angels We Have Heard on High - A Novella** ended with the following conversation at Sherlock Holmes' retirement retreat on South Downs Way in the tiny village of East Dean in Sussex. We begin this story with a recollection of that event.)

Juliet looked at Watson. Nodding toward Holmes, she whispered, "I hope you are watching over him, Doctor. I know his Guardian Angel Ezrafel is."

Watson blew out his cheeks. "As much as his persnickety nature will allow. We have just been arguing about his coming out of retirement."

Ezrafel winced. Director Raymond shook his head. The Baroness looked at him. "Holmes, you're a weary war horse. We all know you're still superior to all of those London hacks who purport to be enquiry agents and consulting detectives. Lord knows (Sorry, Raymond!) Scotland Yard is at a loss now that Lestrade is a Manchester innkeeper. But you were at death's door and you are not getting any younger. Baker Street is no longer available. You've established yourself here and live a fine and worthwhile life. What could get you back to your old haunts and practices?"

"A request from His Majesty!"

She groaned, "Oh Holmes!" and the dog whined.

*****

King Edward VII (Bertie) like his mother Queen Victoria before him, had employed Sherlock Holmes' services in dealing with what we might call 'certain delicate matters.' Watson never knew about them and thus could not record these adventures for posterity but the Great Detective had a clear recollection of the events. Bertie's memory was conveniently clouded and he remembered only selectively. As we noted in our story, **Hymns, Hums, Handel and Holmes**, Holmes also abetted Queen Alexandra's efforts to restore the pilfered manuscripts of George Frideric Handel's works that were purloined by her grandchildren from the Royal library in Buckingham Palace. So, acting on behalf of the British monarchy was well within his remit. He had also carried out missions for sovereigns, royals, heads of other foreign states and nobles.

"Once more unto the breach, dear friends." His announcement that he was coming out of retirement and temporarily turning the care of his bees over to a local farmer left Lady Juliet, Director Raymond, angel Ezrafel, Watson and yes, even Pookie in distress. However, they also knew there was no way they were going to dissuade him from carrying out an assignment from the King.

The celestials withdrew from Sussex to the Elysian Fields and Watson prepared to return to London. The King was sending one of his Daimler autos, of which he was so fond, to transport Holmes to Sandringham, 170 miles away.

His Majesty had not seen fit to enlighten the Consulting Detective as to the task he had in mind. Was this another personal 'delicate matter' or a serious affair of state?

*****

Once back in the celestial realm, Lady Juliet turned to Director Raymond, Ezrafel and Pookie and unleashed an unbeatific rant. "That man is incorrigible. Here I thought we finally got him to settle down and act like a retired beekeeper and he takes on an obligation for Bertie. Raymond, you've become a compadre of his. Ezrafel, you're his guardian angel. Can't you two convince him to relax and let the world of intrigue pass him by? He won't listen to me."

The angel shook his wings in frustration. "He doesn't even _hear_ me. A problem all of us Guardians have. We have to work by indirection. You remember I came to you in the first place to get him to retire. Watson doesn't seem to have any effect, either. Excuse me. I must get back to my protégé before he travels off." He spread his wings and left.

Raymond sighed. "I often wondered whether the Almighty in their infinite wisdom should have given mortals free will but who am I to doubt Them? We can only hope this is a benign task the King has in mind that doesn't involve risk or undue exertion."

They looked at each other, laughed and said, "Sure!" Pookie barked.

Juliet paused for a moment and then said, "I know what I'm going to do. Pookie and I are going to talk with Bertie's mother."

"You're going to approach Queen Victoria?"

"Why not! If a cat can look at a Queen so can a little white dog and her mistress. After all, being an English Baroness must count for something. Maybe I'll appeal to Prince Albert. He's a sweetie."

Raymond smiled. "Let us hope the Empress will be amused."

"Speaking of Empresses, I wonder how Sisi is doing with the Lipizzaners. I'll have to check the stables. Those horses adore her and she adores them. Come on, Pookie. Then we'll go see Mum and Dad. They've really adapted to Heaven. Angelic beings, I shall keep you posted on my audience with Her Majesty Alexandrina Victoria."

"If she gives you one."

"Of course she will. Don't be a spoilsport."

44

Raymond laughed.

Pookie did one of her signature backflips. She loved to be with the white stallions and she was going to meet another empress. Life (death?) was good. How about a Heavenly Chewy snack?

*****

After several stops for fueling, calls of nature, stretching of legs and a pub pint, the King's Daimler entered the 8000 acre Sandringham Estate and moved up the roadway to the House beloved by the King and Queen. A liveried butler met the car and greeted the detective.

"Mr. Holmes, welcome once again to Sandringham. I trust your journey was comfortable. The trains run irregularly and His Majesty felt the car would be a better mode of transportation. He is awaiting your attendance in his personal drawing room. Lord Halsbury, the High Chancellor, is with him."

The Lord Chamberlain Edward Hyde Villiers, 5th Earl of Clarendon who managed the Royal Household joined them. "Mr. Holmes, welcome. Good to see you again. Simms, please have a footman take Mr. Homes' baggage to his room. As usual, sir, you are invited to dinner and to stay overnight here at the Hall. Please come with me."

"Thank you, Lord Clarendon. The last time I was here, it was at Her Majesty's behest."

"She is here and is looking forward to seeing you at dinner. Here we are."

They approached a formal portal bedecked with the Royal Seals. He knocked at the door and a plummy baritone called out, "Enter!"

Dressed in a Norfolk jacket and tweed trousers, the King was sitting in a comfortable Morris chair smoking a cigar and nursing a glass of what looked like cognac. He prefers it to whiskey. His Majesty is a Francophile in many ways.

Sitting opposite him was Hardinge Stanley Giffard, 1st Earl of Halsbury, and Lord High Chancellor of Britain. He is the highest-ranking traditional minister among the Great Officers of State. The Lord Chancellor is appointed by the sovereign on the advice of the prime minister. He is a member of the Cabinet and is responsible for the efficient functioning and independence of the justice courts. The Lord Chancellor is also the presiding officer of the House of Lords, the head of the judiciary of England and Wales and the presiding judge of the Chancery Division of the High Court of Justice.

He and Holmes had a frosty relationship due to a series of episodes in which the detective had conflicts with the courts, They respected but didn't much like each other.

The detective entered the room, bowed to the King and said, "Your Majesty, I am here as commanded. Thank you for providing transportation and lodging."

He turned to the Chancellor. "Good to see you again, milord."

The king waved a cigar laden hand at Holmes and said, "Welcome Mr. Holmes. Thank you for coming to Sandringham. Love this old place."

"My pleasure, Sire. I believe you know I recently performed a small service for the Queen."

"Please call me Bertie within the confines of these rooms. Yes, Alix told me of the adventure our two grandchildren had at the Royal Library, Scamps! Thank you for restoring their pilfering. Sorry I can't tell that story around but the Queen insists we keep it quiet. She also has a preposterous tale about getting music dedicated to her from the spirit of George Frideric Handel. The blighter's been dead for 145 years. But if it makes her happy, who am I to quibble. Don't believe in ghosts myself. What about you, Clarendon or you, Halsbury?"

The Chamberlain shook his head in the negative and Halsbury replied. "No. I do not, Sire. I have too many issues with the living to bother about ghosts."

"Little do they know." thought Holmes.

The Chamberlain excused himself. "Domestic affairs to tend to, Sire. Goodbye, Milord, Mr. Holmes."

The detective bowed his thanks and with his usual directness turned his attention back to King Edward.

"What is it you wish me to do, Sire, er Bertie?"

"Not me, Holmes, Halsbury here has a problem and I agreed to assist him by calling you in."

The Lord Chancellor did not look very happy at the prospect. He coughed and said, "A delicate and troubling issue. Mr. Holmes. Lord Kenworth, a Justice of the High Court-a Master of the Company's Court actually- has been creating quite a stir by insisting on an investigation of International Metals Ltd. The company produces steel items, armaments and associated ammunition for our military and that of several foreign countries, most notably France. He has been instigating enquiries into the financial condition of the enterprise but has extended his remit to include the firm's customers. He insists that International Metals products have been finding their way into the hands of Kaiser Wilhelm's Imperial German Army. Needless to say, these accusations are causing serious disturbances in Parliament and unfortunately, the press."

The King snorted. "We certainly don't want to aid or abet Cousin Willie's war machine."

Holmes replied, "I see the issue but surely, Sire-Bertie-your government has more than sufficient resources to probe these accusations. The Home and Foreign Offices, the Army and Admiralty, Scotland Yard, even a parliamentary investigation."

Halsbury replied, "Those are precisely the activities and agencies we are trying to avoid. You see, both His Majesty and I have significant personal investments in International Metals. Your pardon, Sire but _we_ have a problem,"

Holmes whistled, "And you both may be accused of conflict of interest. Your Majesty, I am willing to assist in any way I can but I will do nothing to extricate you and Lord Halsbury from your investment missteps. I suggest you divest yourselves of your International Metals shares as rapidly and quietly as you can."

The Chancellor replied, "We have already set those wheels in motion. Our investment firm is busy at that task. However, there remains the question: Are International Metals products finding their way into the German war machine? Kenworth is hardly a friend of the Monarchy or my Offices. We want you to investigate his accusations. If they are true, I shall take steps to stop the misdirection and bring the culprits to book."

The King shifted uncomfortably and nodded. "Given the Germanic background of my family, the

House of Saxe-Coburg and Gotha, there are many who are more than willing to put the worst possible face on this whole affair. Once again, I am calling on your discretion and skill, Holmes. Please don't disappoint me."

"I shall give it my utmost attention and effort, Majesty."

*****

Back at Lady Juliet's stables, the Baroness joined Austrian Empress Sisi who was just finishing brushing *(and caressing)* the gorgeous white Lipizzaner stallions and mares. Pookie had pattered over to her Saintly Spectaculars co-star, Der Alte and the two of them were engaged in an animals-only conference which neither Juliet nor Sisi could understand. The horse whinnied and the dog barked, sharing no doubt, some joke or planned prank for their next performance.

Juliet told Sisi of her intention to speak with Empress Victoria about Holmes' derailed retirement. It was unclear exactly what she wanted the Queen or her Consort to do but they may have some ideas on reining in *(no pun)* Edward VII's future calls on the Great Detective.

Sisi remarked, "Victoria may or may not respond to a mere baroness by marriage but I am perfectly willing to intercede for you – Empress to Empress. Oh, dear. This is Heaven. We really should get rid of all this royalty and nobility nonsense. After all, there is really only one Authority we all owe our fealty to and they are quite democratic."

"Would you do that for us? Pookie and I'd be most grateful."

"Ah yes, you and your impertinent little dog. I'm sure she'll charm the Queen."

"Thank you. I'm off to see my parents and brother. Feel free to ride Der Alte if he is willing."

"Oh, that lovely horse and I have spent many an afternoon cantering around the Elysian Fields. Then I will see Victoria with your request."

The Baroness and Pookie flitted over to her parents' villa. Her brother Arthur had just returned triumphant from the Rugby field and was describing the details of the match to his father and totally confused mother. She looked up and smiled. "Juliet, how nice to see you. Arthur was just telling us about his sporting exploits. Alvin understands but I must confess I didn't fathom a word. How are you and dear little Pookie?"

The dog put her paws up on Lucinda's lap and cocked her head. The little actress was giving it her all. "Oh, you sweet little animal. I wish we had a doggie."

Juliet laughed, "Nothing easier, Mum. Come with me over to the Meadows beyond the Rainbow Bridge and take your pick. There's an absolute army of canny canines waiting for someone to adopt them. Unfortunately not all of their earthbound masters or mistresses make it to Heaven. But they're happy enough. Mr. Sherman and his team take loving care of them. He'll help you make a match."

"Oh, that would be wonderful. I do so admire how you and Pookie flit about. Do you have any new adventures on tap?"

"In a manner of speaking, yes. Miss Dog and I are planning to visit Queen Victoria and Prince Albert,"

"The Empress? I thought she and the Prince were keeping private."

"They are but I have a friend who is going to get us an audience."

"Why do you want to see the Queen?"

"To get Sherlock Holmes back into seclusion."

"I don't understand."

"The Queen's son, King Edward VII, summoned Holmes from his sheltered retirement farm and beehives on some job or other. He couldn't refuse. I want the Queen's help in getting Holmes released from his obligation."

"But she's dead, here in Heaven and the King is not. How will she speak with him."

"Oh, Mum. If a lowly Baroness can communicate with the living, an English Empress certainly should be able to. I'm sure Mr. Raymond can arrange something."

Her mother sat wide-eyed.

*****

Dinner at Sandringham was an informal but elaborate and lengthy event – informal because Holmes had not brought a dinner suit with him. Elaborate and lengthy, because the King loved to eat. His expanded waistline was the subject of much palace gossip. Chamberlain Clarendon, Chancellor Halsbury and Queen Alexandra completed the party, carefully picking at their food while Bertie devoured every edible item in sight.

A small dog sat at the Queen's feet, daintily accepting small snacks from the regal table. The queen smiled, "This is Turi, a Pomeranian. One of the few of Queen Victoria's extensive menagerie of animals who are still alive. He's getting on in years. I hope the deceased members are with her in Heaven. Turi was on the Empress' deathbed at Victoria's request. Now he has attached himself to me."

The Queen rose and went to her harpsichord and played a piece with which the detective was not familiar. "You may not recognize this Mr. Holmes. It's Mr. Handel's *Incidental Music for Queen Alexandra*. I'm sure you delivered it but probably never heard it."

53

The King chortled, "Come now, Alix. Not going to repeat that ghost story, are you? What do think, Holmes? Do spirits exist and do they interact with us?"

"I am inclined to be a believer, Sire." *(Little did His Majesty know how soon his own opinion would change.)* The queen smiled and ran the keyboard.

Halsbury harumphed and turned to Holmes. "What are your plans for our little project, Mr. Holmes?"

"I have not yet formulated a program, milord. This seems to be a three pipe problem. However, I shall certainly seek out Lord Kenworth as early as I can when I return to London."

*****

Empress Sisi was still in the stables with Der Alte when the Baroness and Pookie flitted in. "Did you two have a nice ride?"

Sisi glowed, "Oh indeed we did. Der Alte is a such a gentleman. I stopped by my mansion and I have news for you. You can expect a distinguished visitor."

"Who?"

"None other than Alexandrina Victoria; Queen of the United Kingdom of Great Britain and Ireland and Empress of India."

"I was willing to go to her. But she's coming here? Why?"

It seems the Queen shares our affection for animals. During her reign, she owned twelve dogs, three ponies, a herd of goats, a donkey and two parrots as pets.

She has a special love for Pomeranian dogs. One was settled on her deathbed. But her favorites included a spaniel, greyhound and deerhound. She had a full stable of Windsor Grey horses as well. She wants to see the Lipizzaner stallions and she is fascinated by your canine companion, Pookie. Be careful, she may try to steal your little lady away from you. Victoria's two major interests are her husband, Prince Albert and the animal kingdom. Frankly, she's not the least bit interested in you although she has heard of your partnership with Sherlock Holmes, whom she very much admires."

Juliet huffed, "Queen or no queen. She can just keep her imperial hands off Pookie. Maybe I can get her interested in The Meadows and Mr. Sherman's wonderful efforts. I'm taking my Mum there so she can adopt 'a doggie' and bring it into Heaven and her villa."

"Most of the Queen's pets, the dead ones, of course, are with her at her mansion. She also loved horses. You and I will have to be careful she doesn't try to capture the Lipis"

The Baroness stared off. "I'm beginning to think approaching Her Majesty wasn't such a heavenly idea."

Sisi laughed. "I think the two of us can hold her off, if necessary. We can also call on Mr. Raymond for support. I'll call him."

"When is she coming?"

"Shortly."

"I guess curtseys and court manners are de rigeur."

Sisi giggled. "If you can remember how."

"It's all so silly. You're an empress. You don't require all that folderal."

"Yes, but I'm a sweetheart." She broke out laughing.

Juliet pondered. "I'm not being at all charitable about Victoria, am I? Hardly befitting a saintly person and British subject. I'm surprised the Committee hasn't kicked me out."

Sisi responded. "You may not believe it but the Committee and the Almighty are very fond of you. You're incorrigible and you provide variety. Not much of that here in Heaven. I like to think I might be one of the odd ones, too. I've stopped wearing those plain white robes. Actually, as you can see, I'm wearing a red sash on the white, like the Austrian flag."

The Baroness chuckled, "I noticed. Oh, we're certainly odd. Look, here comes Raymond."

*****

Morning came to Sandringham and Holmes began his journey in one of the King's Daimlers back to London He would be staying at the Claridge's hotel. Mrs. Hudson in Baker Street had a new tenant and Holmes was disinclined to stay with Watson. His wife was not enamored of the Great Detective. Regardless, he would have to involve Watson. His guardian angel Ezrafel, who was sitting next to him in the auto, shook his wings in frustration. Holmes was at it again. Hopefully, violence would not be involved. The angel would have to confer with the Baroness. She would be pressing for information. So would Raymond.

The detective's first order of business was to visit Lord Kenworth at the Royal Courts of Justice on the Strand in the City of Westminster. He had secured an evening appointment while at Sandringham. Wonder of wonders, the judicial bureaucracy responded favorably on the basis of Holmes' reputation. He did not reveal that he was calling on behalf of the King or Lord Halsbury. The Chancellor and Kenworth were not friends.

The journey from Sandringham to London was mercifully shorter than his trip from Sussex and he arrived with ample time to change clothes, eat and take a cab *(the third one)* to the Strand. He was greeted by

Lord Kenworth's secretary and was led into a large and ornate office that reeked of pomp and circumstance and the authority of the High Court.

Kenworth was a short, generally unimpressive individual whose height was difficult to determine since he sat at his desk and did not rise to greet Holmes. Solemnly dressed, dark of hair with a carefully trimmed moustache and beard, he squinted from behind his monocle. Overall he exuded an unfriendly attitude.

Before the Great Detective could say a word, the Justice opened the conversation. "Mr. Holmes, is it? I must confess you have piqued my curiosity or I wouldn't have granted this interview. Rumor hath it that you have retired to some apiary in Sussex yet here you are in my office. I doubt you wish to discuss bees."

"No Milord, I do not. Forgive me but what manner of address do you prefer."

"Milord, Mr. Justice, Master. I answer to them all."

"Well. Milord, I am here at the behest of individuals who wish to remain unidentified but have asked me to enquire into the International Metals situation. Dare I call it an affair? I understand that you believe certain of their armaments have fallen into the hands of the German war machine either deliberately or through incompetence on the company's part. They have asked me to determine the truth of that accusation and if so, uncover how it has come about. I hasten to add that in no way do I intend to interfere with any enquiries you may have initiated."

"Are you in the employ of International Metals or the German government?"

"No, certainly not! As of the moment, I am completely neutral on the subject. I have spent my entire career uncovering facts and then letting the authorities deal with them as they see fit."

"Your clients must be indeed influential if they could persuade you to abandon your beehives."

"I fall back on that saying of so many domestics – 'I really couldn't comment, sir.'"

"Well, I have sufficient evidence to support my investigation. International Metals weapons have been found in an overturned German Army lorry near Hamburg. One of our Foreign Office operatives serving undercover arrived at the scene of the accident in time to witness several broken crates full of rifles and ammunition being hauled away. It seems the Germans are filing off the serial numbers and identification upon arrival at their storage locations. The fact that this shipment was not yet neutered suggests that it was stolen or misdirected."

"I cannot believe the management of International Metals, if they were deliberately involved, would be foolish enough to sell their wares to the Kaiser without removing identifying marks. They strongly protest their innocence. I would certainly welcome your confirmation that the company has not been engaged knowingly in an act of treason. If theft or hijacking is involved, we need to find the culprits. Thus far Scotland Yard and the Home and Foreign offices have come up empty."

Holmes replied, "If you don't mind my asking, sir, how did you become concerned in this matter?"

"As part of my responsibility as a Master of the Companies Court, I review commercial organizations considered to be key to the Empire's welfare. The defence industry is high on my list for scrutiny. During a somewhat routine enquiry, I came across discrepancies between IM's records of sale to our military and the corresponding receipts by our Army's Quartermaster units. The shortages were large enough and recent enough to warrant further investigation. And then I heard of the Hamburg incident."

"Who is aware of your search?"

"Besides your unnamed individuals, high level officials of International Metals, the Home and Foreign Office, the Army and Admiralty, Scotland Yard and of course, my own staff. I do not know if the King has been informed." At this last mention he squinted at Holmes from behind his monocle. Holmes showed no facial or verbal response.

"With your permission, Milord, I should like to interview the appropriate members of International Metals management. At the moment, I have no idea where that may lead me but I'm sure that you are aware that I have many contacts in all of the organizations you mentioned. If you could have your secretary give me a list of the specific individuals involved, it would be quite helpful. Please do not inform them of my participation in this search until I request it. By the way, I am a signatory to the Official Secrets Act."

"I hoped as much, Mr. Holmes. The Act does indeed apply. I shall arrange the appropriate interviews at IM Ltd. for you in the morning. You are staying at Claridge's?"

"Yes and thank you for your cooperation."

He gave a near-smile and said, "Thank _you_ and tell your mysterious clients I am grateful for your help."

*****

A mature couple in their forties, dressed in heavenly white robes with red, white and blue sashes approached Lady Juliet, Baroness Crestwell's mansion and stables. Several dogs and a pony accompanied them. Juliet looked at Sisi. "Who are these two?"

Empress Elisabeth (Sisi) laughed. "Don't you recognize your former sovereign?"

"That's Victoria and Albert?"

"Yes, she's invoked the celestial privilege we all share and reverted to her younger self when she and Prince Albert were still a couple. He died in 1861 at age forty two, you remember. She lived forty more years and died in 1901. She appears now in her 1861 persona."

"We all share that privilege? I didn't know that."

"Oh, Juliet. Don't even think of it. Everyone loves you as you are. I haven't changed either. Here they come."

Queen Victoria, who was not known for her pleasant visage, smiled broadly at the two ladies and said, "Empress Elisabeth, Albert and I have come as you requested. Baroness Crestwell, we have met before at Windsor. You were presented to us. We are most interested in your little dog and the Lipizzaner stallions you both have adopted."

Did she include Albert or was she using the royal 'we' ? Juliet curtseyed. Sisi did not.

"Your Majesty and Your Highness. Welcome! *(She omitted the bit about her 'to her humble abode' which her mansion certainly was not. Actually, given her history and nature, she felt she should be living in a celestial shack. She wondered about the level of grandeur of Victoria's or Sisi's palaces. She meant to speak to Raymond about Heavenly Real Estate's*

62

rankings. Weren't all of the celestials equal in God's eyes? She hoped so. They should all occupy similarly glorious abodes, should they not? What does the Committee think? What does the Almighty think? Questions for another day. Right now, she should be gracious unto her former sovereign and her consort. She wanted to beg a boon.)

Pookie, sensing the Queen's attention, stood on her hind legs, swayed and rotated, finishing with her signature backflip. The royal dogs and pony looked on in amazement and yes, some little jealousy. Albert laughed and the Queen clapped her hands in delight. "Oh, what a wonderful performance. She is quite adorable. Is she available?"

Juliet was wary of refusing the Queen so she replied, "I believe that is up to Pookie herself, Your Majesty. She is quite independent."

The Bichon stared at the royals and their animal entourage and then turned and sat down next to Juliet. She had made her choice.

Seeing the Queen's disappointment, Juliet promptly added. "I'm sure we can arrange a program of visits and private performances for you as you desire."

Sisi added, "That applies to the performing horses as well, Victoria."

Prince Consort Albert who had remained silent up to this point said, "I believe that will be most satisfactory, ladies." He was not enthused about adding to the sizeable menagerie already living with the royal couple. Twelve dogs, three ponies, a herd of goats, a donkey and two parrots *(There was no partridge in a pear tree.)* to say nothing of the Windsor Grey horses.

The Queen pouted momentarily but resumed her smile. "That will do. But now, we should very much like to see the Lipizzaners."

Juliet returned her smile and said, "Most certainly, Your Majesty, but where are my manners?" She snapped her fingers and a table loaded with delicacies appeared. " May I offer you both a spread of nectar and ambrosia before we go to the stables and meet Der Alte and his beautiful associates. By the way, they too are independent. Empress Sisi and I support them and love them but we do not own them. They perform in the Saintly Spectaculars with Pookie at our request but of their own volition. They spend much of their time here in our stables but also love to gambol with other equines in the Meadows beyond the Rainbow Bridge. Have you visited the Meadows? As an animal lover you will be entranced by the array of creatures located there. They are principally the ones who have not yet been admitted to Heaven proper but who enjoy the freedom, fun and comforts of near Heaven. The

Peaceable Kingdom. I'm sure Mr. Sherman, their caretaker would be delighted to welcome you."

"The Queen sat and daintily took up a cup of nectar. "I went to the Meadows once to meet some of my pets who were waiting for me to emerge from Purgatory. Some were with Albert but not all. One or two are still on earth with Alexandra. She is a very sweet woman."

Juliet almost choked. Victoria had been in Purgatory?! Not for very long, it would seem. A nation's prayers probably helped. She looked at Sisi. The Empress smiled and mouthed, "Oh, me too."

The Baroness had often wondered about her own case. She had been 'directly admitted' to Paradise. She was hardly a true saint like Cecilia or Francis. Their holiness and humility outweighed any worldly rank or privilege. Queens and Empresses went to Purgatory like many of the commoners. What about a Baroness? She needed to add the question of her immediate heavenly entry to her list of discussion items with Mr. Raymond.

The Queen rose. "We are ready to see these equine marvels." *(She was either using the royal we or had taken to speaking for Prince Albert.)* Her dogs and pony surrounded her. Several statues of Prince Albert as an equestrian are distributed throughout Britain. His interest in horses almost matched that of the Queen.

They flitted out of the building and around to the stables where a group of gorgeous white stallions were gathered. Empress Sisi and Pookie went immediately to a large, well- proportioned and obviously senior citizen – Der Alte. *(The Old One)* He had led the Lipis for close to thirty years before being shot by a rogue estate manager who had captured him for a spoiled 12 year old Countess. She and her parents were banished from Vienna by the Emperor Franz Joseph who loved the horses. The estate manager was never found.

Victoria was entranced by the vision of these spectacular equines with their pure white hair, manes and tails. The horses were similarly attracted to the diminutive woman who seemed to carry herself with the same pride as they did. They were used to royal environments, personages and attention. So was she. Instant mutual attraction.

"Oh, one would dearly love to ride one of these magnificent beasts." She clearly meant Der Alte. Juliet walked up to the horse and whispered in his ear. He whinnied and shook his head up and down.

The Baroness smiled. "I believe Der Alte would be pleased to accommodate you, your Majesty." She walked over to a tack room and returned with a side saddle and reins. She and Prince Albert adjusted the saddle, stirrups and pommel and assisted the five foot Queen onto the seat. Der Alte gently strode out of the enclosure and proceeded to slowly but deliberately execute a series of tightly choreographed maneuvers. The Queen was ecstatic. Albert was amazed.

Mr. Raymond had arrived earlier and was observing the petite Queen sitting atop the significant girth of the pure white stallion as they progressed around the stable yards. He looked at the Baroness, Empress Sisi and Prince Albert. "Her Majesty seems to be enjoying herself."

When she and the horse returned, Victoria was reluctant to leave her seat but finally allowed herself to be lifted down by her Prince Consort. "Good day, Mr. Raymond. We are pleased to see you."

The angel nodded. "Ma'am!"

Back on her feet, dwarfed by Der Alte, she regained her Imperial mien. "Baroness! Please arrange to have these noble equines visit us as soon as possible. I understand they and your dog perform for The Heavenly Theatre Guild's Saintly Spectaculars. We would greatly appreciate a private showing."

"Certainly, your Majesty. Empress Sisi and I will speak with the horses and Pookie and make the arrangements. Tell us where and when."

"Delightful. You shall be informed, Is there anything we can do for you in return?"

"In fact, Ma'am there is."

Holmes got a message next morning from Lord Kenworth setting up an appointment with Sir Ronald Bakersfield, Managing Director of International Metals Ltd. and certain members of his staff. IM's manufacturing and shipping facilities are located in Sheffield but its executive offices are in London near the War Office in Whitehall.

He stepped from a cab in front of a nondescript greystone building. A polished brass plate on an oversized entrance door was the only identification that the industrial giant's executive cadre was in residence. Clearly Industrial Metals Ltd. wanted to present a subtle image closer to a gentlemen's club than a vibrant commercial organization. Probably in tune with the look of other Whitehall establishments representing His Majesty's government.

He entered and was greeted by an attractive but conservatively dressed receptionist of middling age. "Good morning, sir. May I be of assistance?"

"Sherlock Holmes to see Sir Ronald Bakersfield. I have an appointment."

The receptionist's eyebrows rose momentarily. "Certainly, Mr. Holmes. Sir Ronald is awaiting you in the Board Conference Room with several of our other executives. If you would follow me." She walked to a well concealed lift, opened the gate and instructed the operator to take the detective to the top floor. "Sir Bakersfield's secretary will be there to meet you."

As indeed he was. "Mr. Holmes, good morning. I'm James Eliot, the Managing Director's secretary. Welcome to Industrial Metals Ltd. The Director has just finished a meeting with members of our executive committee. They are all eager to make your acquaintance. As I'm sure you know, your fame precedes you."

"Thank you. I am looking forward to meeting your management team, as well. Shall we?"

Eliot knocked on the conference room door and was greeted by a tall, bearded individual who said nothing but stood aside to let the two of them enter. There were four men in the room. From the far end of the long paper-laden conference table a smiling, distinguished figure rose. Sir Ronald Bakersfield, obviously the Managing Director, clad in a well-cut, certainly bespoke grey business suit, raised his arm in greeting. He was slightly taller than the detective, clean-shaven with piercing grey eyes that almost matched his clothes. A large diamond stickpin was nestled in his cravat. "Mr. Holmes, I presume. Ron Bakersfield here. Pleased to have you join us. Come in, come in." He pointed to an empty chair next to him. "Would you care for a coffee. We are trying to get away from the English passion for tea. *(a chuckle)*"

Holmes sat, declining the offer. "Thank you for agreeing to see me, Sir Ronald. I had not expected to meet with your executive group."

"Oh, well, we were together for our monthly business review so I thought we would all join in. Any request from Lord Kenworth is bound to get our attention and when a famous detective is involved, you can see how our interest would be piqued. *(another chuckle)* Let me introduce the members of our party. You have met my secretary. The gentleman on your right is our Corporate Comptroller and Financial Officer, Stanley Foster. Next to him is our Steel Works Director, Charles Stanwick. He's down for the day from Sheffield. Over here is our Vice Director in charge of Sales and Marketing, Harland Brownley. And last but certainly not least is our Director of Military Materiel and Development, Joshua Clemmons, also from Sheffield."

Cordial greetings and smiles. Of the group, only Clemmons seemed uncomfortable but the subject of the discussion was obvious and it was in his bailiwick. Holmes as usual was direct. "I have come out of retirement and am here at Lord Kenworth's request. *(He deliberately did not mention the Chancellor or King.)* He has ample evidence that guns and ammunition made by your establishment have found their way into the hands of the German military."

Bakersfield responded, "We are aware of the incident and are cooperating with His Majesty's authorities in every respect."

Clemmons interjected. "We have tracked all recent shipments and agree with the Royal Quartermaster that there is a serious discrepancy between our records of transfers to the Army and their records of receipt. We are joined by Scotland Yard, the Home Office, the Army's Investigatory Group, the Admiralty and the Foreign Office in our efforts to determine where, how and by whom those armaments made their way into Fritz's hands. Frankly, Mr. Holmes, I think your presence in this matter may amount to overkill. The process is well in hand. You may be wasting your time."

The Marketing and Sales Vice Director chimed in. "I can assure you we have assiduously checked our highly controlled sales channels and have no record of any transactions involving the Germans. The materiel has been stolen, misdirected or highjacked in transit. While we welcome someone of your talent and reputation, I am not sure what you will bring to the party."

"Gentlemen, I have spent my professional career discovering things that others know nothing about. I intend to do the same in this instance. I propose to answer your questions, Mr. Clemmons and determine where, how and by whom those munitions made their way into German hands. I assume all your armaments traffic is controlled out of Sheffield."

"Correct!"

"Then may I accompany you and Mr. Stanwick back to your facility when you return?"

"That will be tomorrow morning. We shall be on the 8:35 train from St. Pancras. First class."

"Holmes turned to the Managing Director's secretary. "'Mr. Eliot. Could you book a reservation for me on the same train, please? I will bear the expense."

Sir Ronald Bakersfield laughed. "No need for that, Mr. Holmes. International Metals Ltd. can surely stand the cost of a first class return ticket to Sheffield. Is there anything else we can do to assist you in your search."

"Not at the moment. I have several appointments here in London that will occupy my time. I shall bid you all a good day. Mr. Clemmons, Mr. Stanwick. I shall see you in the morn." He left the room with Eliot.

Stanley Foster, the Comptroller, who had not participated in the discussions looked at the Managing Director and said, "Unusual chap! Bit of an egotist. Is he really that good?"

Sir Ronald nodded, a frown blanketing his features. "Better than good. We must be very careful. You especially, Clemmons."

*****

"Let us make sure we understand, Baroness. After you, his guardian angel and his companions finally convinced Sherlock Holmes to take up retirement in Sussex and adopt beekeeping, my son Bertie called him out of seclusion to pursue a personal task for him. Is that correct?"

"It is, Ma'am. As Mr. Raymond will attest, it was a near miracle to get Holmes to abandon his dangerous lifestyle and now I fear that once he is back in the saddle, so to speak, he will be reluctant to return to his new retreat. His guardian angel is quite upset as am I. His associate, Doctor John Watson has also retired. I hope Holmes doesn't entice him to once more join in the fray."

"As you may know, Bertie and I have never gotten along, even when he was a youth. Unmanageable lad! I hold him responsible for my dear Albert's premature death."

Albert intervened. "Now Vicki, it wasn't the boy's fault that I contracted typhoid fever while I was there with him in Cambridge."

"Oh, indeed it was. In spite of your illnesses, you travelled to Cambridge to see our son and discuss his indiscreet and scandalous affair with that hussy, Nelly Clifden. It did you in."

The Prince Consort shrugged. She would not be convinced otherwise.

The Queen looked at Juliet. "We are not sure what can be done about Holmes. The damage seems to be committed already. Besides, how are we to communicate with Bertie?"

"I think Mr. Raymond has the solution to that. The Angelic Postal Service delivers messages to the living on earth. I use it. If you could send a communication to the King asking him to relieve Holmes of his obligation, it might do the trick."

"Ask him? Nonsense, We shall command him. Mr. Raymond, how does one invoke this postal service of yours. Won't King Edward be surprised to receive a missive from his irate and very deceased mother!"

*****

"Pardon, your Majesty, I'm sorry to disturb you." The Lord Chamberlain, Edward Hyde Villiers, 5th Earl of Clarendon entered King Edward VII's drawing room carrying a silver tray with a sparkling white envelope precisely centered on it.

The King chuckled, "What's this, Clarendon. Have you decided to take up butlering?"

"Hardly, Sire, but this missive is so unusual, I decided to deliver it myself. It is directed to you."

"I receive tons of mail as you well know. What's different about this one?"

The Chamberlain laid the tray on an end table next to the King. "The envelope practically glows. You will notice the address consists of one word written in purple, 'Bertie.' On the reverse side emblazoned in gold is the phrase 'Via the Angelic Postal Service.' I have not opened it, Sire."

"Is this someone's idea of a joke? As my mother used to say, 'We are not amused.'"

"Perhaps you should look at the envelope's contents."

The King took up a paring knife he had been using on a collection of apples and pears he had been consuming with a hefty tot of cognac and slit the flap of the envelope. He pulled out a single pure white card emblazoned with the combined crest of his deceased mother, Queen Victoria and her Prince Consort Albert of Saxe-Coburg and Gotha.

On it, written in purple ink in classic copperplate script was the following:

"To King Albert Edward VII: You are commanded to immediately relieve Mr. Sherlock Holmes of all current and future obligations to you and your associates and allow him to return to his retirement residence forthwith. Signed: Your mother HRH Victoria Regina."

The King snorted. "What foolishness is this, Clarendon?"

"I don't know, Majesty. I shall investigate immediately. Shall I contact Mr. Holmes?"

"No, not yet. Find out what you can about this jape. My mother is quite dead." He took another healthy swig of his cognac. "Isn't she?"

*****

Deep in the Halls of New Scotland Yard, there is a unit known simply as Special Branch. Originally set up in 1883 to deal with Irish anarchists and revolutionaries, it has extended its responsibilities to include matters of national security and intelligence in British, Irish and other Empire arenas. It acquires and develops intelligence, usually of a political or sensitive nature, and conducts investigations to protect the State from perceived threats of subversion, particularly terrorism and other extremist political activity. In 1903, its commander is Detective Superintendent Patrick Quinn.

Sherlock Holmes approached the office of his professional friend and colleague. "Ah, ha, the beekeeper returns. Come in, Mr. Holmes. Sure, I knew you wouldn't stay retired for very long. Has the country air proved too much for you? Have you uncovered dangerous aliens among your honey makers?"

"No, Superintendent, but I have discovered how excellent a quaff of mead can be distilled from their honey. Here, I have brought your some." He extended a small jug to the policeman.

"Are you offering a bribe to a member of His Majesty's Constabulary?"

"Hardly, I am offering to cooperate with Special Branch in the matter of Industrial Metals Ltd. armaments finding their way into Germany. I am engaged by Lord Kenworth to join you in your search. *(Once again, no mention of the King or Chancellor.)* I suspect you are probably getting more help than you want or need from the Home Office, Foreign Office, War Office, Army and Admiralty."

"Indeed, but if you are becoming involved, I will at last get some help that is useful. The military and the politicos are more trouble than they're worth and your client, Lord Kenworth, is heating the pot to a boil, demanding instant and full results."

"He has made a similar demand of me. I'm sure we both share his concern."

"Of course. The Kaiser and his boyos are getting more and more active. It seems IM Ltd. produces a better field gun than the Germans so they have resorted to a little shoplifting to assist their war plans. I'm sure their technologists will shortly reverse engineer the guns and produce their own weapons but in the meantime, they've upped the threat by using our own firearms. Not much we can do to recover the armaments but we can stop the flow and arrest the traitors responsible. We're following a chain of clues. Have you learned anything useful?"

Holmes shook his head. "I've been on this only a day. I called on the Industrial Metals executive group earlier and I'm heading up to their Sheffield works in the morning with their Steel Works Director, Charles Stanwick and their Director of Military Materiel and Development. Joshua Clemmons."

The Superintendent frowned. "I've met them. Clemmons gives me a real itch. He may just be nervous because all of this is happening in his backyard but you know how, over time, you develop a sixth sense about blokes. My sixth sense is running overtime with him."

Holmes chuckled. "Great minds etc. I share your reaction. He tried to wave me off the investigation. I plan to give him very careful scrutiny. Their Marketing Director was also very defensive. Forgive the pun. But he's no doubt, sorely concerned about the firm's reputation and future business. IM Ltd isn't the only arms supplier in the Kingdom and if Whitehall goes shy on them for future contracts, his job will be very difficult indeed. In all of this, he and Clemmons have the most to lose personally."

"Unless either of them has a hidden personal financial agenda. The Kaiser can be very generous to his friends."

"On the other hand, his minions are not above applying extortion and blackmail."

The policeman nodded "No, and let's not overlook the possibility of some reprobate gang making a few quid by hijacking the weapons on commission. I wouldn't put it past the Fenians. They have a lot of German connections. With the amount of shipping that goes on in Sheffield, it's not at all unlikely that a boatload or lorry or two could have been commandeered."

Holmes returned the nod. "Do you have any record of a hijacking in the Sheffield area?"

"More than a few but none directly related to Industrial Metals. Of course the shipment may have been disguised."

"Have you eliminated the military from all this. A shipment missing from the Army's storehouses is not out of the question."

"We've pursued that angle. The Army Quartermaster's records show that several of IM's listed shipments never reached their destination. Of course, the records could have been fiddled."

The detective sighed. "It would seem we have too many options to consider and very little evidence to eliminate any of them. Have you heard anything from your intelligence operatives inside Germany? Can they tell how the weapons got to Hamburg?"

"We have a few contacts within the Imperial German Army and are plowing those fields as we speak. Hamburg, of course, is a major sea port and the intelligence consensus is that the weapons had been offloaded from a ship onto the ill-fated lorry that crashed. We have narrowed the identity of the ship down to three. One is a large native German fishing boat. Another is a small freighter out of Liverpool. The third is a passenger vessel out of London that also carries cargo. We have boarded and are questioning the captains and crews of the two British ships. We're employing more subtle methods on the German fishing boat. It may have rendezvoused with another vessel somewhere in the North Sea and taken on the loot. A female barmaid in a dockside pub is working the problem for us."

Holmes stood and said. "Well, you seem to have many irons in the fire. I shall be aboard a train to Sheffield in the morning with Messrs. Clemmons and Stanwick. I'll inform you of any significant information I unearth. I hope you enjoy the mead."

*****

King Edward sat pondering and re-reading the mysterious missive supposedly from his mother. He looked over at his Chamberlain, Lord Clarendon who had delivered the envelope and said, "Clarendon, please summon Queen Alexandra." He demolished another cognac while waiting for his consort to appear.

"Ah, Alix. Here you are. What do you make of this?" He handed her the card.

The Queen read it and laughed. "I knew Victoria wasn't going to go quietly."

"You believe it's from my mother?"

"Of course, Bertie. I received my incidental music script from George Frideric Handel through the same Angelic Postal Service. Thanks to Sherlock Holmes."

"The dead really communicate with the living?"

"I'm not sure how widespread the practice is. It seems only denizens of Heaven can use the service and then only very infrequently but that's all I know. I suggest you speak to Mr. Holmes. He seems to be an authority on the subject."

"He was noncommittal when I asked him if he believes in ghosts.

"He does. Take my word for it. Are you going to obey your mother's command?"

"I may not have to if Holmes solves this problem rapidly."

"What problem is that?"

"Oh, some cock up in the War Office. Some missing weapons, Nothing to worry about."

"It must be serious if you've called in Sherlock Holmes."

"He knows some of the players. Makes it easier to solve. I wonder how Mother found out he was involved."

"Heaven sees all and knows all. I thought you knew that."

"Never thought much about it."

Alexandra, well aware of the King's philandering, said. "Well, maybe you should. Are we finished. I have some letters to write."

"Hmm? Oh, yes! Quite! Thank you. Please don't mention the War Office thing to anyone."

"To whom would I mention it? Good Day, Bertie! Good Day, Lord Clarendon! Thank you. I shall see you at dinner."

She swept out of the room, chuckling to herself.

*****

As the 8:35 train for Sheffield pulled out of St. Pancras, Holmes settled himself in his first class seat opposite the International Metals executives. "Good morning. Gentlemen. A bit brisk for this time of year. How are you both faring?"

Joshua Clemmons responded, "Well enough, I suppose. Look here, Mr. Holmes. Just what do you expect to do when you get to our armament works? I don't want you disturbing all of my staff with your impertinent questions."

Stanwick, the Steel Works Director, looked at him. "Steady on, Josh, old boy. We all want to get to the bottom of this poser, what? I for one, want to know how our Teutonic brethren got their paws on our equipment. We need to put a stop to it chop-chop."

"Well, yes but…"

Holmes intervened. "Thank you, Mr. Stanwick. Mr. Clemmons, I shall be as quietly efficient as possible in my enquiries. I'm sure the police and the military have already swept through your works and none too subtly."

"Exactly! How many more rounds of questioning will we have to go through? Quite frustrating!" He turned away.

Holmes persisted. "Perhaps we can facilitate things a bit by using our travel time to discuss the situation. What do both of you think happened?"

Stanwick responded first. "I believe the weapons changed hands at sea. Britain is supplying Norway with armaments, as you may know. Our ships and Norway's cross the North Sea with regularity. We have no record of hijacking or illegal boarding. If it happened, it was a cooperative effort.

"No. I wasn't aware. "Have you been able to trace the serial numbers of the wayward weapons, Mr. Clemmons. Were they destined for Norway?"

"We don't know yet. Shipping records are damned complex and bothersome. We don't keep them down to the individual items like shells or bullets."

"Even when the individual items are field guns?"

"I don't know. You'll have to check with our shipping department,"

The conversation turned to the Steel business in general. IM was facing more competition from firms on the continent and one or two upstarts in Britain. They had recently lost a major bid to provide rails for a new spur to be developed between Brighton and Southampton. The Board of Directors was not happy. Holmes was somewhat surprised at Stanwick's open willingness to discuss business issues and his theories on the missing shipments. Clemmons on the other hand, was increasingly tight-lipped.

The conversation turned to their impressions of Sheffield. Stanwick was a native. Clemmons was from Manchester. Both had spent time in the military as officers. Each regarded Sheffield as an up and coming city and a good place to live. They both belonged to the Chamber of Commerce and individual men's clubs. *(But not the same one)* Neither had any desire to transfer to London but would not pass up an opportunity for promotion.

Stanwick was married for the second time. His first wife had died in childbirth. He had two teen aged children - a boy and girl. Clemmons' wife was especially fruitful. They had six children ranging in age from six months to thirteen. Holmes got the impression they were just getting along financially.

The train pulled into the station and they were met by a liveried coachman in a black growler bearing the company's logo and name in small letters. "Good morning, gentlemen. The train was on time today. Miracles are still possible. You must be Mr. Holmes. I was told to expect a third passenger. Have you no luggage?"

Holmes told him he intended to return to London on the evening express. Could he arrange a return transfer to the station? Clemmons seemed visibly relieved to hear the detective would only be at the manufactory for an afternoon. Stanwick showed no reaction. They arrived at the buildings. An office complex attached to a large fabrication plant. A smaller unit stood in the rear of the property. Holmes assumed this was the armaments wing.

Deafening noises from the works echoed throughout the surrounding area. The occasional blast from a molten steel furnace merged with the syncopation of stamping machines. Sheet and rail metal crashed on the floor. Impossible to converse until they were well inside the offices.

Stanwick laughed. "Welcome to the Sheffield Philharmonic, Mr. Holmes. Guaranteed to deafen a person in record time. As you can see, the steel works are running at full throttle." He turned to Clemmons. "Not so, our defence manufactory. We have delayed our military shipments until we solve this problem with the Huns. I'm going to my office. Good luck, Holmes."

Clemmons nodded "And we better solve the problem damn fast. The interruption is costing us heavily. We've already built for inventory. We need to get those guns and ammo on their way to the Army – our Army, or the armies of our allies and get some coinage in the till."

"What other countries do you serve besides Norway?"

"Primarily France, Denmark and Sweden, although Sweden has a flourishing steel business of its own. At one time, we were supplying Italy until they joined up with Germany and Austro-Hungary in that so-called Triple Alliance."

"Do you think any of those weapons in German hands came from those countries?"

"I doubt it. I still think a Norwegian shipment got waylaid in the North Sea. I've sent for Amos Smith, he's our Military Materiel Works Manager. He can give you more detailed information."

*****

Queen Victoria had asked Mr. Raymond to stop by her mansion. She suddenly found herself facing an individual who had not been there a moment ago. In the form of a middle-aged male, tall, dressed in morning *(mourning?)* clothes, clean shaven, not a hair out of place, dark eyes, color undetermined. But, he seemed to be floating inches above the ground. Mr. Raymond, is a high ranking angel and Senior Celestial Director, charged with keeping Paradise in heavenly shape.

Momentarily taken aback, the tiny Empress regained her composure and asked, "Are you sure my missive was delivered to King Edward."

"Most assuredly, Ma'am, The Angelic Postal Service has an unsullied record of on-time and complete deliveries. His Majesty has your note in hand."

"Well, I hope that rascal calls Sherlock Holmes back and permits him to retire once again."

"I suspect the damage has been done Ma'am. Holmes is like a hound who has once again picked up the scent. In spite of the Baroness', Ezrafel's, Watson's and your efforts, little or no time will pass before he has once more emerged onto the crime scene. A bit slower perhaps and more selective but that war horse will be back in the battle. Take an angel's word for it."

"I suppose you're right. It's in his blood. He served us several times. Flawlessly, I might add. Speaking of horses, those Lipizzaners are wonderful animals. They will be performing for us shortly along with that clever little dog, Puck."

"Pookie, Ma'am. She has been the baroness' staunch companion for fifteen earth years and now in heaven. She is an intrepid performer, aerobat and clever detective in her own right. She and Lady Juliet are inseparable."

"A pity. We would have liked to have her here in our mansion along with those spectacular equines. Our Windsor Greys are lovely but the Lipis are extraordinary. We shall see them frequently. The Baroness is an interesting chit. Quite impertinent, sassy and bold. Very unusual for a heavenly denizen, is she not."

"That's what makes her so charming to the Almighty and I should say, to all of us. She is a special favorite of the angels and even the Committee. I assume you know that she and Sherlock Holmes are working partners. They have had many adventures on Earth and even one or two in the celestial realms."

"So that is why she is so worried about his retirement."

"Indeed! She, Dr. Watson, Mrs. Hudson and his guardian angel, Ezrafel are all concerned with his continued welfare."

"Well, so are we. I hope Bertie does the appropriate thing."

"So do we all, Ma'am"

*****

Amos Smith came into Clemmons' office. The Works Manager was tall, red hair, heavy beard and moustache, steel rimmed spectacles surrounding deep blue eyes, He was dressed in his shirt sleeves. Ink stains on both hands. "You wanted to see me, Mr. Clemmons?" A mild but apparent brogue.

"Yes, Amos. This is Mr. Sherlock Holmes, the famous detective. He's here from London to investigate the weapons shipment that fell into German hands, Give him all the assistance he needs,"

"Sure, Good to meet yer, Mr. Holmes. How can I help?"

Holmes had been studying him. Not much of his face was apparent behind the beard, moustache and spectacles but the eyes were a giveaway. So was his name. Smith. A popular Irish name. A popular name, period. Too popular. Mr. Smith was an imposter. Holmes had met him before. From his reaction, Smith recognized the detective. He was not comfortable.

"I'd like to see the invoices, manifests and shipping records for the last six months, if that's possible."

"If you'll come with me, I think we can help yer out."

They walked out of Clemmons' office and down a long hallway to a smaller space. Desk, several chairs, telephone, file cabinets and stacks of paper on every horizontal surface.

"Thank you. Have you been with IM for a long time?"

"Four years. Man and boy."

"But you're not a native of Sheffield. Your Celtic brogue gives you away."

"Northern Ireland, I'm an Ulsterman, Born and raised in Antrim. Tough to find decent work in the old country. That's why I moved to Sheffield."

"Wife and kids?"

"Nope, I'm a bachelor. No woman will have me." He laughed. "Here's the paperwork you'll be wantin'. I'll leave you to it. I'm going down to the shop floor. Have to follow up on some ammunition. We're still producin' although the demand has dried up. That German mess has given the military a bad case of nerves. I'll be back shortly."

Holmes watched him leave. He searched his memory. Amos Smith is not who he says he is. He needed to get back with Superintendent Quinn in Special Branch. He was up on all the Irish revolutionaries and trouble makers. Holmes was convinced Amos Smith was one of them and he did not hail from Northern Ireland. Meanwhile, let's look at the paperwork.

As he expected, there was little to be gained from the pile of manifests and shipping documents. He looked over a list of production statistics and tried to match them against shipments. A lot more was built than showed as shipped. Could all of it be in inventory? He doubted it. Some weapons and ammunition were being shipped and the paperwork altered or destroyed. He would strongly recommend that Judge Kenworth commission an on-site audit.

An hour passed and Smith did not return. Holmes went back to Clemmons' office. He told him of Smith's departure. The Director responded. "I was just coming to get you. Amos fell down in the shop floor and left to go to the doctor. Did you find what you wanted?"

Holmes was suspicious that Clemmons and Smith were colluding but lacked sufficient proof. He temporized. "I found nothing in the paperwork. Perhaps you can arrange for me to be picked up soon. There's an earlier train back to London I'd like to take."

Smith's real identity had finally dawned. Seamus Corcoran, a captain in the Irish Republican Brotherhood. The Fenians. Holmes had briefly been part of a sweeping arrest in London. Corcoran had escaped but not before he and Holmes had faced off against each other. The IRB had established a partnership with the Germans and had been involved in joint anti-British activities for quite some time. So Corcoran had disappeared to Sheffield, changed his name and appearance and was engaged in pro-German espionage and conspiracy. Kenworth and Quinn needed to know immediately. Corcoran, no doubt faked his fall and was on his way out of Sheffield for parts unknown, probably across the Irish Sea.

The receptionist came to Clemmons' office and told Holmes the coach was ready for him. He shook hands with Clemmons and headed down to Stanwick's office to say good-bye. The Director asked if he had made any progress. The detective said, "There are several issues that require follow up, Mr. Stanwick. You will be informed shortly as will Mr. Bakersfield. Thank you for your hospitality."

He told the coachman to stop at a telegraph office. He pretended he wanted to tell London of his early arrival. He sent a wire to Quinn and Kenworth identifying the fugitive Corcoran, strongly suggesting an audit of IM's military subsidiary and his suspicions of Clemmons.

The issue was now in the hands of the proper authorities. On the train, he composed a letter to the King and Chancellor reporting on his work and respectfully withdrawing from their assignment. Back to his bees.

*****

Pookie and Der Alte had just completed their leaps to the delight of the celestial Royals and nobles. Victoria and Albert has issued invitations to all of their former associates *(now deceased)*. Juliet and Sisi, dressed as equestriennes, worked with the horses and tried out a few new maneuvers and stunts – all successful and enchanting. Raymond was in attendance and so, surreptitiously, was the Committee. Queen Victoria came over to the Baroness and Empress. "Thank you. We are most pleased. Are you sure you would not like to pass these noble animals on to us?"

"I'm sorry, Your Majesty, but the horses and dog have decided to remain with us. It is their wish."

They were interrupted by the arrival of Ezrafel, Holmes' guardian angel. Raymond joined them. The angel said. "I am pleased to inform you that Sherlock Holmes is back at his cottage in Sussex and tending to his bees,"

"Good. My dictate to Bertie did the trick. Now his mother is dead, he listens to us."

Ezrafel was about to tell the Queen that Holmes had resigned from the King's service on his own but was forestalled by Raymond. Let's not disillusion

Victoria. Juliet, Sisi and Raymond just smiled at the Queen.

*****

Special Branch operatives caught up with Corcoran at the Liverpool-Dublin ferry and placed him under arrest for espionage and conspiracy. Under intense grilling, he finally admitted to his involvement along with a group of pro-German Irish revolutionaries.in supplying British armaments to the Kaiser's war machine. He also implicated Clemmons who was being paid to turn a blind eye to his activities. He, too, was arrested.

Judge Kenworth conducted an audit of International Metals Ltd which resulted in the resignation of Bakersfield and several other members of the Executive Committee. IM was deleted from the "preferred vendor" list of the British military for five years.

The King and Chancellor had managed to dispose of their International Metals shares before the news broke but certain members of Parliament were sore upset and called for an investigation. Nothing came of it.

Juliet's mother now has a terrier as a canine companion. The doggy's name is Tinker.

Holmes' beehives prospered mightily and he made a substantial income from selling honey, beeswax and high quality mead to London and Brighton vendors. He also made small gifts of the delicious substance to Sussex locals. Watson visited several times and the two spent their time reminiscing.

Ezrafel relaxed. *That is, until the next time!*

The Adventures of Sherlock Holmes and the Glamorous Ghost

Volume Four

Bye Bye Bees - A Novelette

The End

The Adventures of Sherlock Holmes and the Glamorous Ghost

Volume Four

The Weary War Horses

Gentle Reader! If you were to wander by The Green in East Dean, Sussex Downs in March 1904, you might come upon a most unusual sight. ***Sherlock Holmes on crutches sporting a cast on his left ankle.*** A bone break resulting from a fall in his rustic cottage severely reduced his mobility and significantly increased his irritation. Initially tended to by Doctor Ferguson, a local physician, he was now being advised by his long term colleague, Doctor John H. Watson. *(This of course, was before the X-Ray tube machine was in common practical use and the MRI was undreamed of.)*

"Well, old chap, I'm afraid Ferguson is right. Good news and bad news. The break was clean and you should fully recover. You'll be walking with a cane in six to eight weeks and unaided in several months. The bad news is you'll be stuck in a sedentary lifestyle in the interim. The baroness and your guardian angel will be pleased that you must take it easy. It's a good thing you have Marion to tend to your needs and her father to tend to your beehives. You have quite a growing business."

"You can safely tell the King if he sees fit to call on you again that you are hors de combat for the foreseeable future. Although you tell me his mother, the deceased Empress Victoria, put paid to his disturbing your retirement again. Good for her! I shall call back on you this weekend. Don't do anything to cause further injury. Stay off the cocaine. It will not help your situation. You'll be fine shortly without the use of drugs."

"Your sanguinity is most annoying, Watson. I am still the intense, high speed problem solving machine I always was. Only now with a broken part. I thought I would be able to retire serenely but now I find myself bored to my limits to say nothing of an aching ankle."

"Apiaries and bees, wonderful creatures though they are, have their limits. I need motivations and incentives. The criminal world provided that. Whoever thought I would miss murderers, thieves, traitors and other assorted villains. Or Scotland Yard, for that matter. That exercise in Sheffield with the misdirected armaments was like a drink to a thirsty horse. A war horse put out to pasture."

His one-time partner laughed. "Oh, Holmes. I'm sure a clever boots like yourself will find much to do in your disabled state, Read! Write another book about something besides bees. Or more of your endless monographs. Organize your files. Write letters."

> (*Little did he know. Arriving in the next morning's post.*)

G. Lestrade

The Jaunty Brigadier

Manchester, England

9 March 1903

Mr. Sherlock Holmes
The Green
East Dean, Sussex Downs
England

Dear Mr. Holmes:

It has been several years since we have been in direct contact. During that time we two weary war horses have both retired, much to the relief of the criminals who ply their trade in London and all of England. In your case, I suppose it is most of the civilised and uncivilised world. Many a story can be told of our mutual triumphs over evil. But time moves on.

From what I have heard, you have taken on the role of gentleman farmer and beekeeper. It sounds quite restful. May I make bold to interrupt your rest and ask you to come to my aid?

98

I am under suspicion of having committed murder!

In fact, that is the purpose of this letter. To invite you to come here to Manchester. I am in need of your outstanding assistance. I would like to invoke our old camaraderie and friendship.

You may be aware that my wife and I are now the co-owners of an inn– The Jaunty Brigadier – where we provide fine food, exceptional drink and outstanding hospitality while earning a substantial living – considerably better than the pay and pension of a Detective Chief Inspector of Scotland Yard. Yes, I did make Chief Inspector before I retired. But now, I am an innkeeper. If you are willing to venture north, we would be more than willing to welcome you to our establishment – free of charge.

I know it sounds ridiculous that a former Chief Inspector of Scotland Yard is being looked on as a possible killer but believe me, Mr. Holmes, it is not funny. My wife and I have (or had) a silent partner, Captain George Munro (RN retired) who made a moderate cash investment to help finance The Jaunty Brigadier. He was a former naval officer who left the service under somewhat dubious circumstances. Nevertheless, he was eager to invest and we negotiated an arrangement with him to assist us in financing the hostel. In return he lived here at the inn but was not active in the day-to-day management. We paid him interest and a modest return on his principal as well as providing him with room and board and the occasional tipple. It seemed to be a satisfactory arrangement for all parties.

Until recently! The Captain decided that his dividends were insufficient for his needs. (He was known to gamble rather heavily and lose quite frequently.) He approached my wife and me and demanded that we increase the terms of our agreement. It still had two years to run. He threatened legal action if we didn't. Needless to say, we were hardly pleased and refused. We thought that was the end of it. Instead he hired an aggressive London attorney, Simon Foster, Esq., to represent him. Events turned sour almost immediately.

Our first meeting with this attorney took place in a side room at the inn. The lawyer, the Captain, my wife and I were in attendance. I foolishly did not seek my own legal representation. A mistake! Munro and his solicitor alternated in bullying and menacing us. They threatened to force us into bankruptcy and shut down the inn. The meeting rapidly disintegrated into a shouting match. I'm not sure who was loudest – the Captain or his solicitor. I know Munro is a violent man and I take his warnings seriously. He threatened me with physical violence. "Beware, me lad. I'll not be trifled with. A bruise or two or a broken arm might change your mind."

A number of our patrons in the pub heard the noise and intimidating exclamations. One went to call the local constables. That ended the session with bellowed warnings, I'm sorry to say, by both sides. My wife was in hysterics. The Captain stomped off to his room shaking his fist at me as he went. The lawyer left and took up rooms at a neighboring hostel.

Next morning, our maid went up to Munro's bedchamber as usual to clean, tidy up and change his bed linen. She opened the door, looked at the battered body on the floor and screamed. My wife heard the commotion and went to see what was wrong. She joined in the screaming.

I was out of the hotel at the time ordering supplies from our local provisioner. When I returned, I observed a police waggon and an ambulance at the door and several members of the constabulary keeping back the curiosity seekers.

I nodded to the constables whom I know quite well. They spend time and some of their pay in our bar although they are not above accepting a few pints on the house – courtesy of an ex-lawman. I went up to the room. The Captain was, indeed, dead. The back of his head had been bashed in. A bloody fireplace poker rested on the floor. The doctor was examining the body. He acknowledged me. The officer in charge – Detective Inspector Amos Watts – looked my way uttering that famous 'copper comment' –"This is a bad business, Chief Inspector, and no mistake."

He was right. It is a bad business. Our argument of the previous afternoon was duly reported by several of the pub crawlers. Inspector Watts thought there was insufficient evidence to warrant my arrest but enough to put me high on a list of persons of interest. I immediately contacted my local solicitor who in turn called up a London specialist in crimes of violence – Mr. Charles Quimby, Esq.

As of the moment, the investigation is getting on with a coroner's inquest due later in the week.

As you might expect, the press has made a circus of the whole sordid affair. The local and London tabloids have had their exercise. "Former Scotland Yard Genius Suspected of Murder." "Is Lestrade of the Yard a Killer?" "A Retired Sea Captain is Dead. Is Lestrade Guilty?" There are more but I suspect you no longer take the lurid periodicals at your seaside retreat.

The Captain was hardly popular with the locals and few tears are being shed at his demise especially among the many to whom he owed money and the women he brazenly pursued.

Needless to say, business at the Jaunty Brigadier has fallen off dramatically. Curiosity seekers fill the bar but few people want to stay at a hotel owned by an innkeeper who some believe may do them in while they sleep.

So, may I call on you to turn your bees over to a local farmhand and join me here in Manchester at my expense? I am in great need of your supremely perceptive mind. Being under police suspicion, I am somewhat hobbled to act on my own. Although, as you know, I have never been reluctant to do battle, there is only so much investigation I can legitimately do by myself. Thus far I have had little support from my former colleagues at the Yard. Disappointing! Hoping to hear favorably from you and to welcome your assistance in the immediate future.

I remain,

(Signature)

G. Lestrade, Chief Inspector, Scotland Yard (retired)

G. Lestrade
The Jaunty Brigadier
Manchester, England

15March,1904

Mr. Sherlock Holmes
The Green
East Dean, Sussex Downs
England

Dear Mr. Holmes:

A broken ankle! You have my sympathy.
Fortunately, they no longer shoot us wounded and
weary war horses – at least not yet. However, the
authorities may be of a mind to hang me. I fully
understand why you are unable to travel, but I am
grateful for your willingness to provide your
advice via the post.

I have taken the initiative in my own defense
and am amassing evidence to solve this grim
situation. I have asked both Inspector Watts of the
Manchester police and my crime solicitor, Mr.
Charles Quimby, Esq., to contact you. You should
hear from them shortly. You may also hear from
Scotland Yard.

The coroner's inquest took place yesterday.
The medical examiner's finding was unnatural
death caused by an attack with a blunt instrument.

Time of death: Between midnight and 4 a.m. The police determined that a fireplace poker was the weapon used. Analysis proved the blood on the poker was the Captain's. No useful fingerprints besides the victim's and the maids' were found.

Several of the pub crawlers testified to the sounds of our argument in the side room earlier in the afternoon. I was called to give evidence as to the nature and participants in the confrontation. I described the character and circumstances of the disagreement in which Munro and his lawyer made their demands. My wife was not called. The Captain's lawyer, Mr. Simon Foster, was not available at the inquest. He is based in London and ignored or didn't receive the summons to testify.

All told, the inquest was a long drawn out affair with a number of interventions from the jury and the attending public accusing each other. It was quite a circus. Matthew Cashman, a local farrier, had previously attacked Munro in a drunken rage and was just released from detention. He said he was glad the "bastard" was dead.

Several women spoke of unwanted predation on the Captain's part. Their husbands were called to testify. Their statements were vociferous and hardly charitable. Our barmaid, Rose Latham, told of Munro's offer of marriage and then his breach of promise. She had not yet entered a legal suit but had planned to. Her brother, Edmund, was outraged and leading the charge on that front. That threat may have motivated the Captain to seek further income from us to pay her off and then move elsewhere.

Long story short, the coroner left the case open with a finding of murder by person or persons unknown and instructions to the police to pursue the killer or killers with all due dispatch. I am considered a person of interest but was not taken into custody since there is no reasonable evidence that I entered his room or attacked him. I was serving in the pub or with my wife all evening and in bed at night.

As I mentioned, I have informally joined the police in my own defence. We are actively searching for the killer's or killers' identity. There are many to choose from. The Captain was not a popular character with the alehouse regulars or many of the citizens of Manchester. He was a surly, opinionated, argumentative boor and in debt to practically everyone. He had a hair trigger temper. He was a large, burly character, well-schooled in the art of fisticuffs. Several times he was involved in gambling altercations about cheating that resulted in blows. He often ended up before the magistrate.

In the Navy, he had advanced from a common seaman to his command position in record time. He saw action in several major wartime skirmishes, rising through the ranks and authority. One would have expected him to live in a substantial home rather than an inn but his wagering and other habits put paid to that. He owed substantial sums to a London gambling syndicate headed up by the infamous Gentleman George Carter. You may remember him from your Baker Street days. George doesn't tolerate non-payment.

Munro was also in debt to a group of locals. Ranging from his personal gambling associates to shopkeepers like Lucas O'Neill, a wine merchant and Isaac Meyrowitz, a jeweler and goldsmith. They now refuse his custom. The Captain enjoyed luxuries and also used them in pursuit of the gentle sex. Frankly, I am happy he's gone.

He never married but if our barmaid is any indication he did dally frequently and substantially. I'm not sure who, if anyone, will be burdened by his debts and lay claim to his investment in the Jaunty Brigadier. My local solicitor will have that as one of his assignments. Speaking of solicitors, the police are also searching for the Captain's attorney - Simon Foster. As I mentioned, he failed to appear at the inquest and a citation for contempt has been issued. I have finally heard from the Yard. They have assigned a junior investigator to assist Inspector Watts of the Manchester CID. How generous!

G. Lestrade,

(Signature)

Chief Inspector, Scotland Yard (retired)

*****

On receipt of this second letter, Holmes decided he needed his own neutral investigator on the ground to pursue some of the evidence. Scotland Yard seemed reluctant to invest much time or effort in the inquiry. So much for support of their alumni. Because he was a 'person of interest' Lestrade himself was limited in how far he could become involved. Any evidence he uncovered would be subject to suspicions of bias.

Holmes resolved to contact Inspector Amos Watts, Criminal Investigation Department of the Manchester Metropolitan Police. But he also wanted someone else not affiliated with the police. Watson would have filled the bill nicely but he was heavily committed to his growing medical practice and had limited time.

An interesting idea occurred to him. The Baroness and Pookie. They had certainly assisted in unraveling a number of cases and were usually more than eager to play sleuths. He would contact Heaven's Director Raymond and see what he could do to get the Committee to agree to Lady Juliet's return to Earth. She liked Lestrade. Perhaps he was the only member of the Yard she and her dog were partial to. She regarded Tobias Gregson as something of a dolt and absolutely detested Athelney Jones. She was not familiar with Inspectors Hopkins or Bradstreet, the only others besides Lestrade that Holmes respected.

He used his special channel to Raymond, a process they had set up early in their relationship. A deep baritone responded. "Mr. Holmes. God's blessings upon you. I have heard you have a broken ankle. We will pray for your swift and total recovery. How are you?"

"In need of a favor, Mr. Raymond. I am engaged in a case involving a former associate, Chief Inspector Lestrade."

"I know of him. Is he still active? I thought, like you, he had retired."

"He is not on the case. He is the case. He has been accused of murder and I have agreed to bring about his exoneration. Unfortunately, I am currently disabled and my associate, Dr. Watson is not available to assist me. "

"I think I know what you want. The services of Lady Juliet and Pookie."

"Spot on! As Usual."

"I think, under the circumstances, we can accommodate you if the Baroness and her canine sidekick are available and willing. I'll have to persuade the Committee to allow them to go back to Earth yet again but that shouldn't be too difficult. I'll be back to you shortly. Take care of yourself. I'll give your guardian angel Ezrafel special instructions to keep you from further harm, if he can. It took a lot of effort to get you retired in the first place. It seems we have not been completely successful."

"An old war horse senses battle."

"And may get killed in the process. I'll be happy to welcome you to Paradise at some point but not yet. I'll contact the Baroness.

*****

Juliet, Empress Sisi, Pookie and the Lipizzaners were rehearsing a new routine for an upcoming Saintly Spectacular. Her mother, Lucinda, with Tinker, her newly adopted dog, were watching in sheer delight as the horses maneuvered and pranced in close synchronization. Pookie was riding on Der Alte's back and performing acrobatic stunts as they circled the pasture. Lucinda laughed, clapped her hands but then looked up. Standing in front of her was an individual who had not been there a moment ago. In the form of a middle-aged male, tall, dressed in morning *(mourning?)* clothes, clean shaven, not a hair out of place, dark eyes, color undetermined. But, he seemed to be floating inches above the ground. Mr. Raymond, high ranking angel and director of the celestial expanses.

"God's blessings on you, Mrs. Armstrong. Those horses are wonderful, are they not? I am here to speak with your daughter and her dog. But I see they are busy."

Luci smiled. "Oh, I'm sure she can be available for you, Mr. Raymond." She shouted, "Juliet, dear. You have a visitor."

The Baroness turned and waved at the Director. She signaled to Empress Sisi to take over and flitted over to the ornate grandstand on which a small audience was gathered. "Thanks Mum! Hello Raymond, here for a preview performance of our new Spectacular ?"

"No, unfortunately. I have some serious business to conduct with you."

"Oh, oh, what did we do this time?"

"It's what you are being called upon to do. Were you aware that Sherlock Holmes is laid up with a broken ankle?"

"No. I haven't communicated with him in a while and I haven't seen Ezrafel either. Is it very serious."

111

"He'll recover but for the moment he is out of action. But nonetheless he is working on a case."

The penny dropped. "And he needs assistance! Why am I not surprised? What happened to Dr. Watson?"

"Demands of his practice. He cannot get away to travel to Manchester and London."

"But Pookie and I can. What's in Manchester?"

"Chief Inspector Lestrade, retired. He's running an inn. He's accused of murder."

"Lestrade? What nonsense! I see why Holmes is involved. What does he want?"

"He needs you to do some investigating on his behalf."

"Right down Pookie's and my alley or street or lane. Wait, what about the Committee?"

"I will speak with them. I wanted to get your agreement first. No point in using credits with them if you're not willing to go."

"Of course we're willing, aren't we Pookie? Sisi can manage the horses. Oh, we'll have to be both corporeal and transcendental if we're going to do interviews and surreptitiously gather evidence."

The Director shrugged. "I know. I worry about you two in the flesh."

"Oh, don't be such a fuddy duddy, Raymond. We'll behave. After all, we're saints aren't we? Let us know when we're free to go and then warn Holmes that we're coming."

*****

Marion had gone home after leaving a dinner in the stove and Holmes had settled in with a pipe and a tot of mead. He was re-reading the two letters he had received from Lestrade. It seemed this Captain Munro was quite a reprobate. Any number of people might have been pushed beyond their limits. Unfortunately, the only way he was going to acquit Lestrade was to find the true killer. And here he was, stuck with a broken ankle in his Sussex cottage when he should be prowling the streets and lanes of Manchester.

A telepathic growl and whine. Shimmering in front of him was a sassy white dog and a sassy scarlet arrayed Baroness. *"Hello, Holmes. We've been here for a while. I thought your maid would never leave. I doubt she understands about ghosts. Well, Pookie and I are reporting for duty. You poor soul! How did you manage to break your ankle? You were supposed to retire to avoid doing yourself any harm. We thought your adventure with the gun makers would be your last but here you are trying to get Lestrade out of the soup. If it wasn't a sin, I would despair."*

"Thank you, Baroness and you too, Miss Dog. I had a brief set-to with a loose carpet. The rug won.

Watson and the local sawbones both think I'll be more mobile in a few weeks and completely back in shape in a couple of months. Meanwhile, Chief Inspector Lestrade is under suspicion for murder. The evidence is not strong enough to indict him but his business and his reputation is suffering. Do you and Pookie feel up to snooping and prying? Can you become physical? I think you're going to have to pursue this in both your states."

In response, the two of them took on solid bodily form. "Ta Da!" The Bichon did one of her back flips and landed firmly and noisily on her extended paws. "Does that answer your question?"

Holmes handed her the two letters from Lestrade. "Read these and tell me what you think."

Juliet took the letters and scanned them. Then she re-read both. " This Captain was quite a character. No wonder someone killed him. Fine, what do you want me to do? And by the way, who am I?"

"I'd like you to start with the women in question. Begin with Rose Latham, the jilted barmaid with the aggressive brother. I believe she'll respond to another female more readily. Interview Lestrade's wife and any other women they may refer you to. As to who you are, you are a practicing enquiry agent, one of the few women in the profession. Come up with a name that you're comfortable with. You'll also have to trade in your scarlet gown for something that says, 'Detective.'

Perhaps a tweed suit. Pookie will be a good touch. Everybody trusts a woman with a clever dog."

"I hate tweed but oh, well. Needs must! What about Lestrade and the local police?"

"You are an associate whom I have employed from time to time. Lestrade knows I'm laid up and I believe he informed Inspector Amos Watts of the Manchester CID of the situation. Neither of them knows you will be acting for me. I'll send them wires and then leave the actual introductions up to you. Ever been to Manchester?"

"Once while I was on tour with my Jolly Juliet show. Big city, bit of a cultural backwater but getting better. I gather Lestrade's Inn - what is it? The Jaunty Brigadier is rather popular or was before this incident."

"Yes, but as long as this suspicion hangs over him, his business will hurt. That's one more reason we have to find the killer. You and your dog follow your capable noses." Pookie barked and wagged her tail furiously.

"Well, you know how much I enjoy playing parts. Let me see! Rose LaTour won't work. The French accent won't play. How about Miss Phoebe Farnum, ace detective? We'll leave Pookie as Pookie, She gets confused with aliases."

"Fine. I will tell them Miss Farnum is on her way to Manchester. I assume you know how to get there."

"Of course, we flit. See you soon."

They both discorporated and left the house. Pookie took time to chase a squirrel. "Come on girl. Time for some detecting." The dog reluctantly joined her.

*****

First stop, The Jaunty Brigadier. Clad in a tweed ensemble, complete with steel rimmed spectacles and a fashionable toque set upon her shortened dark hair, Miss Phoebe Farnum and her curly white dog entered the snuggery of the pub and took a seat near the bow window that looked out on the busy street. No one else was there at the period after luncheon and before late afternoon brought on the serious drinkers. The barmaid, Rose Latham, had just come on duty and approached the tall visitor and her dog. Animals, mostly dogs and cats were not unusual in pubs. "What may I get yer, dear?"

"A pot of tea and some biscuits which Pookie and I will share. Perhaps a bowl of water for her as well. Is the proprietor about? Would you tell him Miss Farnum would like to speak with him."

This got a raised eyebrow out of the barmaid and she said, "I'll see if he's available. Miss Farthing, did you say?"

116

"Farnum, Miss Phoebe Farnum from London." Another raised eyebrow and off she went to the kitchen stopping first at the office where Lestrade and his wife were going over the previous day's takings and discussing the current lodgers. The Inn was half empty. Rose looked in and addressed Lestrade. "There's a rather posh bird from London who'd like to speak with you. A Miss Barnum. She's in the snug."

Not a name the inspector recognized. And then it dawned. Rose was terrible at getting names straight. Was this the associate Holmes had wired him about? He'd go see this Miss Barnum or Farnum, as he suspected.

The lady was sitting with a small but lively dog waiting for their tea, biscuits and water. Actually. Pookie would have preferred nectar but she doubted this place would have any. She hoped the Baroness had packed some Heavenly Chewies in her sizeable reticule. She looked up as a slight individual with a rodent-like face entered the room. Before he could say anything, Lady Juliet extended her gloved hand. "Chief Inspector Lestrade. I am Miss Phoebe Farnum. I believe Sherlock Holmes informed you I was coming."

"Yes, Miss Farnum. Welcome to the Jaunty Brigadier. I must confess I was a bit taken aback when Holmes told me he was sending a woman associate to help investigate this murder."

117

"Is that a typical male reaction Inspector?"

"No! Holmes has always been arms-length with women with perhaps one exception. It struck me as unusual on his part to take a woman on as a partner."

"Let me assure you that Sherlock Holmes and I have a highly cooperative and mutually respectful relationship. We have worked on many cases together. We have refrained from letting Scotland Yard know too much about me. I am familiar with some of your former colleagues. Gregson and that idiot Athelney Jones. Pardon my frankness but I wonder how he keeps his job."

Lestrade laughed. "We all have from time to time."

"I have seen copies of your letters to Holmes so I am somewhat familiar with the situation. My job is to interview some of the principals and retrace the evidence. Unfortunately, as you well know, there are far too many suspects. All with motives, some with means and a few with opportunity. I will attempt to narrow that population down and hopefully produce our villain. For no other reason than they are currently here at your establishment, I'd like to start my interviews with three women. Your barmaid, Rose Latham, your wife and the house maid who discovered the body. After that, I have an appointment to introduce myself to Inspector Watts of the Manchester CID. I understand this is his case. Then I'll go on to meet the local men you and the Inspector have identified as possible culprits. There are also several in London. Busy, busy! Oh, I am remiss. Let me introduce you to my canine companion, Pookie. She may look like a frivolous little thing but I assure you, she is a skilled detective in her own right. Do you have any questions?

Lestrade was amazed at this feminine whirlwind who was definitely all business. He shook his head.

"No, well let's get started. May I speak to Rose before the bar gets busy. Oh here she is with our tea, biscuits and water."

Lestrade introduced Phoebe Farnum and explained what she was about. Somewhat reluctantly the barmaid agreed to speak with the detective, little realizing she was talking to a ghost who had been murdered. She acknowledged her affair with Munro and his breach of promise. She was ready along with her brother to pursue legal recourse but now, of course, with his death, that was pointless. And no, neither she nor her brother killed the Captain although she applauded whoever did. She had no idea who did the swine in.

Juliet thanked her and asked if she could speak to Lestrade's wife. Dubious at first, she finally agreed to talk with Miss Farnum. She repeated the story of the argument with the Captain over his demands for more income from his investment. She described Simon

Foster, Munro's so-called lawyer. She didn't trust him or even believe he was a solicitor. Funny how he just disappeared at the time of Munro's death. But why would he kill him?

The Baroness' last interview of the day was the house maid. She had discovered the body, went hysterical and promptly quit. It took some careful persuasion by the Lestrades to get her to return. She just remembered that the window to the Captain's room was open and a breeze was blowing papers and other articles around. She didn't stay in the room long enough to get a good look at the body and didn't want to. Like everyone else, she didn't much like Munro but couldn't think of who might have killed him. It could have been anyone.

Phoebe finished her tea and biscuits which she shared with Pookie and got ready to leave for her appointment with Inspector Watts. She promised Lestrade she would return next day and offered to pay for their refreshments. Lestrade thanked her and said the tea was on the house. She said she would be in contact with Holmes and keep him apprised of her progress *(if any.)* Little did Lestrade know she and Pookie would flit down to Sussex for the evening and confer with the wounded consulting detective directly. On to the Manchester CID.

The Baroness introduced herself and Pookie to Inspector Watts. The following letter to Holmes outlines their conversation.

*****

Inspector Amos Watts
Criminal Investigation Department
Metropolitan Police
Manchester, England

16 March, 1904
Mr. Sherlock Holmes
The Green
East Dean, Sussex Downs
England

Dear Mr. Holmes:

I am writing to you on behalf of the Criminal Investigation Department of the Manchester Metropolitan Police and at the request of former Scotland Yard Chief Inspector Lestrade. I am sorry to hear of your accident. I was anticipating meeting you in person and watching you in action. However, your lady associate and her dog seem to be quite a skilled and unusual combination. You and I will have to rely on the post and my conversations with Miss Farnum. I am giving her a copy of this letter.

I am the lead detective charged with investigating the murder of Captain George Munro (RN ret.) at the Jaunty Brigadier Inn. Your former colleague, Chief Inspector Lestrade has been designated a person of interest in the case. He is well known to us and it is difficult for us to believe he may be guilty of the Captain's death. Nevertheless, we must proceed wherever the evidence leads us.

Chief Inspector Lestrade tells us that he has reported all he knows of the circumstances of the Captain's demise to you and your surrogate. He has requested that I contact you and involve you in our inquiries. To the degree my superiors will permit it, I'm happy to do so. Your reputation is well known to all of us here at CID and any assistance you can lend in solving this crime will be much appreciated. Unlike some of our colleagues, we harbor no distrust or resentment of a famous consulting detectives such as yourself or your associate. What follows may be a repetition of what you and Miss Farnum already know.

The coroner and his jury found that in the case of Captain Munro, murder had been committed by person or persons unknown. It is my responsibility to identify and arrest that individual or individuals. It will not be easy.

As you've been told, the Captain was a difficult person. He had a reputation for engaging in physical dustups with any number of local characters. Constables from the Manchester Met have been called in several times in the past year to break up fights in which he was involved.

He was known for running up debts and refusing to pay. Shopkeepers would no longer extend him credit. Several of them engaged a collection agency run by a pair of rough characters, Dan and Elmo Pargeter. Their motto is "We collect and correct." A few of our citizens have had the experience of the Pargeter's 'correction' methods. We have had the brothers up for assault on quite a few occasions.

Munro was unmarried but quite an active womanizer. Although we have no concrete proof, Inspector Lestrade's wife is said to have been one of his targets. The Inspector and his wife were estranged for quite a while but reunited after they opened the Jaunty Brigadier Inn. She too is a person of interest but low on our list of suspects.

As I said, the Captain was hardly popular. He made enemies easily and we have a number of possible candidates who would be motivated to do him in. However, anyone actually taking him on usually regretted it. Several residents have tried. Matthew Cashman, a local farrier, has permanent scars from his encounter. He found the Captain together with his wife and attempted to thrash them both. He landed in hospital for his trouble. He has just emerged from gaol where he was being held in custody for assault on his wife and the Captain. He may have gone back for a second try.

Munro was also suspected of theft. A local pawn shop was broken into recently and a substantial amount of cash taken. The security guard was overwhelmed and claims the villain closely resembled Munro. The pawnbroker, Mr. Clive Milton had been badgering us to arrest him and recover his money. Seven hundred pounds! Unfortunately, we had insufficient evidence to establish proof of the Captain's guilt.

As to the murder itself, we have determined that the poker found in his room was the bludgeon used to do him in. It was part of his fireplace equipment. The doctor believes the blood on the weapon was the Captain's. No usable fingerprints. I find it peculiar that the poker in its bloody condition was left behind by the killer. The window to Munro's room was open. The maid swears he usually keeps it closed at night. His room was unsettled but not tossed or disrupted. His wallet and a small amount of cash were untouched. He had a modest collection of medals from his war exploits and a few pieces of personal jewelry – all undisturbed. Robbery does not seem to have been a motive.

We strongly suspect he knew his attacker. Strangely, no one in the inn reported hearing any unusual noises or raised voices during the period in question. The bar was closed and the front office shut. The upstairs hall was empty. The door to his room was unforced. He probably admitted his assailant. There was no sign of a prolonged struggle or wreckage. He was struck forcibly several times.

We believe his assailant was a man but a suitably enraged woman might have had sufficient strength to strike him down. Several local women come to mind including Rose Latham, the barmaid at the Jaunty Brigadier. I understand the Captain promised her marriage and then reneged. Several witnesses reported that she loudly berated him that night in the barroom for being a treacherous swine and a liar. She threatened him with breach of promise and said he would have to deal with her brother. Half drunk, he shouted back that he would soon be gone and she would get "nary a penny" from him.

We have no witnesses to the actual killing and no one remembers seeing any strangers in the upstairs rooms or corridors during the hours of midnight and 4 a.m. when the medical examiner believes the event took place. You may conclude that we have no suspects or more likely, far too many suspects.

I am told Chief Inspector Lestrade informed you of the medical examiner's and coroner's statements and opinions. The coroner's jury was unanimous in deciding to leave the case open with a finding of murder by person or persons unknown. It is now CID's burden to track the culprit down. I appreciate any help you and Miss Farnum and her dog may supply.

We and Scotland Yard have also sent out a warrant for the Captain's London-based attorney - Simon Foster. He failed to appear at the inquest and a citation for contempt has been issued. Chief Inspector Lestrade and I both have our suspicions about Captain Munro's lawyer, if he is a lawyer at all. His disappearance and failure to appear at the inquest raises our hackles. He is certainly aggressive enough. We believe he is leading a double life and may even be tied to London racketeers.

However, he is not alone on our suspect list. There are several more irate husbands whose wives have been approached by the captain and he was in debt to a number of local tradesmen as well as known gamblers like Bertie Fisher and Ernie Wilder, both of whom are on our list of recurring bad 'uns. In spite of their sordid reputation, they insist they have no knowledge of what happened to Munro. We are looking into it further.

Several additional pieces of information have since crossed my desk. A more thorough search of the Captain's room uncovered an unsigned, partially burnt note in the fireplace. The fragment read, "Pay up now." We are aware that the Captain was deeply in debt to a gambling syndicate based in London with branches around the country including Liverpool, Sheffield and Manchester. He owed them thousands. But he also had debts galore here in Manchester.

We also found an envelope under a loose floor board beneath his bed *(The carpenters of Manchester have much to answer for.)* In it was a stack of notes amounting to over seven hundred pounds. Was it the pawnbroker's? An interesting coincidence?

On the morning of his death, Munro had a train reservation to Liverpool. He was also booked on White Star Line's RMS Celtic to New York. We're sure he wanted to evade the syndicate as well as any number of other parties seeking his skin. Rose Latham and her breach of promise suit comes to mind. Obviously, if he could afford trans-Atlantic passage, he was not as bankrupt as he pretended to be. We do believe he got the cash from the pawnshop robbery but lack proof. Clive Milton is harassing us to recover his money.

The Manchester, Sheffield, Liverpool and London press have all been baying at our heels. They seem to take great pleasure in the prospect of a former Chief Inspector of the Yard being guilty of murder. "A policeman's lot is not a happy one."

I hope the information I have supplied will provide you with some insights into this frustrating crime. Your advice will be most welcome. I look forward to hearing from you.

Your servant,

(Signature)

Inspector Amos Watts

G. Lestrade
The Jaunty Brigadier
Manchester, England

17 March 1904

Mr. Sherlock Holmes
The Green
East Dean, Sussex Downs
England

Dear Mr. Holmes,

Happy St. Patrick's Day! Not celebrated widely here in the UK but nevertheless.

I hope your broken ankle is well on its way to healing. I assume you are listening to Doctor Watson's advice and staying off it.

In addition to your associate, Miss Farnum, I have had several conversations with Inspector Amos Watts of the Manchester CID. I understand he has been in communication with you. A Scotland Yard investigator has also joined the case and has uncovered several useful facts which I will outline in just a moment.

My criminal case solicitor, Mr. Charles Quimby, Esq., has also been in contact with me. He doesn't know Simon Foster and cannot identify him as a member of the bar. He confidently states there is insufficient evidence to bring me before the Bench but that still leaves us with the question: Who did the Captain in?

I am happy to report that the Manchester CID now agrees with me that my wife is above suspicion. The fact that Captain Munro was a well-known womaniser and that my wife and I had once been estranged gave the local gossip mills a major source of grist to create scandal. Other than hotel business activities, she has had nothing to do with Munro and actually despises him. She has also berated him for his attempts to seduce one of our domestics and deceiving our barmaid Rose into believing they would wed.

Rose and her brother are furious that they will not be able to bring her breach of promise suit. She is a formidable woman and he is a vengeful individual. I am told this is not the first time she has sued someone for breach of promise. I despair of her wedding prospects.

Some of the locals to whom the Captain owed money have banded together in an attempt to garnish his estate, such as it is. I don't think he left a will and as his business partner in the Jaunty Brigadier, I am being subjected to their attempts to seek restitution. I am told by my local attorney that their suits are without merit, but it is another example of Munro's troublesome existence. I am reluctant to admit it, even to you, but I am glad he is gone. Unfortunately he has left a mare's nest behind him.

My Scotland Yard investigator agrees with Mr. Quimby and your associate. . He suspects the Captain's "attorney" – Simon Foster – is not who he claims to be. There is no record at the bar of a solicitor with that name. Who is he? The London Met and Manchester CID has been searching for him to charge him with contempt of judicial process for failure to appear at the Munro inquest. Several customers of the Jaunty Brigadier described him as a party to the shouting match at the Inn involving him, myself, my wife and the Captain.

The Yard has also unearthed and recorded a long history of violence on the part of Gentleman George Carter and his syndicate. His tentacles extend from London to most of the major cities in Britain. I'm sure you will remember that we have both had dealings with him and his minions in the past.

Inspector Watts has been most helpful in trying to untangle the knots in this affair and I am grateful for his trust and assistance. I am also most appreciative of your willingness to become involved in spite of your injury. Thank you once again for Miss Farnum. She has been extremely helpful.

I hope, notwithstanding your disability, you and Miss Farnum will be able to cast a bright light on this situation and help bring it to resolution.

Give my best to Doctor Watson when next you see him and get well soon.

I remain,

(Signature)

G. Lestrade, Chief Inspector, Scotland Yard (retired)

*****

"Pookie and I found him." With that pronouncement, Juliet Armstrong, Baroness Crestwell, aka Phoebe Farnum, appeared in Holmes cottage. "We flitted to London, located and infiltrated Gentleman George's gambling den. We watched as Simon Foster, whose real name is Sebastian Flood, tried to explain why and how he killed Captain Munro. George was not happy. Not only would he not get his money from the Captain but he and his syndicate would attract law enforcement's further attention. Flood realized his days were probably numbered and fled the premises before George could wreak vengeance.

He holed up in a flat in Croydon. I re-established myself as Miss Phoebe Farnum, Private Detective and passed on the information to Scotland Yard. I didn't tell them how we gained our knowledge."

"They now have Flood in custody and he is singing. Better the rozzers than George's hitmen. He admits to killing Munro. He swears it was self defence. I leave that to you and the police. Pookie and I have an appointment with Empress Sisi and the Lipizzaners. See you again, Holmes. Give my best to Lestrade."

Mr. Sherlock Holmes
The Green
East Dean, Sussex Downs
England

19 March 1904

To:

Chief Inspector G. Lestrade (ret.)
The Jaunty Brigadier
Manchester, South Yorkshire, England

Inspector Amos Watts
Criminal Investigation Department, Metropolitan Police
Manchester, England

Gentlemen:

133

Thank you for your concern for my damaged ankle. It is improving steadily. I shall soon be off my crutches. As you suggest, Lestrade, it is a sign of our advanced civilization (and our advanced age) that they no longer shoot wounded war horses such as ourselves and I am pleased to hear that you are no longer in danger of being hanged.

Of course, the true resolution to this situation was to discover Captain Munro's murderer and turn the villain over to the judicial process. We invoked your own skills, the skills of Miss Farnum and her dog, the good offices of Scotland Yard and Manchester CID in achieving that end.

As always, there are some fundamental questions that must be raised in dealing with murder or assault.

Let's take the questions one by one.

Was this victim the intended target? It certainly seems likely. Who else?

Why? Captain Munro, through cheating, debts, raw aggression, theft and sexual predation had managed to accumulate a small army of enemies or disgruntled individuals who would be happy to see the last of him even though he owed them significant sums of money or legal restitution.

Why now? From the evidence uncovered by Manchester CID it seemed likely that Munro was about to do a bunk, as they say, and head to America, leaving debts unpaid. probable thefts unresolved and lawsuits unsettled. He needed to be stopped.

Why this method? I believe the use of the poker may have been in self-defense by the individual accosting Munro. When he or she attempted to force the Captain to stay in Manchester and face the music, Munro once again attacked as was his wont. He was struck several times by his prospective victim.

Who had motive, opportunity and means? Motive: Anyone seeking to get redress from the Captain and prevent his disappearance. Opportunity: Late at night in his room with no witnesses. Means: The poker conveniently available to subdue the Captain

Who did it? Certainly not Inspector Lestrade who would have been relieved to have Munro disappear to the New World and certainly not his wife who shared his sentiments. Could it be Clive Milton, the pawnbroker; Rose Latham, the barmaid or her brother; or the farrier, Matthew Cashman? What about local gamblers Bertie Fisher or Ernie Wilder? And of course, the fraternal owners of the collection agency, Dan and Elmo Pargeter. Possible but not all that probable. Each of them had motive but the timing is questionable.. Most of them despaired of recovering anything from him. One major possibility remains. Gentleman George Carter was a different matter. He wanted action and turned to his lackey, Simon Foster.

Now, let me share a few facts we have jointly uncovered: As reported by the police, the Captain was deeply in debt to Gentleman George's gambling syndicate based in London with branches around the country including Liverpool, Sheffield and Manchester. Through an informer, they determined Simon Foster aka Sebastian Flood is an enforcer for that organization. Posing as the Captain's lawyer, Flood attempted to browbeat the Lestrades into increasing their dividends and payments to the victim. It didn't work!

Flood has since been tracked down and captured hiding away in Croydon. He had been charged with ignoring the coroner's summons. Now they have also added a murder charge which you, Inspector Watts and Miss Farnum have aided in bringing forward.

After he was taken into custody, Flood finally confessed to hearing the Captain drunkenly bragging about his plan to abscond to the New World and decided to prevent his disappearance. He had been staying in a nearby hostel hoping to get Munro to pay up. He approached the Captain on the night of his death and tried once more to get money out of him. He had heard of the pawn shop theft, suspected that's where the Captain's passage fees had come from and threatened Munro to reclaim the money owed Gentleman George.

This led to a major argument and fisticuffs resulting in the sudden, emotional and unplanned violence in which Munro was killed. Flood claims self-defence. Perhaps or perhaps not. The courts will make that determination. The syndicate would gain no advantage from Munro's death. But Flood didn't think that through. He reacted to the Captain's attack. He's not the brightest star in the sky.

The poker was a weapon of opportunity. Flood says on hearing someone coming down the corridor, he dropped it and escaped through the window. A mistake on his part but no useful fingerprints were found on the bludgeon.

Flood's confession has produced evidence tying the gambling syndicate to repeated acts of violence and extortion, carried out by him and other enforcers. Several new investigations have been launched by Scotland Yard and local police. My former associate, Chief Inspector Lestrade is no longer a person of interest in the death of Captain Munro and has been exonerated of all potential charges. I hope this will be given full coverage by the press.

It has been a pleasure to assist my old friend as well as the Manchester police in this endeavor. Miss Farnum accepted my thanks. She has been called away on another assignment. Lestrade, I hope to be able to discard my crutches in short order and accept your kind invitation to join the good cheer at the Jaunty Brigadier – two "retired" war horses celebrating yet another successful campaign.

Sincerely,

Sherlock Holmes

The Adventures of Sherlock Holmes and the Glamorous Ghost

Volume Four

The Weary War Horses

The End

The Adventures of Sherlock Holmes and the Glamorous Ghost

Volume Four

Horseplay

Sherlock Holmes, recovered from his broken ankle, was settled in his retirement retreat on South Downs Way in the tiny village of East Dean in Sussex. He had just returned from a tour of his beehives and was about to indulge in a bracing cup of tea and a honey covered scone provided by his part time domestic, Marion. She lives on a nearby farm with her parents and brother and tends to Holmes' household needs several times a week.

"Excuse me, Mr. Holmes. This came with the morning post while you were tending to your bees. It's quite peculiar."

She extended a glowing white envelope in his direction. On the front was a name written in a feminine hand in scarlet ink. 'Sherlock Holmes,' no address, no stamp. On the back flap, in sparkling gold, 'Via Angelic Post.' Holmes smiled -The Baroness. "It's all right, Marion. I know who it's from. An acquaintance of mine."

The girl raised her eyebrows but said nothing further. She was still getting used to his oddities. Lovely man but strange. Her Dad said he was a retired consulting detective, whatever that was. He didn't seem retired to her. She returned to the cottage kitchen and set about preparing lunch. She wasn't sure whether he'd eat it or not. He insisted her cooking was excellent but his appetite was unruly. As she said, 'strange.'

Holmes took up his jackknife and sliced the envelope flap. He pulled out several sheets of pure white paper covered in scarlet ink. A signature – Juliet Armstrong, Baroness Crestwell - and a pawprint, Pookie - her extraordinary Bichon Frisé.

He read: "Hello Holmes. Glad to hear you're off the crutches and no longer wearing a cast. You can probably get rid of the cane shortly but you may want to keep it as a sign of upper class stylishness. I'm happy we were able to get Chief Inspector Lestrade out of the soup. I don't know who was worse. That horrible Captain Munro or the toady who killed him. I hope the Jaunty Brigadier is doing door busting business."

"Pookie, the Lipis, Empress Sisi and I have created a whole new Equine Review for our next Saintly Spectacular. That's why I'm writing to you. We have a mystery on our hands. While we were rehearsing with the Lipizzaners, they suddenly became quite excited. Standing in their midst was a white horse of similar size, splendor and girth as Der Alte. But he had large beautiful wings. When Der Alte performed his famous leap, this horse spread his feathered pennons, rose and flew above the stables, circled my mansion and returned to the group. Sisi and I were slack jawed. The Lipizzaners gathered around him, curious but welcoming. Der Alte nickered and butted heads with him in a friendly fashion. Was this the mythical stallion Pegasus?"

"We summoned Director Raymond, Mr. Sherman and the heavenly zoologists but they are unable to offer any help. They don't know who he is or where he came from. The consensus is that he flew in over the Pearly Gates, saw the stallions and decided to join them. But where did he come from? Mythology has it that Pegasus existed with the Greek gods on Mt. Olympus. While there are monuments and shrines spread across the numerous peaks that make up the Olympian Range, there are no signs that Zeus and his eleven companions ever really lived there or much less existed at all. Pegasus was supposed to be keeper of Zeus' thunderbolts. Now here is a horse we assume is he with immense wings but no flashes of lightning. Is he dead? Is this his spirit? We've asked many of the angels. They have wings but they can't explain who this animal is. No relative of theirs. Perhaps he's related to the birds or the dinosaurs. I'm sure the Almighty knows but they are not sharing and the horse isn't telling. "

"Can you shed any light on this? You have made studies of some esoteric subjects. Was Greek mythology one of them?"

Holmes smiled. An interesting problem *(at least three pipes)* A visit to the British Museum is called for. Professor William Hobson, historian and curator of early Graeco Roman artifacts was an old friend. Holmes had worked with him on the disappearance over time of several valuable pieces from the Museum's massive collection. He wired the professor and asked for an appointment. Meanwhile, a visit to a classical studies bookstore in Brighton was next on the agenda. He sent a note back to the baroness via Angelic Post. " Re: Pegasus? You have piqued my interest. I am dealing with it. Back to you soon. SH."

Sisi went to the stables and prepared a stall for the winged creature. She spoke to him. "Pegasus? Is that your name?"

The horse snorted and flashed his wings. Sisi laughed. "I'll take that as a yes. Did you live with the gods on Olympus?"

Another snort, a wing flash and a head bob.

"Where are they now?"

This time he pawed the earth.

"Oh dear. Have they gone? Are you all that is left?"

Another head bob.

"I'm sorry but you are safe with us."

Pegasus spread his massive wings and nuzzled the Empress.

*****

"I say, Watson, the baroness has presented me with a bit of a poser." Holmes was on his way to the British Museum and decided to stop off at Watson's surgery/home on Queen Anne Street.

The doctor looked at Holmes. "How is the ankle. You seem to be getting around pretty well."

'Not badly for an old war horse. But that's what I'm here in London about. Heading for the British Museum to do a little consultation and research for the Baroness. It seems the heavenly climes have a new visitor. A flying horse. They don't know where he came from."

"Could it be good old Pegasus?"

"Possibly. That's what I mean to find out. I have an appointment with an old friend, Professor William Hobson, historian and curator of early Graeco Roman artifacts at the museum. Would you like to accompany me?"

"It so happens I have finished my calls and patient appointments for the day. I always find the museum a place well worth visiting. Who is this Professor Hobson?"

"You may recall the disappearance several years ago of two Greek funerary stelae from the museum's Graeco-Roman wing. It turned out to be a prank by a pair of disgruntled curators who hid them in a store room. I found them with the help of Professor Hobson. We have communicated ever since. He has agreed to give me a short tutorial on the gods and goddesses of Greek mythology including the elusive horse Pegasus or Pegasos as he was known in ancient Greece."

"Good! I could stand a little cultural updating and so could you."

"Touché! Allons vite."

"Showing off your French connection cuts no ice here. All right. Let's go!"

The British Museum on Great Russell Street is a monumental Greek Revival Style building in the heart of London's Bloomsbury district in the West End. For many years it was the largest museum on the world. It is still the largest in the United Kingdom. The Bloomsbury district is the location of numerous cultural, intellectual, and educational institutions. We entered the impressive portal and asked for the professor.

A short, rotund individual with steel rimmed spectacles and short white beard, clad in intellectual tweeds approached Holmes with his hand extended. "Sherlock Holmes, so good to see you again. And you must be Doctor Watson. Delighted to meet you. I must admit that your enquiry about Pegasus has me intrigued. Surely, you haven't encountered the wily flying horse."

We certainly were not about to tell the professor of our connection to Heaven and the arrival of a winged horse at the Elysian Fields.

"No, professor, we are engaged in an enquiry for an international organization that must remain confidential. It concerns the gods and goddesses of Greek mythology. Pegasus is one of our primary subjects."

We reached his modest office which was crowded with books, papers, statuary and paintings. He cleared two chairs, offered us tea which we declined and settled behind his desk.

"First, I must disabuse you of one idea. Pegasus was not a god. He supposedly existed with the Olympians and was the caretaker of Zeus' thunderbolts but he was not a deity. He is, however, one of the best known creatures in Greek mythology. He is a winged stallion usually depicted as pure white in color. He was sired by Poseidon, in his role as god of horses, and foaled by the Gorgon Medusa who was decapitated by Perseus. Graeco-Roman poets wrote about his ascent to Mt Olympus and his obeisance

145

to Zeus, king of the gods, who instructed him to carry lightning and thunder."

"There is the tale of Bellerophon, a mortal, who captured Pegasus and rode him to slay the Chimera, a monstrous fire-breathing hybrid creature, composed of different animal parts. It is usually depicted as a lion, with the head of a goat protruding from its back, and a tail that might end with a snake's head. After killing the Chimera, Bellerophon then tried to reach Olympus on the back of Pegasus and become a god. That act of hubris angered Zeus and he sent a gadfly to sting Pegasus. The horse bucked, causing Bellerophon to fall back to Earth. Pegasus completed the flight to Olympus where Zeus used him as a pack horse for his thunderbolts."

"As I'm sure you know, The term 'chimera' has come to describe any mythical or fictional creature with parts taken from various animals, to describe anything composed of disparate parts or perceived as wildly imaginative, implausible, or dazzling."

"Now. all of this is the product of the highly imaginative poets, painters and sculptors of the early Greek and Roman eras. Not a word or image has any historic facts to support it. It is, in truth, myth but a very colorful, complex and fascinating myth."

"If you're still interested, I can give you some more information and images of the twelve Olympians as described by both the Greek and

146

Roman poets. Different names, same mythological deity. Each representing some aspects of human experience or personality.

- Zeus (Jupiter, in Roman mythology): the king of all the gods (and father to many) and god of weather, law and fate.

- Hera (Juno): the queen of the gods and goddess of women and marriage.

- Aphrodite (Venus): goddess of beauty and love.

- Apollo (Apollo): god of prophesy, music and poetry and knowledge.

- Ares (Mars): god of war.

- Artemis (Diana): goddess of hunting, animals and childbirth.

- Athena (Minerva): goddess of wisdom and defense.

- Demeter (Ceres): goddess of agriculture and grain.

- Dionysus (Bacchus): god of wine, pleasure and festivity.

- Hephaestus (Vulcan): god of fire, metalworking and sculpture.

- Hermes (Mercury): god of travel, hospitality and trade and Zeus's personal messenger.

- Poseidon (Neptune): god of the sea.

147

Other gods and goddesses sometimes included in the roster of Olympians are:

- ☐ Hades (Pluto): god of the underworld,

- ☐ Hestia (Vesta): goddess of home and family,

- ☐ Eros (Cupid): god of sex and minion to Aphrodite,

Holmes leaned back and said, "So Pegasus was, according to the poets and artists a mortal creature. I wonder what happened to him."

The professor smiled. "He may have been mortal but there is no mention of his dying. In that sense, he may be immortal. He's certainly not transporting thunder and lightning anymore. Of course, I doubt he existed at all. I certainly believe the Olympians passed on when the poets who created them died off."

"I have a colleague at the Acropolis museum in Athens who has chosen Pegasus (Pegasos) as one of his areas of specialization. Doctor Constantine Dimitriadis. You may wish to contact him."

"Well, thank you, professor. You have been quite helpful. Our clients will be most interested. I'm sorry I can't identify them for you but you know how secretive foreigners can be."

We rose and took our leave.

Once past the museums' portal, I turned and asked. "Well Holmes, what's the next step?"

"I return to Sussex and report back to the Baroness. It's been good to see you again, old chap. Thanks once more for helping me through my convalescence. When you have a free moment, come down to East Dean. My bees and I will reward you with some exquisite honey…and mead."

*****

Over the celestial fields a winged horse, a scarlet clad beauty and a small white dog were cavorting through the heavens. Of course, the Baroness and Pookie were members of the True Angels Aerobatic team and could take flight on their own but riding a flying horse was a special treat. Empress Sisi had just surrendered her seat on Pegasus to the Baroness who was expressing her delight in a song she had just made up. Her sparkling contralto rang out, echoing over the Paradise and Meadows landscapes:

"Pegasus, Pookie and Me, Oh My!

Floating around the celestial sky.

Twirling aloft in the clouds so high.

Pegasus, Pookie and Me, Oh My!"

"Watching the angels go winging by.

Here on a horse that knows how to fly.

Look at the birds giving us the eye.

Pegasus, Pookie and Me, Oh My!"

Down in the pasture, St. Francis with a group of animals had stopped by to see the new sensation. He was delighted. The Lipizzaners were casting jealous eyes on the soaring trio and their airborne frolics. Der Alte reared back and did his signature leaps as did several of his companions. Sisi applauded them. "Bravo, my stout fellows. Bravo! You're still the stars of the Saintly Spectaculars. We all wish we knew if that is really Pegasus and where he came from. You probably know but you can't tell us. Maybe Sherlock Holmes will find out."

When the Baroness, Pookie and the winged horse ended their aerial jaunt, Pegasus *(if it was he)* entered the stall that Heavenly Real Estate had created for him and worked his way through a feed of succulent oats. Like all of his fellow animals he ate earthly foods.

Lady Juliet and Pookie returned to her mansion where an Angelic Post missive was waiting for her. Sherlock Holmes! Short note. "Contact Doctor Constantine Dimitriadis at the Acropolis Museum in Athens. He is the world's leading authority on Pegasus."

"Pookie, let's find Raymond"

*****

Outside a small building next to the Parthenon on the Acropolis of Athens, a tall, very attractive dark haired woman dressed in a scarlet business suit and matching hat stood looking at the former temple of

Athena. Next to her was a small white dog sniffing at the tourists who flocked awestruck to the ancient shrine. Lady Juliet had persuaded Raymond to let her return to earth in corporeal form to interview Doctor Constantine Dimitriadis about Pegasus. The Director and all the angels were highly interested in just who this flying equine is and how he got into heaven. The Baroness hoped to find out. Holmes had wired an interview request to the professor for Juliet. Posing as a writer intent on recording the history of the winged horse, she and Pookie flitted to Athens armed with a list of questions about the historic *(mythological?)* equine. She also came supported by the celestial language facility that allowed heavenly denizens to converse in any earthly language.

A tall, slim *(almost cadaverous)* individual of an uncertain but advanced age greeted her at the door of the modest Acropolis Museum. It was packed floor to ceiling with artifacts, paintings and manuscripts, all thousands of years old.

She smiled and Pookie extended her paw. In perfect modern Greek, she introduced herself. "Doctor Dimitriadis. Thank you for agreeing to meet with me. I am Lady Juliet Armstrong, a British author and amateur historian. This is my canine companion, Pookie. We are inseparable. I hope you are not allergic to dogs.

He returned her smile and stooped to ruffle the dog's ears. Juliet continued, "I have been fascinated for a long time by the stories of Pegasus. My good friend Sherlock Holmes suggested that you are the font of all knowledge about the winged god."

The professor shook his head. "No, no, milady. A common mistake. Pegasus is not a god. He is a mortal horse. He supposedly lived among the gods and goddesses and was a servant of Zeus. He had extreme longevity of life."

"You use the past tense. As far as I can discover, there is no record of his dying."

"That is true. Until recently. He roamed the earth on his glorious wings for centuries well after the Olympians faded away and much of the world turned to monotheism."

"Explain, please."

"You have to understand that the Greek, Roman, Egyptian, Eastern, Norse, Teutonic, South American and other polytheistic gods of mythology were invented by humankind to represent and assist them in their lives. As a result, the polytheistic gods and goddesses developed according to the images of humankind with all their faults and foibles. Zeus was not a particularly likeable individual. Neither was Ares, Hera or Dionysus. Feuds and outright murder were not uncommon.

By contrast, monotheists believe that humans are created in the image and likeness of God and destined to be redeemed in heavenly bliss. Perhaps you are familiar with the concept. See the Bible or Quran."

Juliet thought, "Little does he know how familiar I am with heavenly bliss." She pressed on. "But what happened to Pegasus?"

"It is my theory that finally the image of the winged horse providing flight to his human passengers is no longer necessary."

"Why not?"

"You are aware that in the United States, a powered flying machine has just been invented. Balloons and inflated airships are appearing more frequently. Humankind has turned to technology in order to fly. Daedalus and Icarus are finally coming of age. In the process, Pegasus is released from his obligation as the servant of human flight and is free to climb to Heaven, not Mt. Olympus but true Heaven. Forgive me. You probably regard my rant as the ravings of an old man who has spent too much time among his museum artifacts."

"To the contrary, Doctor. I am quite inclined to agree with your analysis. I can well believe that Pegasus is in Heaven. Thank you so much. You have been most generous with your time and knowledge. I hope your museum expands and prospers. I shall have a contribution forwarded to you. *(Think Sherlock*

Holmes.)   Come Pookie, let us tour Athens and go home."

*****

Director Raymond, Empress Sisi, Mr. Sherman and the angelic zoologists were gathered in the Baroness' mansion. The winged horse was flying overhead. She had just finished sending her report to Sherlock Holmes. Raymond and the zoologists smiled, "So you believe he's the real thing. We agree." Sisi concurred. "God made him one of a kind and wanted us to solve the mystery. Well, you and Holmes did, Juliet." Mr. Sherman sighed, "Fine, that's settled. Now what do we do about the unicorn that just arrived?"

The Adventures of Sherlock Holmes
and the Glamorous Ghost

Volume Four
Horseplay

The End

The Adventures of Sherlock Holmes and the Glamorous Ghost

Volume Four

A Hare Raising Adventure

PART ONE

Narrated by Doctor John H. Watson

18 January 1891 - London-221B Baker Street

I had just joined Sherlock Holmes for breakfast served by our long-suffering landlady Mrs. Hudson. As usual, he toyed with his food and took only small sips of his coffee while I devoured the rashers of bacon and eggs laying before me. A light winter snowstorm had coated the surface of Baker Street and other roads below and an occasional blustery gust set the windows of our rooms to chattering.

He looked to the ceiling. "I have a presentiment, Watson. This is going to be an unusual day."

I laughed, "Oh come, Holmes! Most of your days are unusual." Sherlock Holmes was establishing himself as London's - nay, England's - first and only consulting detective. His reputation was spreading among the minions of Scotland Yard, the scribes of Fleet Street and members of the criminal class. He was sought out by nobles and paupers alike. His name had reached the Continent and perhaps even North America. Thanks in part to me.

Besides pursuing my growing medical practice *(and a lady who had struck my interest)* I had taken to scribbling notes about his adventures as he related them, thinking about further formalizing them into more stories for public consumption. At times I partnered with him as he pursued a villain, found a missing child or recovered an article of great value. Lost animals and marital infidelities were below his consideration. He actually liked dogs and cats but usually had less sympathy for their distressed owners.

We were just completing *(or at least, I was completing)* our repast when Mrs. Hudson knocked on our door. "I'm just finishing, Mrs. Hudson. You may take the tableware away. I don't know whether Holmes here will be making any more progress in consuming your delicious repast."

"Thank you, Doctor, but I'm here to bring up a visitor. She's in the hall below. Shall I call her up? She's a bit strange."

Holmes laughed, "Aren't they all? Many of my clients are strange, especially the females. Show her up."

She closed the door and the sound of footfalls and thumps was heard on the stairs. The door opened again and to our joint surprise, a large white rabbit with enormous ears pointing vertically hopped through the entry, stopped, peered at us and crossed the room to where Holmes was seated. A short woman of indefinite age wearing a tweed suit and matching hat on her pepper and salt hair followed him. Her headgear was not unlike Holmes' deerstalker. Her piercing grey eyes peered at the hare through her steel rimmed spectacles, "Grover, behave yourself."

The animal emitted a grunting huff, flicked his ears and stamped his hind leg. It was unclear whether he was pleased, irritated, questioning or just making conversation. Holmes looked at him and said, "Hello, Grover. Welcome! And welcome to you, madam. I am Sherlock Holmes and this is my associate, Doctor John Watson. And your name is?"

She replied in a twangy Yankee accent. *(I guessed New England.)* "Thank you, Mr. Holmes. My name is Mrs. Patience Morrigan. I am employed by the Pinkerton Detective Agency, female branch.

I reacted, "A female Pinkerton. I didn't know such people existed.'

"Oh, indeed, Doctor Watson. Since 1856 when Kate Warne convinced Alan Pinkerton to hire her as the first woman detective in the United States. She was a huge success. Since that time, women have had an active and growing role in fighting crime in America and elsewhere. I'm a New Englander, you know. Salem Massachusetts. I'm sure you've already determined that from my speech."

Holmes replied, "In fact I have determined a number of things about you, madam. You have been with the Pinkertons for seven years and have a highly successful arrest record. You have recently traveled here in pursuit of a serial murderer from Boston. You and your lagomorph associate arrived in Southampton several days ago and promptly traveled by train to London where you are staying at Brown's Hotel. You are a widow with no offspring.

I complained, "I say, Holmes. There you go again. Doing your identification party game. How did you make all those determinations from just looking at this lady for the first time?"

He chuckled. "I didn't, Watson. I got all that information from Inspector Stanley Hopkins at Scotland Yard. Mrs. Morrigan here registered with the Yard yesterday and described her mission. Hopkins advised her to seek me out. He sent me a wire."

"So that's what you meant by predicting this would be an unusual day. You knew she was coming all the time."

"Sorry, old chap, a little play acting on my part."

The lady detective squinched up her freckled nose and said, "Well, Mr. Holmes. There's one significant item I didn't tell your Inspector friend and you didn't deduce. As I said, I hail from Salem, Massachusetts. I am a witch and Grover here is my familiar."

"Oh come, madam! You are stretching your credibility and my patience. There are no longer any real witches or warlocks even though your Yankee forbears saw fit to hang a number of your ancestors for the so-called crime."

"And yours have burned thousands of us here in enlightened England. You may choose to believe me or not, Mr. Holmes. It matters not to me."

I was curious. "Tell me, Mrs. Morrigan. Are you truly a practitioner of the occult arts? Shakespeare's 'Double, double toil and trouble; fire burn and cauldron bubble?' I can understand why you might be reluctant to let many people know of your association with the mystical. Especially in your profession."

"First off, Doctor. I am no more a 'practitioner of the occult arts' than you are as a physician. No bubbling cauldrons, no poisoned apples, no summoning ghosts, no spells, devil worship or any of the other nonsense written or spoken about us. The Brothers Grimm and Shakespeare have much to answer for. Grover and I are as benevolent as you and Mr. Holmes, here."

Holmes intervened, "Then what do you claim as your witching skills? Why are you telling us you are a witch if you deny having any of their so-called capabilities?"

"Because Grover and I have the gift of preternatural knowledge. We discern persons, things

159

and events fully and in advance. It's a talent of great value to a detective and since we are going to be partners, I am putting it before the two of you."

"Now see here, Mrs. Morrigan or whatever your name is. I have no intention of taking you on as a partner. I have a distinct dislike for the Pinkertons, male or female. I have never and will never have a partner. Watson is my *associate* but our investigating relationship is carefully circumscribed."

(This was news to me. I had no idea of what our real affiliation was beyond a growing friendship. He also omitted mentioning Lady Juliet Armstrong, Baroness Crestwell, our ghostly sometimes colleague.)

She laughed, "Your sleuthing history is well known to us and I am well aware of your attitude toward women in general. But take my word. We will be partners, at least as long as it takes to track down the murderous villain who has escaped from Boston to the shores of Old Blighty. Once that has been accomplished, Grover and I will return to the States and bother you no further."

Before Holmes exploded, it was my turn to intervene. "You keep speaking as if this hare is an active participant in your professional activities. You call him a familiar."

"I do indeed and he is indeed. Grover and I are inseparable. Familiars are not just pets. They are the witch's and warlock's truest friends and confidants. They hear and see it all, they understand and know us better than we may even know ourselves. Familiars and their witchcraft partners are psychically connected and telepathically link with each other. I can easily read his emotions, and he communicates with me in so many different and meaningful ways. Just looking at him, we both understand each other without ever using words. He knows all of my moods."

I asked, "How old is he and how did you meet?"

"He is far older than I. He was passed on to me by my late mother who was also a witch. We just found each other. We chose to be each other's familiar and entered a mutually beneficial relationship."

"Grover is a peculiar name. Where did it come from?"

"He's had many names. I named his current manifestation Grover after Grover Cleveland, America's only president who served two separate, nonconsecutive terms. He just lost recently to Benjamin Harrison. My familiar has also served several nonconsecutive terms. My mother, me and goodness knows how many before us. Hence the name."

"Is he immortal?"

"Darned if I know. What about it, Grover, are you eternal?"

The hare stared at her and then at me and thumped his hind foot several times.

"I think that's a yes."

"He's a rather unique all white color."

"That's his winter camouflage. He's a snowshoe hare. White in the winter, brown in the more temperate months. If you look out your window, you'll see it's snowing and hailing. He changes color at will to match the climate."

Holmes was getting increasingly irritated by our conversation. "All this prating about a white rabbit does not alter the fact that I have no intention of taking you on as a partner nor participating in your manhunt, Mrs. Morrigan. I have one supernatural associate and she is more than enough. Sorry, but I'm afraid our brief relationship is at an end."

"He is not a rabbit, Mr. Holmes. He is a hare. There are differences."

She continued, "A short tutorial: Generally speaking, hares are larger than rabbits and have longer legs and ears. Their hearing and sense of smell are extremely sharp. Rabbits and hares also have different diets, with rabbits preferring grasses and vegetables with leafy tops, such as carrots, and hares enjoying harder substances like plant shoots, twigs and bark."

"While both rabbits and hares shed their coat, when it comes to hares they generally have much more dramatic seasonal color changes than rabbits. As I said, the snowshoe hare goes from a brown to a brilliant white come winter in order to provide camouflage appropriate to the snowy season. Since it is winter here in London and snowing, Grover is arrayed in white."

"Rabbits live in burrows or dens. called warrens. Hares live above ground and make their homes in hollow logs or simple nests they create by tromping down grass and vegetation. Hares aren't as sociable as their rabbit cousins. Most rabbits live in what is known as a colony. Hares are generally solitary creatures."

"Hares are one of the fastest moving animals on earth. My friend here can race at speeds of over fifty miles an hour. And beware his bite. It can be fierce. End of lesson!"

"But as far as our relationship is concerned, Mr. Holmes, it is just beginning. Take our word. We shall return. Au revoir! Come Grover!" She rose and walked out the door. The hare drummed his hind legs, hopped up and followed her.

The detective snarled. "That is a most irritating woman! So is that bunny. Almost as annoying as Lady Juliet and her dog!"

*****

Mycroft Holmes maneuvered his oversize frame into a large Morris chair, popped a Turkish Delight into his mouth and scanned the group sitting around the large table in the Stranger's Room at the Diogenes Club - Mr. Paul Edwards, Deputy Envoy of the US Embassy; Superintendent Murchison of Scotland Yard representing Commissioner Bradford; Inspector Stanley Hopkins CID; Sir Walter Forbush of the Foreign Office; Sherlock Holmes and me, Doctor John Watson.

"Gentlemen, thank you for coming this morning. The subject is Eamon Carmody, a known assassin who is believed to be here in England after eluding the police in Boston and its environs. He is suspected of killing, among others, a Senator from Massachusetts. Mr. Edwards, here from the American embassy, has passed on a request from the US Attorney General and their newly created Department of Justice asking for our assistance in capturing this highly dangerous individual. We have agreed to do so."

Sherlock Holmes looked around the room. "With all due respect, brother of mine, should not the Home Office be represented here if such a decision has been made?"

Mycroft smiled. "In this instance, I am the Home Office. There is more to the American request. They have specifically asked for your assistance, Sherlock. Is that not correct, Mr. Edwards?"

"It is, Mr. Holmes. Forgive me, both Messrs. Holmes. The Department of Justice has commissioned the Pinkerton Detective Agency to manage this effort. They have sent one of their most successful agents to partner with you, Mr. _Sherlock_ Holmes. She is Mrs. Patience Morrigan. I wonder that she is not here."

Mycroft interrupted, "My fault, Mr. Edwards, in choosing this venue. The Diogenes Club does not admit women or animals. I understand she travels with a large rabbit as her companion."

I laughed, "Grover is not a rabbit. He is a snowshoe hare. She was at great pains to enlighten us on this fact."

"Ah," said Mycroft, "so you have met this lady detective."

"Yes," said Holmes, "and I absolutely refuse to work with this witch."

"I say, Mr. Holmes!" said Sir Walter, "no need to be insulting especially in front of our American representative. Need to keep the relations cordial, don't you know? The Foreign Office is eager to assist our American cousins and I can think of no one as ideally suited to the task than you."

Holmes was about to insist that the woman characterized herself as a witch but I coughed and caught his eye. For once, the tables were reversed in our relationship. Usually it was me executing the faux pas. She had revealed her and her familiar's true natures in the expectation of confidentiality. We owed her that regardless of how he felt about them. He nodded and kept silent.

Superintendent Murchison picked up the conversation. "Your pardon, Mr. Edwards, but Scotland Yard must approve any foreign agent operating within our purview. That includes the United States. I hope you understand. Hopkins, I believe you have done the research and due diligence on this Mrs. Morrigan."

"Indeed, sir, and she is quite a formidable woman. She's been with the Pinkertons for seven years and has a highly successful arrest record. She is especially skilled in anticipating her target's next moves and foiling their activities. Both Pinkertons and the US Attorney General have nothing but praise for her performance. I believe she will be quite an asset in this investigation. After all, we want to rid our shores of this criminal pestilence as rapidly as possible. Of course, once captured, I hope we can rapidly extradite him back to the States."

The Foreign Office representative and the American nodded vigorously in affirmation.

Mycroft smiled, "So you see, brother mine, your government is asking you to make a substantial personal sacrifice and join forces with this lady. Inspector Hopkins will join you. I know you much prefer to work alone with occasional assistance from the good doctor here but can you swallow your pride and reluctance toward women and partner with her? Who knows? The relationship may be beneficial for all parties except of course, the villain."

Holmes shrugged. "I sincerely doubt it, Mycroft, but far be it from me to refuse a request from such a powerful assemblage."

*****

"Far be it from me to gloat, Mr. Holmes. It is hardly ladylike but did I not tell you Grover and I would be back."

"Yes, yes! Let's get on with it and tell your rabbit associate to get off my foot."

"He's a hare. He resents being misidentified."

"My apologies. Tell your hare to move and let's put all of our knowledge out on the table. Will you take notes, Watson?"

Without any words being spoken, Grover huffed and moved over to a water bowl that had been set out for him. Mrs. Hudson had rapidly fallen in love with "the exquisite bunny" and was supplying him with crunchy snacks and ample liquid refreshment. He, in turn, nuzzled her at every opportunity. In spite of Holmes' attitude, at least one relationship was being cemented. I wouldn't admit it in front of him but I also had taken a shine to the Yankee pair.

"All right, what do we know about this Eamon Carmody and why is Pinkerton's pursuing him?"

"He is a notorious Irish assassin who has been plying his trade for substantial fees over the past five years. His last victim was Senator Charles Avery of Massachusetts. Undoubtedly a politically motivated killing. Other Pinkerton operatives are on the trail of those who commissioned the murder. It's essential we intercept and capture Carmody alive. He will lead us to his patrons. We and the Massachusetts State Police have come close to capturing him several times but in each instance he has eluded law enforcement and the Pinkerton organization. I have been given the assignment to track him down only in the past several months. I am certain he escaped over the US border to Halifax and boarded a fast ship to cross the Atlantic to

Liverpool. Grover and I are sure he is here in England, probably London."

I commented, "Carmody must be an experienced practitioner of the murderer's arts."

She replied, "Yes, Doctor. He is clever, ruthless, elusive, efficient and skilled in disguises. But he also has an ego. *(She gave a sly glance at Holmes.)* Like many of his colleagues, he leaves a token of his activity – a shamrock."

Holmes looked up. "So he is indeed Irish!

"With a name like Eamon Carmody and living in Boston, that's a certainty. But don't jump to conclusions."

"I never do!"

"He is not a rebel. His only political or revolutionary leanings are motivated by greed. He is the classic mercenary serving the latest master who has the coin."

I remarked, "For someone who has only joined the pursuit recently, you seem to know a lot about him."

"There's a reason for that. He killed my husband." There was a pause as she wiped a tear from her eye. "Sorry, I shouldn't have mentioned that. Neither the Pinkertons nor the government knows that Chief Inspector Alfred Drury of the Boston Police and

I were secretly married. We felt concealment was beneficial to our respective careers. Alfred was a gifted warlock and a splendid detective. I lied earlier. Grover was his familiar, not my mother's. Now he's attached himself to me and we continue Alfred's work."

Holmes was silent.

"How did your husband die?" I asked.

"Shot by Carmody during a chase.' She looked at the floor. "Now, I have left myself open and vulnerable to the two of you. If the Pinkertons or US government knew I was on a mission of vengeance, they would immediately require me to recuse myself, even resign. Grover and I have to bring down Carmody, alive."

I was certain nothing would please Holmes more than to have this witch-woman out of his hair but he surprised me once again.

He looked at her, "Your secret is safe with us."

She smiled, "Grover and I knew you'd say that. Thank you!"

The hare put his head up on my knee. I 'booped' his nose and stroked his incredibly soft long ears. He then turned to Holmes who ignored him.

The witch squinted at Holmes but let his attitude pass. She inhaled, "Let's get to work, shall we? What do you suggest?"

He replied, "I have set the wheels in motion for you and Grover to meet an associate of ours. She and her canine companion are ghosts.... I see you are not surprised."

"No, I'm not! Grover and I are aware of Lady Juliet and her dog, Pookie."

I looked at her. "I say, Mrs. Morrigan. How do you know her name? Have you two met?"

"No, doctor, but we witches have contacts in the world of spirits. She and her dog are famous among the supernaturals. I am looking forward to meeting them."

"You'll be able to see them and communicate with them?"

"Of course!"

Holmes intervened, "I've also sent a wire to Inspector Hopkins. He should be here shortly. The Baroness will arrive later. We need to track Carmody's movements since arriving here in England. The Yard is best suited for that sort of work. We need to consider ways to carry out his capture and his return to Boston."

*****

As usual, the heavenly sun glowed benevolently over the celestial landscape as Lady Juliet Armstrong, Baroness Crestwell *(deceased)* and her canine companion, Pookie flitted to her stables where the Lipizzaner stallions and the winged Pegasus took up part time residence. The stallions, including the venerable Der Alte were enjoying a feed of saintly snacks from Mr. Sherman, heaven's animal master. Pegasus was airborne, gliding overhead with Empress Elizabeth (Sisi) of Austro-Hungary poised astride his back.

Juliet was about to join the merry equine gathering when a familiar presence appeared. She once again found herself facing an individual who had not been there a moment ago, in the form of a middle-aged male, tall, dressed in morning *(mourning?)* clothes, clean shaven, not a hair out of place, dark eyes, color undetermined. But, he seemed to be floating inches above the ground. Mr. Raymond is a high ranking angel and Senior Celestial Director, charged with keeping Paradise in heavenly shape. He greeted her. "Milady, God's blessings on you."

"And on you, Raymond. As usual, I conclude this is not a social call."

"Indeed not. I am reluctant to bring up this request for your services, given the Committee's disapproval of your frequent trips to Earth but it comes from the governments of Great Britain, the United States and Mr. Sherlock Holmes."

"Ah, another mystery or crime to be solved?"

"I'm afraid so but this time with an interesting twist. A witch and her familiar is involved."

"A witch? How interesting. Do I know her?"

"Not yet. She is a member of the Pinkerton organization. Mrs. Patience Morrigan and her associate Grover, a snowshoe hare. Pookie should be fascinated. Holmes and Watson await your presence."

"Let's not keep them waiting."

*****

Hopkins arrived at 221B. He greeted me and the Pinkerton detective and then said, "I got your wire, Mr. Holmes. I have alerted Liverpool, Manchester, Southampton, Brighton, Sheffield, York and of course, London. I doubt Carmody's in Scotland and I don't think he's done a bunk to Ireland although I wouldn't put it past him. But we don't know who we're looking for. He has as many disguises as you do. Not that I think he's as skilled as you are in masquerading."

Mrs. Morrigan remarked. "I suspect he's here to carry out another killing! He needed to leave the States but he could have gone anywhere. South America, the Continent, even Australia. Why

England? He's got Irish connections. He'd be safer in Dublin if he was just trying to hide. We believe he's got another assignment here in Britain." Grover snuffled and thumped the floor.

Holmes stared at the hare and said. "It seems your familiar agrees with you."

Hopkins looked over quizzically, "Familiar?"

The witch replied, "An American slang term for 'pet.' The first thing we need to do is deal with Carmody's disguises. Assuming he's still using that name. The last time I saw him, he had a full head of red hair and beard. Probably a wig. He uses steel rimmed spectacles which also may be phony. He was wearing a walking suit, a cane and moving with a limp. The limp, like his appearance, is fake. I assure you he's quite fast on his feet."

I said, "This can't be the first time Carmody has been in Britain. Do we know who his contacts are?"

Hopkins nodded, "Right you are, Doctor. There's a group of Irish boyos he's conspired with in the past. A bit of smash and grab, assault, kidnapping. Not a nice bunch at all. Several of them are doing time in the nick but a few are on the loose. We're rounding them up. I'm not sure we'll get much from them. Being a nark is a serious violation of their strict code. But it will only take one."

Mrs. Morrigan took a silent cue from Grover. "Try Bertie O'Leary. He's been on the outs with the gang."

Hopkins gaped. "How do you know that?"

Holmes chuckled, "Don't ask! But I'd take her advice if I were you."

The Yard Inspector looked askance at Patience Morrigan and her hare familiar, Grover, shrugged and said to Holmes and me. "It's a place to start. We haven't had any hoorah with old Bertie in a while. He's been an informer for a price. Not sure what we'll get from him. He's not the brightest bulb in the chandelier. I'm sure we can find him among his Gaelic compatriots in Seven Dials. I will see you all later." He reached down to pet the hare but the animal backed away. "Doesn't like police, I gather."

Mrs. Morrigan laughed. "Oh no, he loves the police. It's the smell of cigars that sets him off. Goodbye, Inspector!"

As Hopkins left. Lady Juliet and Pookie appeared. She giggled. "You rang, Mr. Holmes? Hello again, Doctor! Where is Martha Hudson? Who is this lovely lady and her companion rabbit?"

"Baroness and Pookie. Greetings! Let me introduce Mrs. Patience Morrigan and her familiar, Grover. Mrs. Morrigan is a Pinkerton detective and a witch. Grover is a very clever and preternaturally endowed Snowshoe Hare. We need assistance from you and your spirit dog. A little invisible surveillance, if you would. Let me brief you. Once more the game is afoot."

Grover thumped his oversize hind paw in confirmation and snuffled at Pookie. The dog barked. Laughter all around.

*****

The Met staged another of its harassing raids on the Irish gangs in Seven Dials, scooping up Bertie O'Leary in the process. Holmes, Mrs. Morrigan, Grover and I joined Inspector Hopkins in the stuffy Scotland Yard interview room. The Baroness and Pookie sat on a cabinet. They were invisible to Hopkins but not to the witch or her companion. Grover snorted in discomfort and hopped onto my lap. I sat fussing his ears when a constable opened the door and pushed O'Leary into the room. He was handcuffed. He recognized Hopkins and stared vacantly at the rest of us. He locked onto Grover. "Blimey, Inspector, can't the Yard sign up any more rozzers. Yer hiring rabbits now?"

"Never you mind, Bertie. This lady is Mrs. Morrigan. She's with Pinkerton's. The hare is hers. This is Sherlock Holmes and his associate Dr. Watson. You've heard of them. We have a few questions for you."

Bertie indeed had heard of Sherlock Holmes and didn't like it one bit. A woman Pinkerton was beyond his limited comprehension – especially one with a snowshoe hare.

"I don't know nothin' about nothin', Inspector. Old Bertie's been out of the loop fer donkey's years."

Holmes smiled. "Oh. I doubt that, Bertie. I'm sure if you try hard, you can answer one question for us. Where is Eamon Carmody?"

"Who?"

The Pinkerton agent shook her head and looked unhappy. "Oh, that's a shame, Mr. O'Leary. We thought surely you would help us. Now we'll have to release you and tell all your friends that we got what we wanted from you."

"Yer tryin' to get me killed, yer witch." *(Little did he know!)*

"Oh, certainly not! We wouldn't want you to come to any harm. I'm sure your associates will understand."

"They'll understand enuff to slit me throat. Just toss me back in the nick with the rest of them. Question all of 'em."

"I guess we could do that, Inspector, if our friend here cooperates."

"Awright, awright. Whadda yer wanna know?"

"Where is Eamon Carmody and why is he here in England?"

The tough laughed, "Why is Eamon anywhere! To kill somebody, yer stupid bint!"

At this insult, Grover jumped down from my lap, hopped over and bit O'Leary fiercely on the leg. Pookie started to solidify to do the same but was restrained by Lady Juliet.

"Oww! Git him off me" He kicked and tried to move his arms cuffed behind his back.

Mrs. Morrigan smiled and said, "Thank you, Grover. That'll do."

The hare reluctantly withdrew, making growling sounds as he moved back.

I looked at Mrs. Morrigan. "Did he just growl?"

"Yes, he did. Hares and rabbits rumble and growl when they're upset."

Holmes intervened, "To repeat, Bertie. Where is he and who is he going to kill?"

"The American Ambassador. Some Yankee muck-a-muck is looking to start a rebellion. They've already killed a senator. He's paying Eamon to start it off here and blame the Brits. Carmody's organizing a gang to cover his tracks. Last I heard, he's staying in

Chiswick but he's probably moving around. And as you know, Eamon's a whiz at disguises."

"Where in Chiswick?"

"I went to one meeting at Mrs. Rogers' boarding house on Lonsdale Road but the gang tossed me. Said I was too friendly with Old Bill. I gotta be careful."

Hopkins reacted, "Well, that gives us a start. We'll pay Mrs. Rogers a quick visit. Bertie, back you go to the cells. We'll interview your chums just to cover your rump and then release the bunch of you unless someone else decides to speak up. Mr. Holmes, Doctor, Mrs. Morrigan! Are you up for a trip to Chiswick?"

Patience gazed at the hare. Grover stared back. They were communicating. Holmes looked on peevishly. She came back from her trance-like state and stared at Juliet and Pookie whom she could clearly see. They nodded. "Yes, we all think it's a good idea. Let's go!"

*****

The late night snow had resumed as our group silently made its way to Mrs. Rogers' boarding house on Lonsdale Road in Chiswick.

Inspector Hopkins had organized a band of constables to surround the house. Knowing that Carmody was no doubt armed, the police had taken the unusual step of carrying weapons. I had my well-oiled and fully loaded Webley Mark I Service revolver at the ready. To my surprise, Mrs. Morrigan was similarly armed with a Pinkerton issued Remington pistol. Holmes was equipped with the Webley.450 Short Barreled Metropolitan Police Revolver that had been issued to him by Scotland Yard. Pinkerton operative Albert Travers had joined us. He too was armed. We were a walking invasion force.

Juliet and Pookie slipped unseen through the front door and did a quick reconnaissance of the rooms. They returned to Holmes and the witch and said, "He's in there. Tell Hopkins and the police to form up."

When everyone was placed with the back door and first floor windows surrounded. Hopkins strode up to the front door, gun extended and shouted. "Eamon Carmody. This is Inspector Hopkins of Scotland Yard. You are surrounded. Leave your weapons and surrender peaceably. You are wanted on several counts of murder by British and American police. Don't make your situation any worse."

A high pitched feminine scream echoed through the front hall of the building and Carmody slammed open the door, emerged holding his landlady by the neck with a gun pressed to the side of her head. "Get stuffed, rozzer, Unless you want this woman dead at your feet, you're going to drop your gun, step back, call off your hounds and let us pass. You know I won't hesitate to kill her and you too, Mr. High and Mighty Inspector. What's it gonna be?"

Hopkins reluctantly ordered the constables to stand down. Holmes, Mrs. Morrigan and I also lowered our weapons when suddenly, at the invisible Lady Juliet's command, two high speed white whirlwinds jumped at the outlaw and bit hard, knocking him over in the process. He lost his grip on his pistol and the landlady. She ran to us and took cover with me. Carmody was lying on the ground with Grover and a solid bodied Pookie growling and biting him repeatedly. He was flailing at the hare and dog but Grover and Pookie both held on. Holmes, Hopkins, Travers and several constables pounced on the villain, handcuffed him and bound his legs. The hare still had Carmody's throat in his teeth. "Get him off me," he gurgled, "What the hell kind of beast is that?"

The witch chuckled, "Pinkerton operative, lagomorph division. Good work, Grover. You too, Pookie. You can let go now. I can see the headlines. *Eamon Carmody, terrorist and assassin, captured by a Snowshoe Hare and a Bichon Frisé.* Your companions and clients will love that."

Carmody let loose a spate of expletives which affected the woman not in the least. I had to restrain myself from laughing as the killer was hustled off to a

Black Maria. His throat was bleeding but no one paid attention.

The witch looked at Hopkins and me, asking. "Can you see to his wounds, Doctor? Inspector, I'm committed to bringing him back to Boston alive although I'd love to deliver his carcass. Mr. Holmes, I assume your brother, our ambassador and your Home and Foreign secretaries can arrange a rapid extradition of this filth. In spite of your gracious hospitality *(another chuckle)* and our new friendship with the Baroness and Pookie, Grover and I are eager to return home. Mr. Travers and I will contact our office here in London to arrange his and our transportation to the States. We'll have him under heavy guard through the entire trip. By ship to New York and then train to Boston. I'm sure he's already planning his escape. I hope he tries, don't you, Grover?" The hare growled loudly and thumped his hind foot.

PART TWO

Narrated by Mrs. Patience Morrigan (and Grover)

7 February 1891 - Aboard RMS Umbria of the Cunard Line – Liverpool to New York

As expected, Eamon Carmody attempted to overpower his captors and flee while being transported from London to the docks of Liverpool where the trans-Atlantic steamer, RMS Umbria, awaited its secret human cargo. Two burly constables and an equal number of Pinkerton agents subdued him in the back of a Black Maria making its way northwest to the Mersey Estuary. A substantial number of bruises were traded but ultimately the constabulary won out. Grover and I, along with our baggage, rode in the forward section of the patrol wagon. The Baroness and her dog flitted along with us.

Under cover of darkness, he was transferred to the Umbria's seldom used prison cell. Two agents from London Pinkertons, Albert Travers and Sydney Furth, were aboard to ensure Carmody remained confined on the high speed voyage over the North Atlantic. Each one alternated with the ship's security team in keeping watch over the elusive killer. I would back them up. The ethereal Baroness and dog were also with us.

With our prisoner tucked away in the ship's brig, Grover and I were comfortably ensconced in a first class cabin, paid for by the Pinkerton's organization. The Chief Steward had graciously allowed me to keep the snowshoe hare in my cabin. We were bringing Carmody back to the United States by way of New York City to stand trial in Boston Federal Court for the murder of Senator Charles Avery. He had also been prevented from staging an attack on the American Ambassador in London.

In New York, Carmody would be transferred to a heavily guarded special train car to take him to Boston. I have been busy trying to get the Irishman to confess to the killings, real and intended, and to tell us who had commissioned him to do the deed. So far, no success. He laughed at the prospect of a woman detective bringing him to book. I pointed out that he was sitting in a not very large or comfortable shipboard brig courtesy of a woman detective and a snowshoe hare. He snickered again and snarled, "But not for long, Missus, not for long."

In turn, I laughed. "You do realize that you are a dead man walking. Your boss isn't going to allow you to remain alive while you're in custody and can betray him. Unless we can reach him first, your days are numbered."

His smile disappeared. I didn't realize it at the time but I had just given him extra motivation to escape even within the confines of a ship speeding over the Atlantic.

Grover and I went down to the dining room. The maitre d' had provided us with a table where my snowshoe hare familiar could join me in demolishing a tasty English meal. Our bearded and mustachioed waiter limped over to our table and offered the menu, suggesting a bottle of wine. "One glass of Merlot will be sufficient, thanks, Mr. Holmes. I must keep my wits about me. Grover doesn't drink alcohol. Some fizzy water for him, if you please."

The waiter smiled and whispered, "How did you recognize me? My disguises are usually highly successful."

"Oh, your appearance is flawless and your demeanor and slight limp is beyond reproach but one thing you have left to chance. Your odor. Not that it's offensive or overwhelming. The average person would never notice it but like most hares, Grover's sense of smell is acute, much more sensitive and discerning than a human's. He recognized your scent immediately and passed that information on to me. Clever boy, Grover! Baroness Juliet is also with us and identified you. Don't worry, Mr. Holmes, your secret is safe with us. I owe you one. Why are you here? Is Watson with you and who else knows you are aboard this ship?"

"Watson is safe in our rooms and his surgery back in London. The Home and Foreign Office and Commissioner Bradford of Scotland Yard all felt the British government's greatest interests would be best served by having an observer, namely me, present on this trip and during Carmody's arraignment in Boston. Needless to say, my brother was highly influential in getting me to acquiesce to their requests – nay, demands. My true identity is known to the captain, the purser and the ship's security officer. I have a cabin in second class unobserved by the rest of the crew. Fear not, I realize this is your party and I have no intention in interfering with your work. But let's not draw attention to our conversation. Juliet and Pookie will join us. We can speak more freely up in the bow after I come off my shift at eleven. Now, perhaps you should give me your order. I have a selection of hearty greens available for your companion."

I ordered a lamb creation that proved to be delicious. I couldn't resist wondering about this peculiar but highly effective consulting detective. In some ways he reminded me of my dear departed husband, killed by a bullet from Eamon Carmody's gun. Grover and I had discussed Holmes several times. The hare liked him. My jury was still out. The Baroness adored him but kept her feelings carefully hidden.

*****

The sea wind was brisk and a full moon lit up the bow of the Umbria when Holmes, Grover, the ghosts and I met later that night. He had changed from his waiter's garb into a rumpled grey suit that had seen better times. The gusts made it impossible to keep our hats so we stood bareheaded, trying to talk over the crash of the waves and blustery howls. Grover had found a relatively quiet spot below the deck rail and sat staring at us with the breeze occasionally flipping his long ears. Lady Juliet and Pookie, in their disembodied states were unaffected by the elements.

The Baroness and I had chatted earlier. She had enquired with the angelic keepers of the Heavenly Register and determined that my husband Chief Inspector Alfred Drury of the Boston Police was now a denizen of Paradise and awaiting my arrival. It seems warlocks and witches are judged on their own characters and not any prejudices or old wives' tales. She also suggested that Grover, whenever his long earthly life terminated would be welcomed over the Rainbow Bridge.

We decided our precarious location was highly unsuited to serious conversation and withdrew to a first class lounge that thankfully was empty. Grover sat with his head on my knee keeping careful watch on the British detective. He had established a genial relationship with the Baroness and her dog. I told them of my unsuccessful attempts to get Carmody to identify his sponsor. I mentioned how I told him his life was in peril.

Holmes reacted, "Madam, you have given our friend major motivation to attempt an escape."

I retorted, "Where can he go. He's trapped aboard this vessel."

"A large vessel that provides any number of hiding places that he can use. Even a sweeping search before we dock may not suss him out. If he can wait us out, the wily Mr. Carmody could escape from the ship once it's tied up in New York. I know I promised you I would not interfere but I believe I should disguise myself and trade places with one of his guards. I doubt he'll recognize me. Two can play the camouflage game. Perhaps I can wheedle out the name of his employer in the process. We have less than forty eight hours before we reach New York. If he doesn't escape on board this ship, he will certainly try while he is being transferred to the secure rail car to take him to Boston. What do you think?"

I looked into Grover's large amber eyes. We conversed and decided that I had activated Carmody's critical survival instincts and could no longer win his trust. Stupid of me! However, Holmes might be able to head off his shipboard flight. The Baroness would keep an invisible watch over him. We had searched Carmody and his cell in the brig thoroughly for weapons but even handcuffed, he could overpower his guards and steal one of their guns. When he ate and drank or answered nature's calls, one of his hands was freed under careful supervision. His Pinkerton watchers, Albert Travers and Sydney Furth, were highly experienced in prisoner restraint but I wasn't so sure about the ship's security crew. Therein lay a vulnerability. I agreed to Holmes' proposal.

Meanwhile, the Baroness and Pookie would keep a watch over the killer.

Next morning, Holmes went off to visit the purser, explained his plan and obtained a security crew uniform. He would substitute for one of the guards who was down with a 'sudden ailment.' The Pinkertons were matched with a ship's security crew member. The purser took the pair aside, introduced Holmes, relieved his now 'seriously ill' security staff yeoman and ensured that Carmody was still cuffed and locked up in his cell. Travers had taken charge of keeping Carmody restrained.

PART THREE

Narrated by Sherlock Holmes

14 February 1891 - Aboard RMS Umbria of the Cunard Line – Liverpool to New York

(Sherlock Holmes was disguised as one of the Umbria's security crew members. Carmody, clever though he was at cloaking and masking, was no match for Holmes skill at deception. The felon didn't recognize him even after the skirmish in Chiswick. All he remembered was being attacked by a vengeful rabbit and dog. He had the scars to remind him.)

"I'm Yeoman McShane, Carmody. Taking over for Hazelett who's in sick bay. My British Pinkerton friend, Albert Travers and I are going to make sure you're well wrapped and ready for your train ride to Boston when we dock in New York in the next few hours. Albert will be traveling with you along with several coppers from NYPD who will be joining him. I'm staying with the ship. Glad to see you off and gone."

"Get lost, McShane. You too, Travers. The city of Boston will never see hide or hair of Eamon Carmody. Take my word for it. I'll make fools of all of yez."

"Brave talk coming from a trussed up turkey."

"Yeah, well, I have some very influential friends who will be seeing to old Eamon's welfare."

"Important friends, eh! Who might they be?"

"Wouldn't you like to know. Don't take me for a fool, McShane. Think you can get me to peach on the old man? I don't even know his right name. I call him The Chief. He pays me well to do his necessary work."

"Like killing and overthrowing governments and starting wars?"

"Not yet but soon. Meanwhile, I have some good Irish pals in the NYPD and the Boston police who will be taking care of me and there's nothin' you can do to stop it. Ye think a pair of handcuffs and a couple of jumped up detectives are going to hold Eamon Carmody. Think again!"

I nodded to Albert. We checked the killer's handcuffs, locked up the cell and stepped out. We went down to the Purser's office. He greeted us expectantly. "Mr. Holmes, Detective Travers. Is Carmody under control? The Captain is very much concerned about the safety of our passengers with that madman on board. We'll all breathe a sigh of relief when he's taken off at New York. We should be there in several hours. I radioed ahead. We have one of the first experimental Marconi ship-to-shore devices on board. Soon maritime communication will be vastly different. Anyway, members of the New York Police Department are standing by to take him to Grand Central Depot and get him locked up on a train to Boston. He'll be somebody else's problem."

Albert Travers laughed, "Yeah, mine!"

I didn't let Travers know I'd also be making the trip with him once again in disguise. This time I'll be pretending to be a local US Pinkerton recruited to join the transport party on the New York and New England Railroad (NY&NE) special train provided by the Massachusetts government. I had to work on my New York City accent.

Lady Juliet and Pookie would be with us. The dog and hare had formed an animal friendship and the Baroness had taken a liking to the Pinkerton witch.

RMS Umbria docked at the city's North River Pier 15 with typical arrival fanfare. The passengers were somewhat taken aback by the presence of a contingent of city police and a Black Maria wagon on the dock. The First Class travelers were exited though a special gangway while the Second Class and Steerage voyagers were held back as a small procession descended from the hold to the berth and onward to the police vehicles. Some of the more observant passengers saw a tall bearded figure in handcuffs, struggling to free himself from the grips of several Pinkertons and NYPD constables. He wasn't succeeding.

Inspector George O'Hara from the New York City Department of Corrections was in charge. He introduced himself to Travers, Mrs. Morrigan and the ship's security officer. I stood by unnoticed. "Well, your prisoner is now in the capable hands of New York's Finest. We'll get him over to Grand Central Depot and you can secure him on your special train. We'll ride the rails with you until we reach Westchester County. Then he's all yours. Get him out of here and on to Boston as quick as you can. All right! Let's go!"

With warning bells ringing, the horse-drawn convoy proceeded northward to 42nd Street and crossed Manhattan Island east bound toward Grand Central Depot – an edifice soon to be replaced by Grand Central Terminal with a more opulent interior, greater safety, less smoke and noise and a much larger collection of tracks and platforms providing considerably more room and passenger capacity and better maneuverability.

A three car special train of the NY&NE line sat on a siding waiting to take its human cargo to Boston. A heavily protected, armored mail car sat between two passenger carriages. It had been converted into a rolling jail cell to hold Eamon Carmody and his guards. Also on board in the leading and trailing cars were several New York and Boston PD officers and backup Pinkerton operatives including Travers, Mrs. Patience Morrigan and Grover. I was with them. Lady Juliet and Pookie flitted between the cars.

While still struggling, Carmody was transferred to his confinement. A separate reconnoitering locomotive left the siding and moved northward from the station. Armed Pinkertons and members of NYPD on board were scanning the right of way for any threats or possible attacks intended to free the assassin. Each switch point was examined as the engine made its painfully slow progress out of the depot. The special prison train with its short series of cars fired up its steam and slowly proceeded up Park Avenue behind the pilot engine.

It had only moved a few blocks when one of the guards from the 'jail car' ran into the forward carriage shouting "stop the train, stop the train." Inspector O'Hara pulled the emergency cord and brought the cars to a halt. "What the hell is wrong,

Murphy? This better be good or you'll be out pounding a beat."

"He's dead, Inspector! Carmody just keeled over, convulsed and died as the four of us watched."

*****

"Ricin! I recognized the symptoms although I haven't seen it in a while. One of the oldest poisons in the world. The ancient Egyptians used it. It's extracted from castor beans. Very painful. Takes an hour or so to work depending on how it's administered. He could have eaten it in his breakfast, had it rubbed on his skin or been injected with it. I'll have to make a thorough post-mortem examination of him." The police doctor who had joined us aboard the train was speaking to Inspector O'Hara, Detective Travers, Mrs. Morrigan and me. I had revealed myself to them when I first heard of Carmody's demise.

O'Hara thanked the doctor. He had earlier ordered the engineer to reverse the short train back into the Depot where an ambulance waited to take the body to the police morgue. He commented. "Now, depending on when he was stricken with the poison, we have a whole different cast of characters to deal with. I've called the Commissioner and he's assigned Captain Reilly of the Detective Bureau to the case. He should be here shortly. I get to deal with live prisoners. He gets the stiffs."

A tall, clean shaven, dark-haired man in a fedora and grey business suit stood at the foot of the platform joined by two constables in uniform. He watched as the ambulance attendants maneuvered the stretcher holding Carmody's body down the railcar steps and off to the waiting horse drawn vehicle. He then turned and walked forward to the rail carriage from which Inspector O'Hara, Albert Travers, Mrs. Morrigan, Grover and I were emerging. He looked half surprised and half amused as the hare hopped up and stared at him with his large amber eyes. His nose and long ears twitched and his hind leg thumped. I noticed that Grover's coat was beginning to change from his winter white to the brown suitable for more temperate weather.

The female Pinkerton reached down and attached a long, lightweight lead to the hare's collar. She looked at the NYPD detective. "Captain Reilly? I'm Mrs. Patience Morrigan of the US Pinkerton organization. This is my companion, Grover. I believe you know Inspector O'Hara of your Corrections Department. This gentleman is Detective Albert Travers of our British branch and this is the famous consulting detective Sherlock Holmes.

The Captain's eyebrows raised when she introduced me. He shook hands all around and beckoning, walked off with me. "I've heard of you, Mr. Holmes. Your friend Doctor Watson spins an interesting yarn. Why are you involved in this exercise?"

"I have the British and American governments to thank, Captain. The late Mr. Carmody was a one-man assassination squad in your country and mine. Actually, that's not quite true. He had colleagues and assistants. He worked for someone he called The Chief who, I believe, is American and quite wealthy."

"Well. It seems The Chief couldn't keep his hoodlum from being killed off.'

"Or perhaps, Captain, he was responsible for it."

"You think Carmody became a liability?"

"It's quite possible. He was attracting a lot of attention in Massachusetts and in London. Attention his employer probably didn't appreciate. When we get a better idea from the doctor as to how long ago he was attacked with the Ricin, we'll have a better idea of who our likely killer is. It could be someone from the Umbria's security staff; the Pinkertons; your own police force. Ricin is not all that difficult to produce. Just some castor beans, a liquid base and some patience. It's not all that difficult to deliver, either."

"And what about you, Mr. Holmes. Should I regard you as a suspect?"

"By all means but I had a rare opportunity recently in a London suburb to do him in and didn't take it. I was charged with bringing him to justice, not killing him off."

"Tell me about this woman Pinkerton and that rabbit of hers."

"Mrs. Morrigan is a childless widow and has been with Pinkertons for seven years. She is a formidable detective with an outstanding arrest record. She is from Salem."

"Ah, the city of witchcraft!"

"Indeed! By the way, Grover is not a rabbit. He is a snowshoe hare. There are significant differences. A very interesting animal."

Of course, I didn't mention the invisible Baroness and her talented dog who were standing invisible in the background. I also avoided mentioning that Mrs. Morrigan was a witch.

I refrained from telling the Captain that Carmody was responsible for killing her husband but I would take it up with the lady in short order. I returned to the subject of the Chief.

"Tell me, Captain. Do you or your colleagues have any clues as to the identity of this so-called Chief."

"Perhaps! Our Federal cousins have been informally circulating data on a very wealthy New York tycoon who has ambitions of establishing a New

World Order with him in command, of course. Not that unusual. We get a lot of these fanatic nut cases with their equally crazy followers. Usually a lot of noise, newspaper reports, even public rallies. This guy, Martin Shreveport, was opposed by the senator from Massachusetts in a recent national party primary election. Our best bet is that Carmody killed the senator at Shreveport's command. Not enough proof to indict or even arrest him."

I replied. "Carmody's next target was the US ambassador to Great Britain. We caught him before he could follow through on his plan."

"That would make sense. Ambassador Jenkins has been rumored as a possible Presidential candidate in the next national election. When Carmody failed, he became a problem to the Chief. He could possibly talk about or even blackmail our ambitious friend. I'll pass on that information to the Federal Attorney General. Now, let's concentrate on our immediate problem. Who did Carmody in? Maybe we should give him or her a medal. One less snake in the jungle. Let's wait and see what the doctor has to say. Meanwhile, introduce me to this bunny."

*****

"It was ricin. Injected in his hip through a sharp instrument. Took an hour at most to work! Probably less." The police doctor opined as to when and how Carmody was done in.

I said, "So. he was likely assaulted while he was already off the ship and on his way to the train station? He was putting up quite a struggle. He could have received the poisonous shot and never even noticed. I'm sorry but I think we have to conclude, Captain, that a member of law enforcement was quite probably responsible for the murder. Pinkertons or NYPD."

The policeman shook his head. "Unfortunately, we have quite a few bad apples in our law enforcement basket. Bribery, missing evidence, false arrests, beating witnesses and suspects. Things I'm not proud of but outright murder is an extreme. I hope it's a Pinkerton."

I turned to Mrs. Morrigan and Albert Travers. "What do you think? Was it a Pinkerton?"

The witch stared at Grover. The hare was obviously communicating with her. He had already conversed with Lady Juliet and the dog. They reached agreement. She turned to Travers. "I think you'd better confess, Albert."

"What? Are you out of your mind? You and that stupid rabbit! Really, Patience, I know your reputation but this is too much. Just like you, I was assigned to bring Carmody to book."

"No, you went further. You were paid to get rid of him. You didn't have a clean shot at him on the ship. There were too many witnesses around. But there was the brawl getting him into the Black Maria and onto the train. That was your chance. Did The Chief contact you here in New York and tell you to get rid of old Eamon? You'll be next, you know. He can't afford to have any loose ends. There's probably a killer on your tail right now. Isn't that right, Mr. Holmes? Captain Reilly?"

I smiled and the policeman shook his head in regret that The Chief obviously had such a wide band of minions at his disposal. I said, "Mr. Travers. For your own safety, I think you should let Captain Reilly here take you into custody. I think he'll find you haven't yet been able to dispose of the surgical needle you used to inject Carmody. Did you prepare the ricin yourself or did one of The Chief's underlings provide it? I'm sure the Pinkerton organization would be happy to surrender you to the New York Police."

Albert brazened it out. "I'm innocent. I'm a trusted member of the Pinkerton organization and a British citizen. Well, Reilly. I suppose this is the time I'm supposed to ask for an advocate."

The Captain frowned, "We call them lawyers here in the States and yes, that would be a good idea. Come along with me. I don't think we need cuffs. First thing we're going to do is search you. Then we'll provide you with protection by several of my trusted officers. Thank you, Mr. Holmes! Thanks, Agent Morrigan and thank you too, Operative Grover!

The hare flicked his ears and thumped his hind leg. The invisible ghost smiled and the Bichon barked.

EPILOGUE

10 March 1891 – On the deck of RMS Umbria of the Cunard Line – New York Harbor

A tall male and a short female stood at the bow of the ocean liner. A snowshoe hare snuffled an invisible Bichon Frisé while a scarlet clad wraith looked on. The Baroness smiled and said, "It's time Pookie and I returned to heaven. The Committee gets upset when we're away too long."

"Thank you, milady and you too Pookie. If you get a chance to meet my husband, please tell him we've been avenged on Carmody who no doubt, is in Hell. Also tell him, I love him and am looking forward to joining him. This detective stuff is getting stale."

The ghosts bid Holmes farewell and flitted off.

"I assume you are happy to return to London, Mr. Holmes. Have a safe voyage."

"Thank you, Mrs. Morrigan, although I will say this episode has had some interest. I assume you will be keeping watch over Albert Travers' situation."

"Oh indeed, as will Pinkerton management. It has distressed our powers that be that one of our own agents has been accused of murder – even if the victim was an infamous killer we had set out to capture.

Captain Reilly and the NY Prosecutor are already building a substantial case against him."

"It's a shame, really. Travers actually did the world a great favor. Has he been of any use in cutting down the infamous Chief?"

"Yes, he has been spewing accusations and information quite freely in exchange for promises of police protection and leniency. Martin Shreveport, if he is The Chief, has immense connections and influence but I hope his days as a criminal mastermind are numbered."

"He's reminiscent of my own nemesis, Professor Moriarty. One day soon, I will bring that Napoleon of Crime his just deserts. Not murder, mind you, unless he attempts to do me in."

"The Napoleon of Crime? He sounds like he would be very interesting. What do you think, Grover?"

The hare grunted and shook his head.

They both laughed. Holmes stared at her. "Mrs. Morrigan, I must confess two things. One: In spite of my insistence on eschewing the mystical and occult, you and Grover have left me more willing to believe in the existence of witchcraft."

"Benign witchcraft, Mr. Holmes, not those horror stories that frighten children."

"Fair enough."

"And what is your second item?"

"For a brief period, I thought that you may have killed Carmody in retribution for your slain husband."

"I suppose I should be shocked or angry at that but I am neither. I'm a professional detective and have learned to follow my suspicions wherever they lead. I'm sure you do the same. Anyway, I hope we have a chance to work together again, either here in the States or in England. Give my best regards to Doctor Watson and your lovely landlady. Come Grover, time for dinner. *Good Night, Mister Sherlock Holmes!*"

Where had he heard that before?

The Adventures of Sherlock Holmes and the Glamorous Ghost

Volume Four

A HARE RAISING ADVENTURE

THE END

The Adventures of Sherlock Holmes and the Glamorous Ghost

Volume Four

Il Genio – A Novelette

"We are almost finished, Baronessa. I think I have captured your rebellious spirit and enigmatic charm as well as your little dog's unique personality." The speaker was Leonardo DaVinci, artist, inventor, scientist and virtuoso. Il Genio - the Genius. He and his model were conversing in the universal celestial language that miraculously enabled all the denizens of Heaven to freely and easily communicate with each other and the Almighty.

"Are you quite comfortable, Baronessa?"

"Oh yes, Maestro. Pookie and I are quite relaxed. As you Italians say, 'Dolce Far Niente."

DaVinci laughed. Yes, we are very skilled at doing nothing."

Leonardo had spotted Lady Juliet Armstrong, Baroness Crestwell upon her first entrance to Paradise and after several attempts, finally persuaded her to pose for him. He was enthralled by her mysterious smile, not dissimilar to that of his famous masterpiece, Mona Lisa. Renaissance portrait painters often included small animals in their canvases along with their female models. Pookie fit the bill, perfectly.

Because Lady Juliet was often away on adventures, the sittings moved along slowly. Leonardo used the interim to capture the images of saints and angels; invent even more startling objects and processes and further his exploration of the Almighty's wondrous creations.

The Baroness waved at the portrait. "May I see it, Maestro?"

"Si. Although it is not quite complete. Some small background details need to be added. Other animals, trees, buildings, fountains. But your likeness and the dog's are finished. I suppose your little Pucci will want to give her opinion, too."

"It's Pookie, not Pucci and yes, she is a most judgmental creature."

"Well, ladies. Here you are." He turned the easel in Juliet's and Pookie's direction.

The Baroness sucked in her breath. "Oh. it's marvelous. I wish I was actually that beautiful but I am willing to be flattered by the greatest painter of all time."

"Oho, Baronessa. Who is doing the flattering now?"

"I mean it. You are truly a genius. What do you think, Pookie?"

The dog jumped down from the couch on which they were both ensconced, ran up to the easel, barked, wagged her tail furiously and finished with a backflip.

They both laughed. "Signore, I think you can take that as a canine seal of approval. I am so pleased. Once you finish it, will it be mine to have?"

"If you want it, Baronessa Juliet. However, I would like to keep it long enough to display it at the next Celestial Art Exhibition, Then I would be most pleased to formally present it to you at the event."

"Of course. How selfish of me to ask for it!"

"Not at all! I am pleased that you desire my humble effort."

"Humble indeed. It's magnificent. Is there anything I can do to reciprocate. Not that I can think of anything in the same class as this masterpiece."

"In fact, there is. I think you know that in addition to my paintings and sculptures, I have also experimented with inventions and made scientific enquiries about engineering, mathematics, anatomy, geology, physics, music, military technology and aeronautics, One of my major interests was in the nature of powered flight. I even produced a notebook or codex on The Flight of Birds in 1505. The Wright Brothers caught up four hundred years later."

"Some of my observations on flight are also contained in a random bundle of notes, diagrams and sketches in what is known as the Codex Arundel after the lord who purchased it. While I was still alive, I planned to arrange the Codex by topic and relationships. I never got around to it. It has been in the British Library. It has recently disappeared. The library is keeping it quiet. I believe the Codex now contains forgeries. One on balloons and airships, for example. I never contemplated that form of flight. Can you and your esteemed colleague, Sherlock Holmes, recover the Codex, uncover the forgeries, and track down the thief and forger? My historical and scientific integrity is at stake."

*****

Sherlock Holmes had just returned from tending his beehives at his retirement home in South Downs, Sussex. He had doffed his protective bonnet and coat and hung them on the rack in the entry foyer when he spotted a bright white envelope lying below the mail slot in his front door. Strange! The postman had been by earlier. This was a special delivery. In fact, he deduced what it was before he even took it up. His name was in scarlet script and on the reverse the legend 'VIA the Angelic Postal Service' in shining gold.

A lengthy message from Lady Juliet:

207

"Greetings, Holmes. I hope you are fully recovered from your broken ankle, fit and of a mind to conduct some explorations on behalf of no less a historic intellect than Leonardo DaVinci. Il Genio - the Genius."

"Leonardo is putting the finishing touches on a glorious portrait of Pookie and me. I feel like Mona Lisa or one of the magnificent Madonnas he crafted during his lifetime to say nothing of his Last Supper. *(Oh, I hope that's not blasphemous. I hope Jesus and Mother Mary will forgive me.)* After showing it at the next Celestial Art Exhibition, he is going to present it to me. I am overjoyed. I believe Pookie is too. She is such a little show off. I asked him if there was any way I could reciprocate his generosity and surprisingly, he said 'Yes'."

"As you probably know, besides his painting, sketches and sculptures, Leonardo created and kept a collection of notebooks in which he recorded images and thoughts on a wide variety of subjects. Each book is called a Codex. A very famous one is the Codex Arundel. It's named after the Earl of Arundel, who acquired it in Spain in the 1630s. He contributed it to the Royal Society and they in turn sold it to the library at the British Museum along with 549 other Arundel manuscripts (half of Arundel's collection) in 1831."

"The Codex Arundel is comprised of 283 loose pages that DaVinci describes as 'a collection without order, drawn from many papers, which I have copied here, hoping to arrange them later each in its place according to the subjects of which they treat.' *He never did!* It contains materials written between 1480 and 1518 on topics such as mechanics, astronomy, hydraulics, geometry, nature, sound, the flight of birds and a variety of machines including a bird-like ornithopter and underwater breathing apparatus. All written in Italian in his peculiar right to left 'mirror' script. ***Unfortunately, according to Leonardo, the current Codex Arundel is missing from the library. He believes it also contains a group of forgeries among its pages.*** The library had been silent about the incident. He wants assistance in tracking the Codex down, finding the thief, dealing with the fake pages and discovering who created them. I volunteered our services. I hope you don't mind. Leonardo got the Committee's permission for Pookie and I to join you once more in England. The Trinity thinks very highly of him."

Holmes shook his head. "That woman is incorrigible but working on Leonardo's behalf will be a unique experience."

*****

"Maestro, I have heard back from Holmes. He is willing to take on your case. Pookie and I are going back to Earth to assist him. Meanwhile I am so looking forward to seeing the completed painting. My mother

209

and father are overwhelmed at the prospect of my appearing in a Leonardo portrait. Have you painted many of the celestial dwellers?"

"Si. I have made sketches and oils of Jesus, Mary, several of the Archangels, St. Francis and his animals. I am flooded with requests, many of which I refuse. But a beautiful spirit like yourself! Mona Lisa or Lisa Gherardini, the wife of Francesco del Giocondo will be jealous. Oh, I forget. Jealousy is forbidden here in Heaven.

The Baroness laughed. "Fortunately, flattery is not. My dog is so pleased. We can't wait for the Art Exhibition. But we must leave. I'll have news for you shortly. We can't have your Codices going astray. Come Pookie. Flit, we must."

Through the Pearly Gates, over the Rainbow Bridge, sharp left turn at the Meadows and a descent to England. On to Sussex and South Downs. "Ah, Pookie, here we are. Nothing much seems to have changed. Let's see how Holmes is doing. He should be off the use of his cane by now."

They flitted into the cottage and came upon the Great Detective sitting in his basket chair, pipe in hand, reading a book. Jean Paul Richter's *The Literary Works of Leonardo da Vinci.* On the floor was a pile of manuscript pages.

"Hello, Holmes! Studying up?" Pookie put her paws on his leg and stared at his face. The two wraiths changed into corporeal state.

"Ah Baroness. Welcome!" He reached down and ruffled the dog's fur "And welcome to you, little Miss. I wondered when you two would appear. It seems the Italian Virtuoso is correct. His Arundel Codex has indeed gone missing from the British Museum library. I shall be making a pilgrimage to Bloomsbury in the morning. Watson will be joining us. The library management has not made the incident public nor have they informed the Met or Home Office. They are trying to avoid scandal while they frantically search. Thus far, there has been no request for ransom. I have been contacted by the Chief Librarian, Mr. Bernard Barham Woodward, an old friend. Of course, you are invited to join me and report back to your artistic sponsor. I understand the immortal Leonardo has fashioned a portrait of the two of you. A shame it cannot be shown here on Earth."

"Yes. It is miraculous! *(no pun intended)* He's lost none of his skills or interests after his death and over the ages. He is a wonder. How are your bees progressing?"

"Wonderfully well, thank you. I'd suggest a visit to the hives but the two of you should turn back into your evanescent selves before you go. The queen is a bit touchy."

"I know another one who is."

*****

The gates to the British Museum were closed as Watson and Holmes approached with the two ghosts. Several constables were posted at the entrance as well as two Scotland Yard carriages. Holmes advanced to a burly sergeant whom he remembered. "Good morning, Sergeant Foster. What is the event?"

The policeman was taken aback. "Mr. Sherlock Holmes, is it? My sainted aunt! I thought you were retired or are you just visiting?"

"Yes Sergeant, I am retired - almost. You might remember my former associate, Doctor John Watson. We are here to meet with Mr. Bernard Barham Woodward. We have an appointment."

"Well sir. I'm afraid Mr. Woodward is tied up momentarily with Inspector Gregson. There's been a murder, ya see,"

(It wasn't clear which upset Lady Juliet more. A murder or the presence of Inspector Gregson. Gregson had declared her own demise as collateral damage when she was shot several years ago. He insisted her husband, the Baron was the intended target. He was anything but and the Baroness resented being treated as an accidental victim. She referred to the Inspector as one of the Yard's jackasses second in stupidity only to Athelney Jones. The one Inspector she respected

was Lestrade who was now retired and running an inn in Manchester.)

Holmes raised an eyebrow and glanced at Watson. "A murder, you say? Might we know the victim's name?"

"Professor George Fisher from the Fitzwilliam Museum in Cambridge. He was working in the library. He was found strangled in Green Park. I'll tell the Inspector and Mr. Woodward you are here. Come inside."

Down the seemingly endless halls of the museum leading to the library, Holmes and Watson followed the sergeant. Juliet flitted alongside with Pookie pausing to sniff at different natural history exhibits. Curiosity satisfied, she ran to catch up with the procession. Juliet chuckled. *"Yes I know, Pookie, some of those bones must be very interesting."*

They arrived at the Chief Librarian's door and the Sergeant knocked and peeked in. "Excuse me, Inspector and Mr. Woodward but Mr. Sherlock Holmes and Doctor Watson are here. I thought you would want to see them."

Gregson looked up in surprise. "Mr. Holmes, I thought you were happily retired in South Downs. What brings you north? Hello, Doctor!"

The Baroness stuck her tongue out at the inspector and Pookie growled. *"Control yourself, Miss Dog.*

213

Although, I'd like to see you bite him. Actually, I'd rather kick him – the idiot - but that's not what we're here for. Let's hear about this murder. Holmes, that's something we didn't expect."

He responded telepathically. *No, but I'm not surprised. Fisher is a well-known expert on the drawings and writings of Leonardo DaVinci. He, no doubt, was investigating the disappearance of the Arundel Codex at Woodward's request. He may have come upon the forgeries."*

He turned to Gregson and the librarian. "I am here at Mr. Woodward's request. He thought: (*To say nothing of Signor DaVinci and the Baroness.*) A missing Codex by the genius Leonardo. Was that why Professor Fisher was here? What happened to him?"

Gregson cleared his throat and said, "Garroted. Found this morning in Green Park. He has been here working with a junior librarian, Miss Grant. No suspicion there. The young lady clearly lacks the strength to strangle the professor and only saw him during working hours. She is recovering from her shock in one of the anterooms. Now, we were just about to discuss this missing code book. What do you know, Mr. Holmes?"

"First off. It's called a codex. One of Leonardo's many notebooks. Correct me if I'm wrong, Mr. Woodward, but this Arundel collection is somewhat random in subject matter and organization."

`"Correct, Mr. Holmes, The Arundel Codex is a 283 page collection of Leonardo's manuscripts originating from every period in his working life, a span of 40 years from 1478 to 1518. It contains short treatises, notes and drawings on a variety of subjects from mechanics to the flight of birds. From Leonardo's text, it appears that he gathered the pages together, with the intention of ordering and possibly publishing them. He never got around to it. The Codex is named after the Earl of Arundel, who acquired it in Spain in the 1630s. The Codex Arundel is recognized as second in importance to the twelve volume Codex Atlanticus in Milan."

"Leonardo customarily used a single folio sheet of paper for each subject, so that each folio presented as a small cohesive treatise on an aspect of the subject, spread in his reverse notation across both back and front of a number of pages. This arrangement has been lost by later book binders who have cut the folios into pages and laid them on top of each other, thereby separating many subjects into several sections and resulting in an arrangement which appears random. This practice has also lent itself to the possibility of forged sheets being inserted. Professor Fisher believed they were."

Watson interrupted. "I say, why would someone add pages to the Codex. I could see them removing some for resale but including spurious pages. It seems strange."

The librarian replied, "An excellent question, Doctor. One that Professor Fisher was pursuing. He was convinced that a section on balloons and airships was not of Leonardo's authorship and several other notes on gasses and metals were anachronistic. Leonardo was a genius with great predictive skills but even he would not have foreseen a few of the recent discoveries on those subjects. The professor believed it may have been a complex and sophisticated prank. And now the documents are gone and the professor has been murdered."

"If the two events are connected, we may be dealing with a prank that ended with him being killed."

"Yes, Mr. Holmes. We may also be dealing with a highly intelligent madman."

"Or a team, Mr. Woodward, A team. Do either of you have any evidence as to what has become of the Codex? I assume it was under careful lock and key."

"Oh, indeed. It disappeared from its case less than a week ago. The case was broken and the lock destroyed. We haven't a hint as to what has become of it or who might have purloined it."

The Inspector stared at Holmes. "Why have you returned from your retirement to deal with this affair?"

"I have a commission from a very important client who will remain nameless, to track down and deal with any changes that have been made to the Codex. I am not at liberty to identify him or explain how he knew about the forgeries. I was not aware of Professor Fisher's activity in this matter nor his death. Who is or was he?"

The Chief Librarian replied. "He is from the Fitzwilliam Museum in Cambridge and a renowned specialist in the sketches and notations of Leonardo. He was examining the Codex for a research project he was embarking on. During his researches he came upon the airship/balloon anomaly. The brothers, Joseph Michel and Jacques Etienne Montgolfier, were inventors of the first hot air balloons in 1783. Fisher insisted that the Master never explored that method of flight and further scrutiny of the drawings and texts led him to conclude those pages were forgeries. Excellent forgeries that only an expert like Fisher would detect but forgeries nonetheless. And now of course, the entire Codex is gone and Fisher is dead."

During all this conversation Lady Juliet and Pookie sat motionless and silent resisting the urge to give Gregson a good swat or bite. *"Oh well, he's better than that fool Jones but not much better. I'll have to report back to Leonardo. Perhaps he will have finished the portrait. I really want to see the end result, don't you Pookie?"* The dog wagged her ephemeral tail but continued to stare menacingly at the Yard Inspector, grumbling doggie threats as she glared.

Holmes heard but ignored his ghostly associates and turned to Gregson. "I should like to interview this librarian who worked with the professor. Miss Grant? Have you spoken to her, Inspector? Where is Professor Fisher's body?"

"I believe it is at the morgue and no, I have not yet spoken to Miss Grant. Do you have any objections, Mr. Woodward?"

"No, but please be gentle with her. She is a very intelligent but sensitive young woman. I'll go with you."

Juliet and Pookie got up and flitted through the door. *"So will we!"*

*****

"You fool, you didn't have to kill him. I was willing to take the risk and engage in some literary larceny for a healthy pile of quid but I'm not going to swing for murder."

"What's done is done. He could have exposed us. I'm afraid your delicate neck and mine were on the line. I sent him an anonymous note telling him he could recover the Codex in Green Park at midnight. He fell for it, literally. Goodbye Professor! Let's just get the bloody notebooks into the General's hands, collect our fee and leave His Majesty's shores for some more genial climes."

The two conspirators, Jessica Morton and Arthur Gage, were sitting in the lowest floor of a Bond Street gallery surrounded by stacks of framed portraits and landscapes laid against the walls. A bound collection of cryptic notes and illustrations *(The Codex)* rested on a table between them. She, a senior librarian at the British Museum Library, he a dealer in art and rare editions. They, the temporary appropriators of the Arundel Codex and killers of Professor George Fisher.

Gage shook his head as he stared at a yellowed page of illustrations and mirrored writing.

"Max is a bloody genius. He captured the master's style and crazy reverse script perfectly and treated the paper and ink to blend right in with the rest of the codex. I couldn't tell the difference between his work and Leonardo's and I'm an art authority. That professor saw through the ruse not so much from the technique and artistry but from the subject matter. DaVinci never wrote about balloons and airships – just those human powered ornithopters."

"What's an ornithopter?"

"It's a mechanical, human – powered, flying apparatus – an aerial machine modeled after the birds. It's in the Arundel Codex but DaVinci never built one nor has anyone else. I personally doubt it would have worked. You need too much strength to offset the weight of the wings, body and tail. I'm not sure how you'd steer it. "

"Sort of like Daedalus and Icarus!"

"Exactly! And you know what happened there."

"But that's a myth. Balloons have been around since the 1780's and the Montgolfiers.

"Ah, you know about them."

She sniffed, "Don't forget. I am a senior librarian at the British Museum. Anyway, I can understand the General wanting a DaVinci Codex. They're worth a mint but why did we add the pages on balloons and airships? And some of the other stuff on metals and gasses."

"Because the General is a fanatic on so-called lighter than air flying. Believes it will revolutionize warcraft. I convinced him that Leonardo had come up with the idea and built a model three hundred years before the Frenchmen. He wants to show DaVinci's writings to the military as proof of concept. I told the General I could produce the pages but he had to purchase the entire Codex Arundel. He agreed. That's how we make our money. He can afford it and he doesn't much care how we acquired it."

"But if he finds out the Codex is stolen, he can hardly use it. "

"He can't use the Codex but he can use Max's wonderful additions. He can claim like many of Leonardo's notes, they were loose and only recently discovered. He's also an obsessive DaVinci collector so he's delighted with owning the Codex even if he can't show it publicly"

"Well, the death of the professor may put him off."

"I doubt it. As I said, the General is a fanatic. What's the life of a stuffy academician compared to owning a DaVinci Codex that supports his belief in airships. Besides, there is no proof that the theft and Fisher's death are related. His body was found where I dumped it in Green Park. The General won't realize the connection and we, of course, know nothing. The bumpkins from Scotland Yard won't be able to put the two events together."

"Don't be so confident. I have a very uneasy feeling about this. We can't trust anyone. What about Max?"

"Max can't say anything without admitting he's a forger. He'd be in the nick right enough. You worry too much. I have things well in hand. Nobody is going to upset our little scheme. Now, I must get over to Belgravia and present our military friend with his prize and you should get back to the library before you are missed."

*****

Arthur Gage was wrong. Gregson wasn't quite the sharpest axe in the Scotland Yard toolbox but he was intelligent and suspicious enough to tie the theft and the Professor's death together. Of course, Holmes, Watson and the Baroness had all immediately come to the same conclusion. The Professor had been on to something and had paid for it with his life.

Miss Olivia Grant was seated in one of the library's many reading rooms, staring off into space. The Chief Librarian, Gregson, Holmes and Watson, plus the two wraiths entered the chamber. The junior librarian had probably not yet reached her twentieth year; petite; slim figure; dark brown hair drawn into a bun; blue eyes that showed traces of tears; dressed in a white blouse and long grey skirt which turned out to be the standard uniform for the female museum and library staff.

Recognizing the Chief Librarian, she immediately rose and executed a half curtsey. "Mr. Woodward. I'm sorry, sir. I should get back to my duties. Miss Morton is away on an errand."

"In just a few moments, Miss Grant. These gentlemen would like to speak with you. This is Inspector Tobias Gregson of Scotland Yard and these two gentlemen are the famous detective Sherlock Holmes and his associate Doctor Watson."

The unseen Baroness chuckled, *"And I am the famous deceased stage star, Lady Juliet Armstrong,*

Baroness Crestwell and this little imp is Pookie, Bichon Extraordinaire." The dog barked, unheard.

Gregson took up the discussion. "Who is Miss Morton?"

Woodward answered, "She is our senior staff librarian. I will arrange for you to meet her on her return. Meanwhile, I trust you have some questions to ask Miss Grant. She was assigned to work with Professor Fisher while he was here at the library."

The girl sniffed, "A fine old gentleman he was. Such a scholar. Why would anyone want to do him in?"

Holmes responded, "That is what we intend to find out, Miss Grant. I understand the two of you were working on the Arundel Codex before it was purloined."

"Well he was. I was only doing 'find and fetch' duty for him. He was off on some research about balloons and airships. I think he was trying to find out if Leonardo DaVinci ever had anything to do with them. He had heard rumors that there were extra Codex pages that proved he had. He couldn't find them and we were researching other sources. Then of course, the Codex disappeared. He was most upset. So was I. So was Miss Morton. And now he's dead." She began to cry.

Holmes waited for her to recover. "Did he think there was some connection between the airship rumors and the missing Codex?"

"I believe he did. He said something about forgeries and possible fraud. I told Miss Morton about it."

"We will speak to her. What do you know about the missing Codex?"

"Well, the Professor was using it in his research. I understand you agreed to that, Mr. Woodward."

"Yes, I did."

"Every morning, I would open the locked case, take out the notebook and bring it to the professor. In the evening, when he was finished with it, I'd take it and lock it back up. Whenever he was away or not needing it, I'd make sure it was safe and locked in."

" You have a key to the case?"

'I did until the Codex was stolen. So did Miss Morton. I gave mine back. I don't know what she did with hers."

"The case was broken and the lock destroyed as I understand it. But we don't know if the Codex was missing before the damage was done."

Gregson looked at Holmes. "You think someone with a key removed the Codex and then did the damage to mislead us?'

"It's possible. Who else had keys to the case, Miss Grant?"

"I don't know, sir. You might ask Miss Morton."

"I will."

Gregson looked to the young librarian. "Tell us, my girl. Did you and the professor have any social connections?"

She frowned,. "If you mean what I think you mean, Inspector, that is the most foolish and insulting thing I have ever heard. We worked together here in the library – period, full stop. He was a nice old gentleman, very skilled and knowledgeable, polite to a fault. We had no mutual interests other than the Codex. He felt he was on to something and was feverishly pursuing a solution. He didn't like London. He was eager to return to Cambridge as soon as he could."

The Baroness cheered. *"That's telling him, sister. These policeman are always suspicious when a man and woman work together. He's such a boob."*

Just then, a tall, well-built woman, also clad in museum/library dress entered. She scanned the room, looking quizzically at Gregson, Holmes and Watson. She wore steel-rimmed spectacles that sat at the edge of her sharp nose. No wedding ring or jewelry of any sort except for a small lapel watch pinned to her blouse. A few grey hairs shot through her dark brown tresses, also drawn up into a bun. The hairstyle seemed to be part of the staff uniform. Pookie sniffed at her with some interest. She smiled at Mr. Woodward and Miss Grant.

"Good morning, Sir. I have completed my errand. A private bookseller eager to pass on what he purports to be a first edition full copy of *Dombey and Son*. As you know, Dickens published much of his work in installments. This volume was missing one or two segments. I had no interest, especially at the price he was asking. May I be introduced to these gentlemen?"

Juliet made a mental note to contact Dickens when she returned to Heaven and check whether he did indeed publish Dombey and Son in serial editions. He probably did. This lady wouldn't lie about it in front of two literary specialists. But was that where she was? The Baroness wondered.

Woodward returned her smile. "Miss Felicia Morton, may I present Inspector Tobias Gregson of Scotland Yard and Mr. Sherlock Holmes and Doctor John Watson. Inspector Gregson has taken over the investigation of the missing Codex and is also enquiring into the murder of Professor Fisher. Mr.

Holmes and the Doctor are also involved in the examination."

She smiled somewhat wanly at the trio. Her blood ran cold at the prospect of Holmes' involvement. So much for 'Scotland Yard bumpkins.' She needed to inform Arthur Gage immediately that the great detective was on the case.

"Such a shock about the Professor. Such a lovely man." She looked at the junior librarian for confirmation. Miss Grant nodded her agreement.

She continued. "I hope the culprits are captured shortly. I'm sure you will. I'm so pleased to meet you gentlemen. She merely nodded at Gregson. I have read several of your thrilling adventures, Doctor. It's a delight to meet you in person. And of course, the famous detective himself. I thought the Doctor reported you as retired to a farmhouse in Sussex, Mr. Holmes.'

Holmes replied, "That is my intent, Miss Morton, but events keep catching me up. I was originally commissioned to look into the disappearance of DaVinci's Codex but now this murder had caught my interest."

"Do you believe the two events are connected?"

"It seems highly likely." He watched her face for a reaction which didn't come.

Juliet chuckled, *"Holmes, take it from a skilled thespian. This woman is an experienced actress. She knows something. She may even be directly involved."*

He replied telepathically. *"Thank you, Baroness. Two great minds arriving at the same conclusion. What say you, Watson?"*

The doctor who was tuned into this ghostly conversation, subtly nodded. Gregson, of course, was out of the telepathic loop.

Holmes continued, *"Lady Juliet, will you and Pookie please keep a watch on the senior librarian? Let's see where she goes and who she meets."*

The wraith replied. *"Assignment accepted."* The dog wagged her tail.

Miss Morton rose and left the room, unaware of being followed by the two ghosts.

Holmes turned to the junior librarian. "Miss Grant, can you share with us what Professor Fisher was researching in the Arundel Codex."

"Well, as I told you, he had heard of some spurious pages in the Codex about balloons but couldn't find them. Da Vinci's notebooks were hardly prime examples of organization or neatness. I imagine he wrote and drew on impulse. As an idea occurred to him, he recorded it. Then there were the bookbinders who tried to create folios out of the pages. I doubt they could translate his reversed writing and only had the diagrams to go by. Their attempts at seeking order only made the confusion worse."

"Was the Professor trying to reorder the Codex."

"No, he felt too much respect for Leonardo to 'trifle with the Master's work' as he put it but he took copious notes and transcribed many of the entries for further study."

"How did he come to believe there were forged pages in the collection?"

"I don't know for sure. I think he had heard of a rich retired General who's a fanatic on lighter than air flight, bragging that he knew of Leonardo's work on balloons. He wanted to use it to promote interest in the military's development of airships although those French brothers had already proven they work. The General wanted to outdo the French. There's a community of academics and military specialists who are engaged in promoting lighter than air flight. There is also a coterie of individuals who are DaVinci enthusiasts. A few well-to-do personalities belong to both groups."

"Who is this General?"

"The Professor never gave me his name but I think he resides here in London. Professor Fisher was convinced no such notes existed and thought the General was an overly eager crackpot. Of course, that wasn't the only item on the professor's agenda. As a DaVinci specialist, he treated the Arundel Codex as the Holy Grail. He even tried to get the Museum to transfer it to the Fitzwilliam Museum in Cambridge. No such luck."

Woodward interrupted. "Much as I respected the Professor, there was no way we were going to give up that treasure even temporarily."

Watson shrugged. "But now it's gone." He looked at Gregson. "Is Scotland Yard involved in the theft or are you only interested in the murder."

"I'm pursuing the murderer. Inspector Stanley Hopkins has been assigned the theft.'

Holmes raised an eyebrow. "So the Yard doesn't think the two events are connected?"

Gregson shrugged. "Maybe! Maybe not!"

"Well, I believe they are. I shall have to contact Inspector Hopkins. I assume you and your staff have been interviewed by him, Mr. Woodward."

"Indeed, right after the theft. He doesn't seem to have made much progress on recovering the Codex, however."

"Gregson, do you have any idea how and why the Professor ended up in Green Park?"

"That's a puzzle, Mr. Holmes. It's not that near the Museum or the Kingsley Hotel where he was staying. We presume he was meeting someone in the Park and ended up being done in. We haven't found any message or appointments in any of his clothing or articles in his hotel. The concierge and the desk clerks couldn't shed any light. Miss Grant, do you know any reason why he may have been in the Park?"

"No, Inspector. I don't. The Professor did not share any of his off hours activities with me. You may wish to ask Miss Morton."

"Thank you, I shall."

*****

Inspector Stanley Hopkins is one of the few members of the Scotland Yard investigative unit who studied and imitated the techniques of Sherlock Holmes. He had worked with Holmes and Watson in several cases that the Doctor had written up as *The Adventures of the Abbey Grange; the Golden Pince-Nez; and Black Peter*. The trio had an attitude of mutual respect for each other.

As they strode the corridors of the offices of the Metropolitan Police on the Victoria Embankment, Holmes said, "I'm glad Hopkins is on the case. He is one of the few Yard denizens with a functioning brain in his head."

The Inspector was seated at his miniscule desk, bowler hat tilted on the back of his head, moustache shrouding his downturned mouth. He looked up in surprise. "Mr. Holmes, Doctor Watson. To what do I owe your esteemed presence? I never thought I'd see you again after you retired. Have you retired as well, Doctor?"

"Not yet, Stanley, and my worthy colleague here keeps entering and exiting the emeritus state. Right now we are looking into the disappearance of the Arundel Codex and the murder of Professor Fisher. We understand you are investigating the theft and Gregson has the murder."

"True. I think that division of labor is a mistake. The two cases are obviously connected but the Super doesn't see it that way."

Holmes nodded, "We agree with you but at the moment, the issue is not worth battling over, Inspector"

He shrugged. "I suppose not. But it's frustrating. Gregson and I get along but all this unnecessary coordination is a waste. How can I help you? What is your interest?"

"We were originally commissioned by a party who wishes to remain anonymous to look into the loss of the Codex but now this murder has put a new face on the whole affair. We have just come from the British Museum Library. We had short interviews with the Chief Librarian Mr. Woodward, Miss Felicia Morton, the senior librarian and the young lady who was working with Professor Fisher, Miss Olivia Grant. We got very little from them."

"Neither did I, Mr. Holmes. It seems the Professor was on about possible forgeries included among the original DaVinci papers in the notebook. He may have made a discovery that cost him his life."

Watson intervened. "Miss Grant seemed to think he had found nothing. His suspicions were raised by a General he met who claimed Leonardo invented airships and balloons long before those French brothers succeeded with their experiments. But so far, they found no references in the Codex."

Holmes thought to himself. "Leonardo makes no such claims. Ornithopters were his subjects."

He turned to the Yard detective. "What do you make of the theft?"

"I believe it's an inside job. The broken case and lock may well be a red herring intended to mislead us into believing someone from the outside did an overnight smash and grab. It's just as likely someone with a key lifted the documents and then broke the case and lock to misdirect our attention and cover up their crime."

"Excellent, Hopkins. I share your opinion. Now, who had the keys?"

"The Chief Librarian, the senior librarian and the junior who was working with the Professor. Those two ladies could have done it or they may have a co-conspirator. I'm not all that sure about this Miss Morton, the senior librarian. Nothing I can prove as yet but I consider her a 'person of interest.' I'm not ready to take her into custody. I'm less convinced about Miss Grant, the junior, as a possible culprit. She seemed to be dedicated to assisting the Professor but you never know."

"However, there may be other copies of the keys. The professor may have had one although Gregson says he hasn't found any on the body or in his effects. It could have been one of the guards although I doubt it. Whoever took it must have contacts willing to pay substantially for it though it will never appear on the legitimate market. A wealthy but obsessive collector. Mr. Holmes, do you have any idea who this mysterious General might be?"

"Not yet but I have a source who may be able to assist. I'll be back to you. I'm also watching this Miss Morton. Once again, Hopkins, we are in accord. Join us in this!"

They rose and left the room.

As they walked down the corridor, Watson looked at Holmes. "Am I correct in assuming who this source is you're planning to call on?"

*****

"Yes, Watson, I think it is time to visit the repository of all London scandal and gossip, the St. James Street Club that accommodates Langdale Pike. If anyone knows this General it will be him. We must stop at a wine shop. A bottle of fine cognac in exchange for information."

"You know how I feel about that rumor monger, Holmes, but I suppose you are right."

"He is the wholesale purveyor and collector of London's gossip. If anyone has information on this unknown military officer, Pike is our man. Our alternative would be a survey of Mycroft's military connections, Pike is more rapid in his responses. He sits in the bow window of his club, apparently immobile and inert and yet he has his antennae sharply tuned for the latest disgraces, rumors, scandals, relationships, transactions, tittle-tattle, crimes and outrages. He filters these and passes them on to the press and chattering classes, all for a price of course. He and I have a reciprocal relationship. If this general exists, Langdale Pike will know who he is."

As Holmes, Watson and Hopkins descended from their cab at the St. James Club, Langdale Pike spied them from his bow window perch. His curiosity was immediately piqued. Holmes never approached the club unless he had some reason to deal with Pike. He was also interested in Doctor Watson and an obvious

Scotland Yard Inspector accompanying the detective. This was no social call.

As they entered, he waved an indolent hand in Holmes direction and drawled. "Mr. Sherlock Holmes. Doctor Watson, greetings. Who is this gentleman?

"May I introduce Inspector Stanley Hopkins of Scotland Yard."

"Always a pleasure to meet another stalwart of law enforcement. So, Mr. Holmes, are you buying or selling?"

"A bit of both, Langdale. Perhaps a swap may be in order."

"Ooh, interesting. Please have a seat, gentlemen. We can speak confidentially here. Perhaps a bit of liquid refreshment to facilitate the discussion?"

Holmes produced the bottle of VSOP cognac. "I am told the quality of the St. James' cellar has gone downhill. This may compensate. Feel free to imbibe. I and my companions will abstain."

Pike was familiar with Watson and knew he was not on the Doctor's Christmas greeting list. He languidly nodded in his direction. "A pleasure to see you again, Doctor Watson. Still writing your exciting tales?"

Watson grunted.

"Ah well! He opened the bottle and poured himself a generous tot and waved his glass at the three. "Are you sure you won't join me? No? Well, on to business. Now, in what way can I make my humble self of use to you gentlemen?"

Holmes responded. "We are in search of a General who is obsessed with balloons and airships and may be involved in the disappearance of a priceless museum artefact – Leonardo DaVinci's Arundel Codex.

Watson coughed loudly. "I say, Holmes! Should you be telling this to a known gossip peddler. The story of the missing notebooks will be in the streets and possibly the press within the hour."

Pike smiled, "Fear not, Doctor. Mr. Holmes and I have conducted numerous highly confidential exchanges and I doubt he would be here if he did not believe in my trustworthiness. Some of our previous transactions would have gotten both of us killed if they were discovered by the wrong persons. Now, I may have some useful information for you, Mr. Holmes but I doubt you are here just for a name provided by a "known gossip peddler."

"I need several things from you, Pike. The identification of this General; his address and direction; and anything you know about him that supplies evidence of his possible involvement with the missing Codex."

"I believe I can be of some assistance. But I think another bottle or two of fine brandy is in order, Mr. Holmes."

"Aha! A three bottle problem. Say on! You know I am good for it."

I believe we are talking about General Wilton Braddock, Lord Eustace, Royal Army Retired. Considers himself an authority on the future of aviation such as it may be. Wherever and whenever there is a conference on the potential of military airpower, you will find Lord Eustace in the middle. Rich as Croesus. He also prides himself as a collector of historical documents, memorabilia and items of wartime history. I would not be surprised if he were connected to this missing Codex. Of course, he could not admit to owning it but he might be able to separate a folio or two and claim it has no kinships with the Arundel notebook. The man's a definite eccentric but a very wealthy eccentric. Lives in a massive pile in Belgrave Square. Widowed, two sons, both in the military. Does that suffice?

"Three bottles of fine cognac on their way to you. Thank you as usual, Langdale. We'll see ourselves out.

Hopkins was flummoxed. As they hailed a cab, he sputtered. 'I say, Holmes. Do you trust his word? How does Langdale Pike do that? Does he really just sit there and sweep up, retain and trade tons of information? From all over London?"

"Oh, not just London, Inspector. He has connections on the Continent. I am led to believe he deals with North America as well. Canada and the United States. And yes, I trust him and no, I do not know how he does it. He stumbles every now and then but on this subject, he is most believable. London's aristocracy seems to be an area in which he is most knowledgeable. He is equally au courant with all the toffs, nobility and royalty. He puts Fleet Street to shame although feeding the press is a major source of his earnings. He is quite unique. Let us see if his lordship is at home to visitors."

Watson demurred. "Count me out. I don't know the first thing about flight. My knowledge of birds is limited to the dining rooms of London's luxury restaurants."

*****

Felicia Morton returned to her office at the library where she nervously opened and closed office drawers, adjusted her spectacles and fiddled with the pens on her desk. She was waiting for an appropriate time to leave the museum without rousing suspicions. She would have been even more upset if she knew that two female spirits were closely watching her – one a saint and the other a celestial canine.

"So, Pookie, we wait to see what, if anything, Miss Morton is going to do or whom she's going to meet."

The dog yawned and shifted in her seat on a file cabinet.

"Yes, yes. I know but that's the problem with stakeouts. Long boring periods of inaction followed by sudden bursts of movement. Oh, oh. It looks like our literary friend has decided on some movement. Let's see what she's going to do. I hope she's not just going for a cup of tea."

Tea was not on Felicia Morton's mind. Sherlock Holmes and Arthur Gage were. She rose, locked her desk and file cabinets, little knowing an evanescent Bichon Frisé was staring at her from atop one of the cupboards. She took up her coat and stylish hat, tiptoed out of her office, securing the door behind her and then strode unconcernedly down the corridors of the library and museum. After all, she was the Senior Librarian and could go wherever she wished. She waved at one of the guards as she stepped out of the employees' entrance and around to a cab stand on Great Russell Street. She was joined by the ephemeral Baroness and her dog. She gave the cabby the address of a Bond Street art gallery and settled back for the short ride.

"Ah, Pookie, Miss Morton is not going for tea. She has an assignation that I find most interesting. Let us see what develops."

The Bichon whined and Juliet reached into her bottomless celestial reticule and pulled out a Heavenly

Chewy snack for her companion. *"Yes, I know. This detective work can stir an appetite."*

The librarian reached her destination, paid the cabdriver and strode into the Gage Gallery along with her invisible entourage. The establishment's assistant got up from her desk to welcome the woman. "Hello again, Miss Morton. I'm afraid Mr. Gage is not here. He left a bit earlier with a package he said he was personally delivering. He should be back shortly. May I get you some tea?"

Miss Morton nodded affirmatively. Lady Juliet chuckled, *"It seems I was wrong, Pookie. Miss Morton is going to have tea after all. I wonder who and where this Mr. Gage is and what he is doing. Our librarian friend seems most eager to see him. Oh well, more watchful waiting."*

*****

They were not the only ones engaged in observing. Holmes, Watson and Hopkins had arrived at Belgrave Square just in time to spot a tall, moustachioed individual in a well-tailored afternoon suit and bowler hat enter the doorway of Major General Wilton Braddock, Lord Eustace, Royal Army Retired's opulent establishment. He carried a moderate sized package under his arm.

"Aha, Watson and Inspector. I believe the General is about to receive the purloined Codex. Why don't we split up. Watson, you follow this mysterious individual when he leaves and Hopkins and I shall beard Lord Eustace in his den. Meanwhile let us take a casual stroll and enjoy the Belgravian scenery."

Meanwhile, inside the mansion, the General's butler had directed Arthur Gage to a luxurious drawing room heavily decorated with war trophies, banners and weapons. Pictures of war machines, weapons and equipment lined one wall including a reproduction of DaVinci's armored fighting vehicle as well as a French self-propelled cannon and a very recent sketch of H.G. Wells' Land Ironclad. On another wall were illustrations of the Montgolfiers' balloons, fanciful airships and Leonardo's ornithopters.

This was not Gage's first visit to Lord Eustace. They had first met at a conference on weaponry held at the V&A Museum. The art dealer had arranged an introduction to General Braddock and over time persuaded him that he could procure for his lordship the original Arundel Codex which the British Library was eager to sell in order to offset some massive reconstruction costs. *(All a lie, of course!)* Lord Eustace's interest was piqued when he was told the notebook contained text and illustrations of DaVinci's concepts for airships and balloons as instruments of battle. *(Max's forgeries.)* With more money than common sense and believing he was helping the Museum to relieve its debt as well as strengthening his arguments for military airship development, the

General had agreed to acquire the Codex for £10,000. *(£1,572,556.00 today.)* This was delivery day!

When his lordship entered the room, Arthur Gage rose and trying not to seem too eager, held his package out to the enthusiastic recipient. "The Arundel Codex, milord, as promised."

Lord Eustace was the "very model of a modern Major General" *(apologies to Gilbert and Sullivan)* Tall and white of hair, clad in a dark morning suit befitting his retirement. Lacking at the moment his sword, plumed hat, sash, medals and red coat, he still radiated military authority, posture, elan and mannerisms. His monocle, furrowed brow and flowing moustache said it all as did his sharp baritone voice.

"Well, unwrap the bally thing, Gage. Let's see what I'm buying."

The gallery owner's smile bordered on a covetous simper as he considered the £10,000 draft he would soon receive in exchange for the pilfered portfolio. He uncovered the Codex and presented it to the nobleman, carefully tugging at a bookmark that revealed the forged notations and diagrams of airships and balloons. Max's marvelous handiwork.

The General chortled with glee. Ah, yes! Wonderful! Wonderful! DaVinci was a true prophet. A seer! An oracle! I suppose the rest of these notes and illustrations are of interest, as well. Why did the man write in that topsy-turvy manner? Right to left?"

"I am told, your lordship, that such writing was not uncommon among the artists and innovators of the 14 and 1500's."

"Well, it certainly makes reading difficult and especially in Renaissance Italian. Damned nuisance. I can understand why the Museum Library was willing to sell it off."

"They are most grateful to you for your purchase. As I told you. This transaction must be hush-hush. No mention of the Museum's need for funds or the sale of the Codex or other assets. Fleet Street would have a field day if it was discovered. Parliament might even get involved. Gage Galleries are acting as the library's intermediary."

"How is the Library explaining its disappearance?"

"It has been withdrawn from view and put away to preserve and maintain it. Museum and library lights and humidity are a great issue. I hope you have made provision here in your home to safeguard your investment."

The General, who hadn't given a moment's thought to the subject, except to order a special safe from Chubb, shook his head. "Of course, of course. I have taken detailed steps in that regard."

"Excellent! Well then, shall we complete our transaction?"

"What? Oh, yes!" He looked at his butler. "Soames, get Forsyth in here. Forsyth is my secretary. He was my batman when we were still in active service."

Gage produced another of his hyena smiles as the General paged through the Codex. Forsyth appeared and anticipating the General's requirement, produced a bank cheque."

The secretary looked solemn "Here is a draft on the National Provincial Bank for £10,000 made out to Gage Galleries. Before it is accepted in your account, it must be countersigned by an officer of the National Provincial Bank. Have your bank's managing director contact them. Large amount, don't you know. Can't be too careful."

Gage's smile hid a twinge of annoyance. Foxy old soldiers! Petty banker bureaucrats! Oh well! He'd have to sustain a day's delay in his voyage to the south of France while the banks carried out their security exchanges. On the other hand, now he had more time to get rid of that pest of a woman. Miss Morton. Expecting a share of the spoils. Hardly! She was useful but certainly not someone he wished to spend any time with. Like the nosey professor, she had to go. He had a plan.

He took the draft from the secretary and placed it in his portfolio, shook the General's hand, wished him luck with his new acquisition, turned and left the mansion. He didn't notice that his departure was being observed by three gentlemen engaged in conversation across the street from the splendid building. One of them parted from his fellows and followed Gage to a cab stand. Taking his seat in the hackney, Watson uttered those oh so familiar words. "Follow that cab."

The short ride past Buckingham Palace took them to Bond Street. First stop, the local branch of the Barclay's Private Bank that served the Gage Gallery. Back and forth with the manager. Hums and coughs as the deposit procedure was put in place. It wasn't as if Gage was not a familiar customer but his transactions lately were seldom of this magnitude. Not unless he was conducting an auction. There had been none recently. The art world was fickle and volatile. Gage was not au courant with the latest fashions and trends and was rapidly falling out of favor. *(In fact the Gallery was in dire financial straits and Gage was faced with possible bankruptcy.)* This sale would allow him to escape all that bother.

On to the gallery to face down that pestilent woman. He did not observe the tweed clad gentleman perusing the racks of bank literature as he passed out the door. Watson waited a few moments and then left behind him. The gallery was only a few doors away. As Gage entered his establishment, Watson was greeted on the street by a snuffling ethereal dog and a beautiful scarlet clad wraith.

"Doctor, I am so glad to see you. I believe the Senior Librarian, Miss Felicia Morton and this Arthur Gage are preparing to do a bunk. Where is Holmes?"

*****

As soon as Arthur Gage had climbed into the cab in Belgravia followed by Doctor Watson, Holmes and Hopkins approached the impressive doorway of the General's mansion. Warrant card at the ready, the inspector rang the doorbell which intoned the first few bars of "God save the King." Soames, the butler, opened the door, prepared to dismiss these intruders, whoever they might be. He was taken aback by the sight of Hopkins waving his credentials accompanied by a tall, hawk-faced man who looked vaguely familiar.

"Good day. I am Inspector Stanley Hopkins of Scotland Yard and this is Mr. Sherlock Holmes. We must see Major General Wilton Braddock, Lord Eustace on a matter of some major importance."

The butler stared at the duo, his mind sorting possible alternatives including summoning Forsyth, the secretary, when Lord Eustace solved the dilemma for him. "Who is it, Soames? Send them away. I'm in no mood for salesmen or charitable do-good solicitors."

Hopkins took the opportunity to seize the high ground. "Lord Eustace. I am here representing Scotland Yard and I am sorry to say that you are about

247

to be subject to arrest for receipt of irreplaceable stolen goods"

The General was aghast. He turned to Soames. "Get Forsyth down here immediately. Come in, come in. Obviously you are mistaken. You know who I am. Never been involved in stealing in my life. Oh, maybe an apple tart or pork pie as a lad. What are you talking about?"

Holmes looked at the General. We have irrefutable reason to believe that you just bought the Arundel Codex of Leonardo DaVinci recently stolen from the British Museum Library."

"Stolen? Preposterous! What, what! Who are you, sir, and how do you know about the Codex?"

"My name is Sherlock Holmes. It is my business to know what other people do not know."

"Yes, heard of you, Holmes. You're that detective Johnny. Read some of that Doctor's stories about you. Didn't know you actually existed. Now, what is this nonsense about the Codex being stolen? Mr. Arthur Gage, a highly reputable dealer in art and artefacts sold it to me on behalf of the British Museum Library for £10,000. He's representing them in a confidential sale of several of their acquisitions to raise money for reconstruction and repairs. Very hush-hush, don't you know. Don't want the press or wild-eyed art or history lovers to know about it. The library is claiming the Codex has been removed for preservation."

Hopkins interrupted, "I'm sorry to contradict you, Milord but that notebook is priceless and it was stolen from its case at the library several nights ago."

The secretary arrived and looked at the assemblage quizzically.

"Forsyth, what do you know about this?"

"About what, milord?"

"These gentlemen of the law insist that Gage has sold me a priceless work of historical art stolen from the British Museum Library."

"I'm sorry, milord, but you will recall that you negotiated the purchase yourself something about balloons and airships by the Great Master Leonardo."

Holmes looked at the General. "We have reason to believe that those pages are forgeries inserted in the Codex after the theft. DaVinci never had anything to say or do about airships. Gage hired a forger to create that content so you would be more willing to buy the notebook."

The General seethed, dropping his monocle in the process. "Don't just stand there, Forsyth. Get a stop order off on that draft from the Bank. That bounder bilked me. I'll see him in irons. Not one penny of mine will he get from his chicanery."

Hopkins turned to Soames. "Are you on the telephone exchange?"

"Yes sir, we are. The General is insistent on keeping up with technical progress."

"I'd like to place a call to Scotland Yard."

"Of course, sir. Follow me!"

The Inspector walked to an alcove in front of Forsyth who was on his way to call the National Provincial Bank and stop payment on the draft for £10,000 made out to Gage Galleries. Hopkins held up his hand and stopped the secretary. "Just give me a few moments. We need to arrest the wily Mr. Gage."

He gave the number to the exchange operator, telling her this was an important police matter. Several minutes passed before the baritone voice of Tobias Gregson came on the line. "'Gregson? Hopkins here. Get over to the Gage Galleries on Bond Street and arrest Arthur Gage. He's the thief who stole the Codex and I believe he's also Professor George Fisher's killer. If that librarian Felicia Morton is there, bring her in, too. Holmes and I will give you the full story as soon as we finish here with Lord Eustace. Good man! Talk to you soon."

Forsyth took up the handset and placed his call to the bank. Meanwhile the General was bombarding Holmes with questions and loud reactions. "What are you going to do about the forgeries. I'm tempted to keep them as a memento of my own stupidity."

"Sorry, milord! I'm afraid they are criminal evidence. We've yet to track down this counterfeiter. He's a brilliant craftsman but operating on the wrong side of the law. Art and literary forgeries are difficult to identify. I suspect Professor Fisher from the Fitzwilliam Museum saw something there that set off an alarm. We are sure the theft was an inside job and the fake entries were placed in the Codex prior to its theft. Probably by this Miss Morton, the Senior Librarian. We know how to reach her but we'll have to hurry. She and Gage are probably in cahoots and planning to disappear once your cheque clears the banking system. A good thing you decided not to pay in cash."

"Never use cash except to pay for cabs. Don't do that often. Travel around London in my limousines most of the time."

Forsyth and Hopkins re-entered the room together. The secretary reported that the stop order had been issued. The Inspector said, "I'm afraid I'm going to have to relieve you of the Codex, milord. It's evidence and eventually has to be returned to the museum library."

"Take the damned thing. Never want to see it again. To think I was buying stolen property. Arthur Gage is a slippery scoundrel."

Hopkins grimaced, "We also believe he's a murderer. Another inspector is on his way to arrest him for the theft. We'll see if we can get him to confess to the killing."

Holmes interjected "Or perhaps his partner in crime will sell him out to save her own neck."

*****

"Miss Morton is inside, Doctor. Gage just returned. I'm going back inside. We'll keep them under observation. Why don't you summon a bobby. We don't want you getting into another 'shoot-em-up' do we?" The invisible Lady Juliet and her dog were ready to gather evidence and pass it on to the Doctor. He in turn could notify the police. They didn't realize Gregson was on his way to the gallery. Watson went off to summon a constable and explain the situation."

In the basement of the gallery, under the watchful eyes of the Baroness and Pookie, Felicia Morton greeted Arthur Gage. "Well, how did it go?"

"The deed is done. The old fool fell for it. Unfortunately, he paid me with a draft on his bank that needs to be countersigned. I deposited it in my bank. They're taking care of the process. Funds will be available tomorrow. I suppose I shouldn't have expected cash."

"Well, then, tomorrow we leave for France."

"No, my dear, **I** leave for France. Your usefulness has ended. Go back to your books and periodicals."

"I was afraid you'd pull something like that. Scotland Yard will soon be receiving an anonymous letter accusing you of murdering the professor as well as stealing the Codex."

"You fool! Don't you realize I can implicate you."

"Me, the highly trusted Senior Librarian of the British Museum? I'll take my chances unless of course you want to cut me a substantial share of that £10,000."

"You'll get your cut, all right." He picked up a nearby packing knife and lunged at her. She screamed but both of them were shocked when a female figure in scarlet grabbed his knife hand and a small white dog sank her teeth into his ankle. The two phantoms had solidified and were making short work of the gallery owner. The librarian cowered in a corner behind a packing case. Gage was lying flat on the floor, unconscious, struck down with a wooden board swung by his mysterious attacker.

The gallery assistant, hearing the screams, raced down the stairs to the basement followed by Watson and two constables. The Baroness and Pookie disappeared. Miss Morton sobbed. "He tried to kill me. Like he did the professor."

Inspector Gregson made his appearance just in time to hear her outburst. He ordered the constables to cuff both of them. Miss Morton struggled. "I'm the victim. He's the killer. Where did they go?"

"Who?"

"The woman in red and her dog. They knocked Arthur out."

The constables laughed, "Now I've heard everything."

Watson smiled as he reached down to check on the semi-conscious killer. He noticed bite marks on Gage's ankle. He murmured under his breath. "Nice work, ladies."

In response, he heard a tinkling laugh followed by a ghostly bark.

*****

Next morning, in Watson's Queen Anne Street offices, Holmes, the Doctor and the incorporeal Lady Juliet and Pookie gathered to review the bidding of the previous day. Holmes summarized telepathically. *"The Codex is in the hands of the police and the library has been informed of its recovery. The fake DaVinci entries about airships have been identified and set aside. Gage, trying to save his neck, fingered Max and he has been arrested. Miss Morton has been pouring out her story, accusing Gage of the theft and murder of the professor. The police have ample evidence of his attempt to kill the librarian. Nobody believes the culprits' story of the mysterious scarlet lady and the dog. They think the librarian struck him with the board. I didn't point out the canine teeth marks in Gage's ankle.* (laughter) *The General is annoyed at the loss of the Codex. Although now that he knows the entries about airships were faked, he's relieved his money has been restored. Gregson and Hopkins are the heroes of the hour. We are forgotten"*

The Baroness laughed, *"Well Holmes. It pains me that Gregson is a fair haired boy. He is such an idiot. I have hopes for Hopkins. I'm sorry I didn't get a chance to meet Lord Eustace. He sounds like a hoot. The Modern Major General. I starred once in the Pirates of Penzance. I was the sweetest Mabel ever to hit the stage. A long time ago. Ah me! I'd prefer it didn't get around that I clobbered Arthur Gage. Unsaintly behavior but necessary under the circumstances. Pookie and I are going back to Paradise. I'll report to Leonardo. I believe the Celestial Art Exhibition is about to kick off. My portrait is supposed to be a feature of the show. We'll see. Come, Miss Dog. Let's return and see everyone. Ta-ta all. See you again, God willing.*

*****

'La Baronessa e il suo Cane.' Leonardo had outdone himself. Beautifully framed and centered in the Celestial Exhibition Hall, Juliet's image glowed with her enigmatic smile. Seated at her feet was a little white dog, head on her paws, looking the soul of innocence. Most of the denizens of Heaven knew otherwise. The show was sensational. Most of the great artists who had made it to Paradise were represented.

Juliet had given a delighted Leonardo a full report on the Codex affair.. She in turn was delighted with her portrait and the fact that it would soon be hanging in her mansion, She and the dog stood by the painting, smiling at the compliments coming from her saintly and angelic friends. Several of Pookie's chums came by wagging their tails in approval. Juliet's mother was beside herself and even her taciturn father was clearly pleased. Mr. Raymond appeared. "Well. It seems the Maestro has retained his touch. The Committee and the Almighty are pleased." A man in his late thirties approached and bowed. "Scusi, Baronessa. I am Raffaello Sanzio da Urbino, known as Raphael, I am a painter, not the archangel. Could I interest you in posing for me."

The Adventures of Sherlock Holmes and the Glamorous Ghost

Volume Four

Il Genio – a Novelette

The End

The Adventures of Sherlock Holmes and the Glamorous Ghost

Volume Four

Confucian Confusion

Barks, howls, whines and growls echoed over the Meadows as the last moments of the Celestial Multi-Dimensional Fetch Championship Tournament wound down. Pookie had scored the winning fetch in a last minute dash, leading the Heavenly Hounds to a victory over the Cosmic Canines. Cheers and groans from the saintly and angelic onlookers almost, but not quite, drowned out the enthusiastic shouts of Lady Juliet, her family and Empress Sisi. The Baroness ran down the sidelines and lifted her heroine dog high in the air in a show of triumph. As usual, Juliet hadn't the slightest idea of the rules of the game but she recognized a victory when she saw one. Pookie jumped out of her arms and executed one of her signature backflips. She was greeted by joyful snorts and whinnies from the Lipizzaner stallions and a thunderous flapping of Pegasus' wings. The unicorn shook its horn in excitement. The celestial referees led by Mr. Raymond and Mr. Sherman cleared the field as the teams headed to their respective locker rooms.

Pookie raced ahead and joined her teammates in a rollicking chorus of winners' yelps. There would be extra rations of Heavenly Chewies for the dogs and cups of nectar and ambrosia for the human spectators. The angels, as usual, abstained.

On the way back over the Rainbow Bridge and through the Pearly Gates, the Armstrong family plus friends bellowed fun-filled songs. Pegasus dived and did a barrel roll in a fly-by. Juliet was distracted and didn't notice the tall, magnificently robed, bearded Asiatic figure who approached her.

"A thousand pardons, Baroness, for interrupting your celebrations but might you spare this humble creature a moment of your time?"

She paused, taken aback but impressed by this far from humble personage standing by her side. She let the procession of revelers pass and turned to the striking individual before her. Seeing her quizzical expression, he bowed and said, "I am Master Kong, commonly known as Confucius."

"A pleasure to meet you, sir. I know you have been here in Heaven for thousands of earth years but I've never had the opportunity to make your acquaintance. I am delighted to do so now. You seem to know who I am. Lady Juliet Armstrong, English Baroness Crestwell, deceased, at your service."

"Thank you, milady. I am well aware of you and your worldly and heavenly reputation. I am also aware of your collegial relationship with the famous earth-bound detective Sherlock Holmes."

"Oh, oh!" thought Juliet, "Here we go again." She had just completed yet another adventure with Holmes at the behest of Leonardo DaVinci, to say nothing of a string of earlier undertakings with the Great Detective. Their mutual fame in celestial circles was becoming excessive but out of sincere respect for this great philosopher she would listen to what he had to say. "Shall we retire to my modest home, and discuss your needs over a cup of nectar?"

"A most gracious offer, milady. I accept."

They floated into the mansion and took up seats in the drawing room. Her visitors had settled in the dining room and library and were demolishing choice ambrosia and nectar. The animals were in the area behind the stables, chasing each other and playing newly invented games while having a go at Heavenly Chewies.

She turned to her guest and said, "Forgive me, Master Kong. I am of English birth and breeding and a Christian. I know little of your Oriental ways and principles."

"Not unexpected, Baroness. First off, over 2000 Earth years ago, I served my Chinese states and families in many ways. At different times, I have been called a politician, teacher, advisor, editor, moral philosopher, and reformer. I and my followers profess the unity of the individual self with what we call Tian. Tian is a place - Heaven; an ethical condition; a blissful state of being and a person, the God of Heaven."

"You might think of Tian as 'fate' and 'nature' as well as 'deity.' It is an extra human, absolute power in the universe aligned with moral goodness. It depends on human agents to actualize its will, and its associations with mortal actors."

"I am not a religious figure. Not a priest, not a prophet and certainly not a god. At approximately the same time as Jesus walked the earth, the Egyptians deified Ra and other godheads, the Hebrews worshipped Yahweh, Muhammad preached about Allah and the Greeks and Romans had their Pantheon, I was teaching in China."

"I taught that human beings are fundamentally good, and teachable, improvable, and perfectible through personal and communal endeavor, especially self-cultivation and self-creation. Confucian thought focuses on the cultivation of virtue in a morally organized world. Some of my basic ethical concepts and practices include 'benevolence' or 'humaneness' and the essence of the human being manifested as compassion. Heaven or Tian is the upholding of righteousness and the moral disposition to do good. I developed a system of ritual norms and propriety that determines how a person should properly act in everyday life in harmony with the law of Heaven. Confucianism is the ability to see what is right and fair, or not."

Lady Juliet sighed, "Your teaching and the principles embraced by your followers make you arguably the most significant thinker in East Asian history."

"Modesty forbids me from commenting, milady. However, perhaps you have heard of the *Analects*, a large collection of sayings and ideas attributed to me and my contemporaries. They are traditionally believed to have been compiled and written by my followers after my death in 479 BCE. I will admit that the *Analects* has been one of the most widely read and studied books in China for the last 2,000 years and continues to have a substantial influence on Chinese and East Asian thought and values today."

"But therein lies my problem. You see, over time there have been several different versions and serious conflicts among my current followers. Asian and non-Asian authorities have arisen with strong opinions about the true meanings of my teachings. I wish to settle these issues and bring tranquility and peace to the millions who embrace Confucianism. I need a disinterested earthly representative to negotiate among the conflicted parties. Not a religious, political or literary specialist nor a Chinese influencer. Although it is not his specialty, I believe Mr. Sherlock Holmes is an ideal person for the task."

The Baroness gulped. "Oh dear, Master Kong. I suspect your confidence is misplaced. Sherlock Holmes is hardly the diplomatic negotiator you believe him to be. In fact, his brother Mycroft might be a better choice."

The philosopher demurred. "He is a seeker of truth and justice who has dedicated his life to the support of virtuous living. Will you at least approach him and seek out his willingness to assist me?"

Juliet decided on the spot to extricate herself from this dilemma by contacting the Great Detective and letting him make his feelings known. "Yes, I will call him and I will present your request in as objective a form as I can. Honestly, I doubt he will feel this would be a fitting assignment for him. He is attempting to retire but requests for his services keep arriving at his doorstep at South Downs in Sussex. However, Holmes is the Master of Surprises. Anyone who believes they have reliable prior knowledge of what he will or will not do is deluding themselves. He continues to amaze me and even his longtime associate, Doctor Watson. I'll send him a missive via the Angelic Postal Service outlining your request."

"I am most grateful, Baroness Juliet. You are truly a noble woman. By the way, your ambrosia and nectar were delicious."

*****

Sherlock Holmes sat in a basket chair at his South Downs cottage, sorting through the morning's correspondence. The traffic at the local post office had increased dramatically since his arrival at East Dean. In addition to the typical advertising circulars and appeals for funds, there were requests for his services, offers to publish his memoirs, an occasional letter from acquaintances and former colleagues and a large collection of what could only be called 'fan mail.' He dealt with most of them rapidly, using the burning flames in his fireplace as his disposal unit, keeping some interesting professional and personal missives for further review. Included in the personal stack was a bright white envelope which had arrived earlier with only his name in scarlet script and the notation on the back - VIA Angelic Postal Service. The Baroness was in contact again.

Settling back with his favorite calabash and a glass of mead at the ready, he read and re-read Lady Juliet's request. It sounded halfhearted at best and she knew well what she was asking was far outside his usual remit, especially since he was trying so hard to finally retire.

Much as he had a sincere respect, agreement and fascination with the thoughts and principles espoused by Confucius and his followers, he had insufficient knowledge and motivation to agree to participate in philosophical debates. He had a strong desire to avoid involvement in metaphysical conflicts. Many a war was launched over religious, cultural and ethical differences and he had no taste for entering the lists to negotiate with or pacify the respective parties. He sent a short reply to her ladyship. "Thanks but not my cup of nectar. Apologies to Master Kong and his followers." He sealed the return envelope, placed it by the mail slot in his front door and watched while the document was invisibly spirited away by an angelic messenger. He once again marveled at the swift celestial service. Thinking the matter was settled, he turned his attention to the latest bulletins from the Royal Apiculture Society. Little did he know.

*****

A flutter of wings and a young looking *(they were all immortal and of the same eternal age)* angelic messenger bowed in the Baroness' direction, reached down and patted Pookie, while depositing an envelope on Lady Juliet's incidental table. "A message from Earth for you, milady. I hope it is good news." He/she flashed away.

The Baroness suspected the angel would be wrong and as she opened the missive, her suspicion was confirmed. Holmes, as she expected, had turned down her request to assist Master Kong. Oh well, nothing for it but to inform the ancient logician. "Pookie, let's go see Confucius. I wonder what the heavenly dwelling of an age-old Asian philosopher looks like."

As they flitted along the golden paths leading to celestial residences, Lady Juliet couldn't help but marvel at the variety of architectures created by Heavenly Real Estate to suit the nature and customs of their occupants. From Greco-Roman to Renaissance European; Art-Deco to Minimalist Modern; Sprawling Campus to Spiraling High Rise; British Manor House to American Colonial; South Seas to Arctic; Indian to Asian and infinite variations. They stopped in front of a simple structure with pagoda-like projections and alternating layers of dark and light sparkling wood. "This is it, Pookie. Just as I expected."

As they turned to the entrance, they were greeted by the ancient sage and a younger Chinese man. The Master smiled. "Ah Baroness Crestwood, Lady Juliet. Welcome to my modest dwelling. It is splendid to see you again. Let me introduce Yan Hu. His courtesy name is Ziyuan. *(A courtesy name is assigned in the Chinese tradition when a person reaches adulthood.)* He is the thirty fifth in one unbroken line of my disciples. His forebears were natives of the state of Lu and he has carried on their traditions and my teachings for the most recent thirty Earth years. Of course, since he is here in Tian with us, you can conclude that he has passed from his worldly life. He has just recently arrived.

The man was of average height for an Asian, with intense dark eyes. He wore a heavenly white robe trimmed with gold. White was also the color of Asian death. His jet black hair hung in a pigtail down his back to his shoulder blades. His eyes flashed. Clearly an individual to be taken seriously.

Juliet returned the ancient logician's smile and lightly curtseyed to the disciple. "Philosopher Ziyuan. It is a pleasure to meet you. I regret that one so young should be deprived of his earthly life although I am sure you will be happy here in Heaven...excuse me, Tian. How is it that you are here with us? You did not succumb from some painful disease or infirmity, I hope."

"No, milady. I was shot."

She winced. "Oh dear, you and I shared the same fate. I too was taken down by poorly aimed assassins' bullets. Do you know your killers?"

"No. That is the subject Master Kong and I were just discussing. He tells me you refused to enter Paradise until the villains were found."

"True. But they were discovered thanks to the efforts of my earthbound colleague, Sherlock Holmes. Which reminds me, Master Kong! I passed on your request for Mr. Holmes to engage in arbitration among your followers. He regretfully declines. He feels his philosophical knowledge is woefully insufficient for him to mediate between rival scholarly groups. It is a skill he admits is outside his repertoire."

Confucius sighed. "A pity. I shall have to look elsewhere. Philosopher Ziyuan, perhaps you might assist, I realize your demise makes it impossible for you to intervene directly but you might be able to help me select an appropriate arbitrator."

"I am willing to use my relationships, what little diplomatic skill and metaphysical knowledge I have, Master Kong, but let me ask you, Lady Baroness. Do you suppose your colleague Mr. Holmes would be able to apply his great talents of detection to discovering who my murderers were? Like you, I strongly desire to bring justice down on the heads of the culprits who left my wife without her mate and our sons without their father."

Juliet realized that given her own history, she could hardly refuse to relay his request to the Great Consulting Detective. "Holmes is retired although I admit he seems to be as busy as he's ever been. Where did the attack take place?"

"London. The Police have done little. Just another Chinaman killed off. Who cares?"

*****

South Downs, Sussex. "Excuse me, Mr. Holmes. This came after the morning post while you were tending to your bees. It's another one of those strange envelopes."

He had just returned from a tour of his beehives and was about to indulge in a hearty luncheon provided by his part time domestic, Marion. She lives on a nearby farm with her parents and brother and tends to Holmes' household needs several times a week.

She extended a glowing white envelope in his direction. On the front was the name written in a feminine hand in scarlet ink. 'Sherlock Holmes,' no address, no stamp. On the back flap, in sparkling gold, 'Via Angelic Post.' Holmes smiled to himself -The Baroness. "It's all right, Marion. I know who it's from."

The girl said nothing further. She was still getting used to his oddities. Nice man but strange. Her Dad said he was a retired consulting detective, or something like that. He didn't seem very retired to her. She returned to the cottage kitchen and finished preparing the meal. She came back in to serve the beef stew she had been working on most of the morning.

Holmes had cut the flap on the envelope and sat perusing the single sheet contained within. Lady Juliet was being persuasive but about a totally different matter. A Murder! This was something he could deal with – something his expertise was honed for.

The situation was becoming familiar. Deceased individuals were admitted to Heaven after an act of violence had ended their lives. Like the Baroness, they didn't know who their killer was. Unlike the Baroness, who had refused to enter Paradise until her murderer was found, this person, Philosopher Ziyuan, was eager to join Confucius in his celestial home. Holmes found the proposition interesting and sent back a post to Lady Juliet, agreeing to investigate. He doubted whether the Heavenly Governing Committee would allow Lady Juliet and Pookie to make yet another journey earthward. They would have to rely on the Angelic Post. He would also contact Watson. Hopefully they would partner again.

Now, who is this Yan Hu, the Philosopher Ziyuan and why was he killed? A deliberate assassination or an accident? What Gregson would call 'collateral damage.' Was Gregson conducting an enquiry? Was anyone from the Yard conducting an enquiry? Please God, not Athelney Jones! My worst nightmare!

Unfortunately, as Holmes was about to find out, his nightmare would come true.

*****

Next morning, Marion was waiting for him with a letter in Cantonese from Lo Sing, the eldest son of Ah Sing, owner of several London opium emporia in Limehouse and elsewhere. *(I present their names in Anglicized format.)*

"Honorable Mr. Holmes. Please forgive this intrusion once more on your praiseworthy and hopefully serene retirement. Kindly permit this unworthy person to inform you of another arrest of his noble father by the Scotland Yard Police. Your long standing friend, Ah Sing, is again in Inspector Athelney Jones' custody charged with the murder of Yan Hu, the Philosopher Ziyuan. This is totally untrue and is a clear injustice. May my righteous father and I once more request your usual splendid assistance in effecting his release and procuring proof of his innocence. As always, we stand in extreme debt to your esteemed self. (Signed) Lo Sing"

Holmes fumed and wired Watson. "A new murder involving Chinese personalities and Athelney Jones. Jones is being his usual peremptory, hasty and dogmatically incorrect self. I was hoping after the Lady Marie Everett, Countess Faulkner incident, he would have been fired from the CID. May I join you at your Queen Anne Street residence?"

(The Countess had been arrested and remanded to Holloway prison to await a coroner's jury in the death of the Dowager Countess, Lady Phyllis Everett. Her incarceration and Jones' idiotic public comments created near riots by a large contingent of Suffragists.

Inspector Jones stated that the Dowager's death was caused by poisoning of her bed time tea. He prattled on. "The Countess and Dowager had a long-standing dislike for each other and had political and social disagreements, especially about women's suffrage. That culminated in this heinous murder. I am sure she is guilty. As is well known, poison is a woman's choice of weapon."

It turned out the Dowager committed suicide.)

Holmes took the train to London and arrived at Watson's office cum residence. They had both left 221B Baker Street months ago. He outlined the situation with the recently murdered philosopher, a disciple of Confucius. They decided to spend an evening together getting caught up on each other's doings including Watson's latest publications. His wife was away with her sister for a few days.

"A shame the Baroness cannot be with us. She and her dog have taken up with a unicorn and Pegasus, no less. I'd love to meet the famous flying horse. This morning, I must be off to Scotland Yard and the office of that idiot Jones. Join us there at your leisure. Oh, would you be kind enough to inform Lo Sing that I am

271

responding to his request. I am sure Ah Sing is not guilty. We can always count on Athelney Jones to jump to the most obvious and erroneous conclusions. He has Ah Sing in a cell at Scotland Yard. I'm going to see him. Jones still regrets he couldn't make his previous arrest of Ah Sing hold water. He has an extreme prejudice against Orientals of all stripes. The man is hopeless. Maybe this time we can get him fired. Next to him, Lestrade was a genius. Ah well, once again, the game is afoot."

*****

At Scotland Yard CID. "This time, you have gone too far, Inspector. Ah Sing is highly respected in the Chinese community, even if you think otherwise. He is incapable of murder or of ordering the death of another."

"Respected, eh? Those heathen Chinese don't know the meaning of the word. Don't get so high and mighty with me, Sherlock Holmes. Your friend, Ah Sing, profits tremendously from those poor opium fiends he accommodates. Perhaps you're one of them or is something else your narcotic of choice? He is hardly the choirboy you make him out to be. One of these days those slack jaws in Parliament will stir themselves and pass an opium control law. Then watch Athelney Jones go into action against your slant eyed companions. I'll bag 'em all. Meanwhile, Ah Sing is my current culprit. This murdered philosopher was trying to stop his malicious trade. You obviously think otherwise. Very well, if you want to see your Oriental associate out of gaol, bring me the true villain. You can't, can you! I'm not surprised because as usual, I am correct. Ah Sing is the murderer. "

"Inspector, You have little or no evidence other than your own prejudices. I shall have a criminal barrister here shortly who will once again re-acquaint you with the contents of a writ of habeas corpus. You seem to have no lasting familiarity with it. I wish to see my client."

"Your client, eh?" He laughed. "Your client! Oh, alright. In the interest of courtesy to the detection brotherhood, amateurs *(a sneer)* as well as we professionals, I'll allow it." *(With his evidence as sparse as it was, Jones was obviously motivated to cooperate to offset the prospect of an expert lawyer descending on him.)* "Sergeant, escort our guest to the cells. Tell your barrister friend not to hurry, Mr. Holmes."

*****

Ah Sing was a dejected figure, sitting in isolation when the sergeant opened the door to his cell. The Asian looked up, spotted Holmes and broke into a smile. "Mr. Holmes! I see my unworthy son reached you. Thank you for coming so promptly to the aid of my undeserving self."

They conversed in perfect Cantonese to keep the sergeant from overhearing and understanding.

"Our camaraderie endures, Ah Sing. I shall have an expert in criminal law here shortly to restore your freedom. In the meantime, what can you tell me, if anything, about the death of Yan Hu, the Philosopher Ziyuan. The murder of whom you are accused?"

"Very little, I fear, Mr. Holmes. I had no part in that tragedy. Unfortunately, Inspector Jones thinks otherwise."

Holmes stared at him. "But you do know why and how it happened. Do you know who did it?"

Ah Sing was a long-time practitioner of Oriental inscrutability. He hesitated but then, faced with his own unjust incarceration, he said, "We Chinese are a very close society, as you know. It has quickly become common knowledge that an untimely death took place. I do not believe it was related to any political or factional conflicts. The general atmosphere has been quiet lately. Master Ziyuan was a man of peace, love and tranquility. He spent much of his time trying to calm the more hot-headed members of our community. Trying to get them to abandon their weapons and dismantle their alliances. He had some success. I, too, look for peace. Inspector Jones thinks that because I deal in opium, I am a villain. I hope your legal associate is swift in making his rounds. This cell is not the most comfortable."

"Have you no opinion as to who the killer is?"

He was about to answer when Watson appeared on the scene. "I say, Holmes. You have put the wind up Athelney Jones. He gave me a sharp lecture on your high-handedness before he would allow me down here to the cells."

"I will give him a sharp lecture on his stupidity, racial prejudices and ridiculous ego. The man is a disgrace. It's a shame the Commissioner retired before dealing with him."

He turned back to Ah Sing. "You were about to give me your opinion as to the murderer's identity."

The old man sighed. "It pains me to say this but I believe it was one of his children. A question of money and inheritance. Ziyuan believed in leading an abstemious life much like Confucius but he had received a small fortune from his marriage. His wife and sons were urging him to allow them to enjoy the moneys she had brought to the marriage. He resisted. I am not sure but I believe his opposition to her spending may have brought matters to a head. I do not believe any of the Confucian factions were involved but you should certainly enquire. Two names dominate. Wong Lee Fang and Chen Xi Zhu. They are firebrands of a sort but more noise than action. "

"Thank you! I shall pursue that advice. Meanwhile, Watson, is the barrister here to get our good friend released?"

275

"I left him in Jones' Office. The Inspector is no match for your legal friend. You should be out shortly, Ah Sing. Stay well! Give my regards to your dutiful son."

Standing outside the Yard Headquarters on the Victoria Embankment, Holmes turned to Watson. "I hope our legal friend's tongue lashing will have Jones retracting his horns but that is probably too much to ask. I think it's time to turn our investigation momentarily over to the Baroness. We need to understand whether Philosopher Ziyuan's domestic life was one of Confucian serenity and harmony or monetary conflict. I also want to know about the philosophic conflicts that Master Kong wanted me to arbitrate. I shall send her an Angelic Post and set her on a voyage of inquiry. I'm sure she's frustrated that she cannot be here in London to participate directly in our enquiries."

*****

Shortly thereafter, in Paradise, Lady Juliet read and re-read Holmes' latest missive asking her to get more information on Ziyuan's family and the rival groups. "Come, Pookie. We have some snooping to do. Back to Master Kong's establishment."

Once more over the golden pathways and on to the pagoda-like structure that housed the Great Master. Ziyuan was in his own pavilion a short distance away. As usual, the Baroness and Confucius invoked the celestial universal language that allowed all heavenly denizens to converse with each other.

"Master Kong! What a pleasure it is to see you again. I am glad Master Ziyuan is not here. Mr. Holmes has asked me to seek some information about him from you."

"If I can, Lady Juliet. What do you wish to know?"

"It is Holmes' fear and belief that Master Ziyuan's murder was done not by a gang or political or philosophical opponents but by a member of his family. He will be checking the opposing learned parties but he feels the villain or villains are closer to home."

Confucius drew in his breath and stared off into the celestial landscape. "I wondered about that. You see, there had been conflict between his family and Master Ziyuan about money. His wife, Huang *(Jade in your language)* brought a very substantial dowry to their marriage. Yan Hu forbade her and their two sons from exploiting their riches. He insisted on a simple, ascetic life. The sons, Bai *(named the Outgoing)* and Caishen *(ironically named after the God Of Wealth)* wanted nothing of this. They saw their contemporaries enjoying a life of opulent comfort and knew it could be theirs. They often argued with their father. However, I cannot believe any of them caused his death."

The Baroness smiled, "Sherlock Holmes has uncovered any number of murderous crimes committed by family members against each other. I have been witness to several of them. As you know, not all humans can be aligned with the objectives of Tian."

"Regrettably, No. I bow to Mr. Holmes' skill and experience. I shall say nothing of this to Yan Hu. If he raises the issue, I shall promptly inform you and you can pass the information on to Mr. Holmes. Farewell, Baroness. Farewell, little dog."

*****

At Queen Anne Street. "Well, Ah Sing is back with his family and Athelney Jones is sorely frustrated." Holmes and Watson shared a laugh. "Now comes the problematic part of our adventure. Who is Master Ziyuan's killer? I have just now received a letter from the Baroness. Amazing how the Angelic Postal Service can track one down! She says Confucius confirms that all was not well in the Ziyuan household. Conflict over spending dowry money between wife and husband. Sons also involved. I plan a call on the bereft widow after I speak to the warring theorists."

Watson frowned. "You would do well to wear something light in color when you do. White is associated with death in China, as in many Asian cultures. Sometimes a white banner is hung above the door of the bereaved household, and mourners often wear subdued colors. You will be arriving while the family and friends are still grieving. A Chinese funeral usually takes place over 7 days, but the period of mourning lasts for 49 days with weekly prayers recited by the family every 7 days. A final ceremony, signifying the end of the period of sorrow, may be held after 100 days."

"You are well acquainted with Chinese funereal practices, Watson."

"As a physician, I have had the sad occasion to see several of my Asian patients pass on."

"Thanks for your guidance. I must first seek out the learned Wong Lee Fang and Chen Xi Zhu and see if their conflicts led to Ziyuan's death."

*****

"I am honored to meet the Great Consulting Detective, Mr. Holmes, but also puzzled. What brings your highly respected self to my modest home?"

The conversation was taking place in Mandarin rather than Cantonese. Holmes was less adept at this dialect which was close to being a whole separate language. Could this be part of the issue between the disputing parties? Language was the lifeblood of theorists.

"Thank you, Philosopher Wong. for agreeing to see me. I shall be quite direct. I am here to enquire about the recent death of your colleague, Master Ziyuan."

"Hardly a colleague, Mister Holmes. Ziyuan and I had strong disagreements on the fundamental meanings of the writings of Master Kong. You know him as Confucius. His ideas and precepts have been passed down for thousands of years and have been subject to interpretation and misinterpretation by generation after generation of thinkers. But let me anticipate your next question. None of this strife was sufficient for us to bring about his murder. Confucianism is a belief based on the highest moral standards and respect for life. Killing a learned opponent is absolutely unthinkable. Neither I nor any of my disciples had anything to do with his tragic and untimely passing. Violence of any sort is contrary to our most basic beliefs. I suspect you will also be calling on Chen Xi Zhu who is a bit more aligned with Ziyuan's thinking than I am. While we disagree on numerous things, I am confident he will concur that neither group had anything to do with Master Ziyuan's death. But of course, it is up to you to satisfy yourself that no guilt lies with us. I believe you will find nothing. May I advise you to look elsewhere?"

"Where is elsewhere?"

"Ah, a good question. We are often betrayed by those 'nearest and dearest' to us. I will say no more. Good day, Mister Holmes."

*****

Chen Xi Zhu lived only a short distance from Wong Lee Fang's establishment as well as the home of the Ziyuan family. Holmes walked the crowded streets of London's Chinatown taking in the noise and smells of the enclave. He came to a small but carefully tended row house. The house boy who greeted the detective bowed deeply and apologized profusely. The theorist was engaged in a tutorial of sorts with several of his students and could not be disturbed.

Holmes introduced himself. The house boy, Ling, was flustered that he was unable to satisfy this famous detective's request to see Master Chen immediately. "The Master will be finished with his scholars in a short while, if you care to wait. Is there any way this unworthy person may be of assistance? May I offer you refreshment? Some English or Chinese tea, perhaps."

Holmes agreed to wait and opted for Chinese green tea. When Ling returned with a small delicate cup of the steaming, fragrant drink and a tray of rice cakes, the detective decided to test the waters. He asked in Cantonese. "I am here to speak with Master Chen about the much lamented death of Master Ziyuan. Are you familiar with the affair?"

The house boy, taken aback with Holmes fluency in the language replied. "Sadly I am, sir. His murder was a terrible blow to our community. The police have

281

been here to question us. I had nothing to contribute but Master Chen spent a great deal of time with an Inspector Jones. A nasty man, if I may say. He clearly doesn't like Orientals. Are you too enquiring into the circumstances of Master Ziyuan's demise. I wonder who would have taken that splendid man's life,"

"As do I." A clear Oriental masculine voice rang out from behind a beaded curtain and a distinguished Asian stepped through. Tall, stern of visage and clad in funereal white with his dark hair speckled with grey, Chen Xi Zhu entered the room. "Thank you, Ling. Mr. Sherlock Holmes? An honor, sir. I am pleased that you are concerned with the death of our revered and well-loved colleague. I despaired of getting any rational response from the oaf from Scotland Yard. Jones, was it?" Ling nodded. "He originally was convinced that Ah Sing, the opium dealer, was responsible but has since redirected his attention to those of us who follow the time honored precepts of Master Kong – Confucius."

Holmes shook his head. "I agree. Inspector Jones is indeed a prejudiced oaf. I hope I can bring some light into this situation. What are your suspicions?"

*****

"What are your suspicions?" Lady Juliet was sitting with the two philosophers, Master Kong *(Confucius)* and Master Ziyuan in the library of the ancient logician's heavenly home. Scrolls and books

282

were everywhere. Pookie had settled on the floor next to the Baroness' feet. She yawned and promptly dropped into a semi-doze. Philosophers were not her strong suit but murder was. She kept one ear cocked for useful information while her eyes were closed. She listened to her mistress and these two Chinese fellows.

Confucius sighed and Ziyuan shook his head. "Suspicions? I have none or many. I was out in the tiny garden behind my house off Gerrard Street performing my morning meditations when I heard a noise and everything went black. I surmise that I was shot and I died immediately. Mr. Raymond tells me a single bullet entered my head. The next thing I remember was standing before the Pearly Gates in this white robe and being welcomed by St. Peter and several angels. Master Kong also greeted me."

"As a leader of a Confucian faction, I have opponents. Philosophical positions can be strongly motivated but we are people of peace. I have great difficulty imagining one of my intellectual adversaries being willing to take a life because of a disagreement."

The Baroness raised her eyebrows. "Were there any substantial conflicts in play between the opposing sides?"

"Nothing new or unusual that I can remember."

"How about a power struggle in your own group. Did someone seem set on gaining ascendancy and you were standing in the way?"

Master Kong intervened, "Unfortunately, even among members of our schools dedicated to peace and tranquility, ambition rears its ugly head. It was true in my day. It is true today."

Ziyuan nodded affirmatively. "I'm afraid that is so, Baroness. Master Kong is correct but no one stands out as willing to do me in to satisfy their political desires."

Lady Juliet shuffled in her place, disturbing Pookie in the process. "I hesitate to bring this up but how about members of your family? Any conflicts that could have led to your demise?"

Both sages sucked in their breaths. Confucius looked to the ceiling while Ziyuan shook his head. "I cannot believe that my own flesh and blood would seek to take my life. I have had conflicts with my sons, Bai and Caishen about money. My wife brought a substantial dowry and has often urged me to permit her and our sons to seek a more luxurious lifestyle. I have refused. As the immortal Master here has taught so forcefully, desiring and seeking wealth is a curse in disguise."

"Have you been subjected to theft or robbery? It must be known that even if you don't use it, you are wealthy."

"All of my wife's dowry is deposited in bank shares. There is little in our home that is worth stealing or killing for."

Juliet thought "Except to get access to those funds."

*****

Back in Queen Anne Street, Holmes and Watson prepared to call on the widow Ziyuan Huang *(Jade)* and her two sons, Bai and Caishen. Lady Juliet had updated them with her most recent message after her interview with the two deceased theorists. *(Angelic Post flies yet again.)* Dressed in light colored suits appropriate for Asian mourning, they took a cab to Gerrard Street and the home of the late moral theorist.

In spite of their abstemious existence, the Ziyuan family had a telephone which the sage used primarily to maintain contact with his disciples. Holmes called ahead and after expressing his condolences, told the widow of his intentions to uncover the murderer of her husband. He avoided saying whom he was representing but assured her there would be no cost involved. She was somewhat hesitant because they were in mourning but she had heard of the famous detective and had also experienced the roughshod treatment of Athelney Jones. Yes, she wanted justice. She agreed to see him. She would summon her sons. 2:00 o'clock!

As Holmes and Watson got out of the cab, they were intercepted by Ling, Chen Xi Zhu's house boy. They lived only a few houses away from the Ziyuan home. "Mr. Holmes. I must speak with you urgently but not here. I have information for you regarding Master Ziyuan's' death. Master Chen will be away this afternoon. May I meet you at the Perfumed Garden Tea Room at 4:00 o'clock?"

Holmes agreed. Watson would not be able to join him. A medical board meeting at 5:00.

They proceeded to their appointment with the widow. The house was draped in white and silent. A young man also dressed in white greeted them at the door. He spoke with a broad 'a' upper class London accent. "Gentlemen, Welcome to the humble residence of the family Ziyuan. I am Caishen, son of Master Ziyuan. My mother and younger brother, Bai will be with us shortly. Will you have some Chinese green tea?"

Holmes gratefully declined as did Watson. The doctor hated the stuff. A rustling sound and a woman supported by a young man entered the room and sat. She wore a simple white robe, hair unset and no cosmetics. Her face was drawn and downcast. The son, Bai, was similarly clad in austere form. The austerity extended to the sparsely decorated home.

With one major exception. White chrysanthemums, the flower of mourning, filled the rooms and portals. The wife wore the flowers in her hair.

Holmes spoke, "Madame Ziyuan, I am Sherlock Holmes and this is my associate, Doctor John Watson. Our sincere condolences on the loss of your husband."

She nodded her head in return and Bai responded. "We have been gifted by the presence of Scotland Yard. The bigoted idiot, Inspector Jones. You have told our mother of your intention to seek justice for our father's violent death. Why is a famous detective like you getting involved?"

Obviously, Holmes was unwilling to explain the otherworldly commission from Confucius and the Baroness. He simply replied, "We have been appointed to pursue this matter by individuals who wish to remain unidentified. Fear not. There will be no fee or costs due from you. Let us simply say they and we wish to see justice done. I agree that Inspector Jones is an incompetent. It is our intention to prove to him who the guilty party truly is and see the wheels of the law turn correctly. I have only a few questions."

The wife, who had been silent up until now looked up and said, "Ask!"

"I understand your husband's body has already been buried."

Caishen replied, "The three days of funerary visitations ended today and his body was commended to the earth from which it came. Confucian disciples from all over England came to share in our grief. We will continue to mourn my father's death for quite some time."

"Your father was shot – once in the head?"

A sob from the widow. Bai answered, "Yes! The Police Surgeon and Coroner attested to that."

"Has there been a Coroner's Inquest?"

"Not yet. It is scheduled for the end of the week.""

"Have the police uncovered the weapon?"

"No! That imbecile Jones has dragged his feet on that too."

"I am sorry to ask this question but although he was a beloved and highly respected sage, did your father have many enemies?"

"Philosophers, sages and historians all disagree on many subjects. Some fiercely. But we do not know of anyone who was so opposed to our father's thinking that they would stoop to murder. Confucianism is a way of life dedicated to peace, kindness and justice."

Watson intervened. "It is that justice we seek in this instance. Were there any other individuals or situations that might have brought about this tragedy? Debts, revenge, jealousy?"

Silence and shaking of heads.

Holmes asked, "May we see the site of the murder? I understand it is a small garden where Master Ziyuan retired to meditate."

Huang *(Jade)* diffidently raised her hand in agreement. Caishen rose and said, "Please follow me. Are you finished interviewing us? May Mother and Bai leave?"

Holmes bowed to the two of them. He and Watson followed Caishen through the house and out to the garden. Holmes looked about, got down on his knees, took out his magnifying glass and ran his long, skilled fingers under the seat the philosopher used as well as the garden grass immediately surrounding it. He pulled an object out from beneath the seat. "A bullet shell casing. From a Webley Mark IV. The Boer War Webley." He snorted, "I wonder if Jones even looked out here after the body was discovered and removed."

Caishen had watched this process with his mouth gaping wider and wider in surprise. He turned to Watson. "That's remarkable. How does he do that?"

Watson laughed, "You're not the first one to ask that question."

"Caishen, did your father or any family member own such a pistol?"

"No, Father detested firearms or any such weapons. Wouldn't allow them in the house. My brother and I pleaded with him to keep one for protection but he was adamant."

Holmes turned. "We shall have to look elsewhere. I think we have seen all we have to see here, Watson. Caishen, thank you for your hospitality. Once again, extend our sympathies to your mother and your younger brother."

They walked through the silent house and out to the noisy jumble that is Gerrard Street. It was 3:15. Watson needed to be at Barts for his meeting so the friends parted. "I wonder what Ling has to say that is so important. He seemed quite secretive."

"I shall find out shortly. Now where is the Perfumed Garden Tea Room?"

The doctor laughed. "The great detective is stumped. It's down the next block. I doubt Ling can wander far from the house even if Master Chen will be away."

"I shall see you at Queen Anne Street and issue a full report. Dinner? Will your wife be home?"

"No. Let's meet at the Criterion Bar instead. I'll go straight there after my meeting."

"Agreed. Now let's see what the mysterious Ling has to say."

*****

The Perfumed Garden Tea Room was a small, non-descript traditional Chinese establishment decorated with wooden panels and dark lighting to create an atmosphere of silent anonymity for the guests. Little or no chatter. Most of the patrons were Asian with one or two London matrons whose laughter occasionally broke the silence.

Ling was seated in the back of the room at a small table on which were two delicate cups, two pots of hot water, small dishes of various Oriental teas and small plates of dim sum and rice cakes. "Mr. Holmes, would you care for oolong, black, green, or silver needle white?"

"I am unfamiliar with silver needle white. Let me try it."

'A good choice. Please try the dim sum. Rice cakes may be too bland for you. I have chosen this place because we can converse undisturbed. I have information to give you about Master Ziyuan's death."

He poured the tea and placed a small plate of delicacies in front of the detective. Holmes took up his chopsticks and adroitly speared one of the dumplings. Ling was impressed. "I see you have some familiarity with our cuisine. Do you have familiarity with Confucian thinking?"

"I have had some exposure to Master Kong's Analetics, his thinking and his ideas as well as the variations introduced by his disciples over the centuries. I am hardly an expert. However, I suspect that you are far more than the traditional house boy."

"Correct. I am a student of the Great Confucius with ambitions to become a Master myself. I earn a living by serving Master Chen. Actually, I am more aligned with Master Ziyuan's philosophies. He was a true ascetic. Chen Xi Zhu is a hypocrite. While preaching and teaching the virtuous life, he secretly lives an immoral self-indulgent existence hidden from his followers but not from me. I stay in his service because he is blackmailing me. My father killed a fellow villager and Master Chen threatens to expose my shame and ruin my chances to advance on the road to spiritual leadership."

"I sympathize with your plight. Blackmail is a terrible crime and sin. But what has it do with Ziyuan's murder?"

"Chen and Ziyuan's wife, Hang *(Jade)* are lovers. They have been for quite some time. They hide it well. I'm not sure Master Ziyuan ever knew. I doubt his sons know but I know. She has a substantial dowry which her husband would not let her or their sons touch. Chen has his lustful eyes on that money. He is unmarried. After an appropriate mourning period, I fully expect them to wed. Her sons may object but Chen is powerful and can be very persuasive."

"That is very suggestive but it still leaves Ziyuan's murder unsolved."

"I have another piece of information for you. Master Chen had a revolver, a Mark IV Webley. I have seen it many times hidden away in his bed chamber. It is now missing. I have not mentioned it to him or anyone else except you. The police never thought to interview me and I have not volunteered. However, I have had enough of Chen's hypocrisy, threats and immorality. I cannot prove he killed Master Ziyuan but I felt in your experienced and capable hands, these facts might lead to a solution."

Holmes has placidly sipped his tea through most of this recitation but realized that a potential breakthrough could be at hand. "Thank you, Ling. You have been most helpful. I shall take your information and study, analyze and pursue it. Pardon my cynicism but I must also ensure that you are not trying to frame your master. You would not be the first servant to take vengeance on an employer he hated."

Ling looked calmly at the detective. "It is as I expected, Mr. Holmes. If I were to tell the same story to that ridiculous Scotland Yard Inspector, I would either be totally ignored or arrested for some infraction - perhaps wasting police time. I trust your skill and fairness in judging my information. Now I must go, Master Chen will be returning soon."

Holmes thanked the houseboy once again and paid for the tea service. He had a dinner appointment with Watson but first he had another missive to send to the Baroness.

*****

"Oh dear, Pookie. Another message from Holmes. More on this Confucian Catastrophe. He wants me to seek out Master Ziyuan and ask him a very sensitive question. Was his wife Master Chen's lover?"

She and the dog flitted over to Confucius' home where she asked the Sage to accompany her to Master Ziyuan's dwelling. They found him taken up in deep meditation. Master Kong interrupted his concentration. "Forgive us, Master Ziyuan, but the Baroness has a very important and sensitive question to ask you relative to your murder."

He graciously turned his attention to Juliet. "Yes, Baroness. I assume you are acting for Sherlock Holmes. I greatly appreciate his and your attention. It seems Scotland Yard has all but abandoned the case. Please ask your question. Over the years, I have developed quite a thick skin."

Juliet ran her hand down Pookie's back. The dog settled at her feet, alert to any change in the atmosphere. She looked at Confucius with her head cocked to one side and then stared intensely at Ziyuan. Pookie understood more than most people were ready to admit.

The Baroness cleared her throat. "Well, you see, Holmes has uncovered evidence that strongly suggests that your wife and Master Chen were lovers. Were you aware of anything that would support that claim?"

Ziyuan looked up to the sky and then bowed his head. "Yes, much to my eternal shame, I suspected that Jade and Chen were having an affair. Most likely they still are now that I am deceased. She was unhappy that I would not allow my family to live a more luxurious lifestyle, especially since she brought a very substantial dowry to our marriage. Our sons were also chagrined at our abstemious life. I do not believe they know about my wife's dallying. It pains me more that she is involved with my philosophical rival, Master Chen."

"Do you believe either of them may have been responsible for your death?"

"I wish not to believe it but it is possible."

The Baroness shook her head. "Paradise is supposed to be the home of perfect joy and everlasting comfort. I am sorry that you are touched by sorrow. Do you wish Holmes and me to continue the investigation. The police seem to have given up."

"Yes, please. I need to know who my killer is."

"I understand. I once shared your situation. We will find him or her. Good day, Master Ziyuan and Master Kong. Come, Pookie."

*****

A rustle of wings and a brilliant white envelope appeared next to Holmes' plate at the Criterion Bar. "Ah, the Baroness is as efficient as ever. Let us see what she has to say, Watson."

He sliced through the envelope with his steak knife, read through the message and passed it to the Doctor. "It seems Ling was being truthful and accurate. Now we will have to create a situation to ensnare the conspirators."

"You believe Chen killed Ziyuan?"

"No, I believe the wife did it. I need to get her to confess. Chen gave her the weapon. That makes him an accomplice. No doubt, he urged her on to free herself of the ascetic life Ziyuan imposed on her and her sons. He has designs on her dowry. But first, much to my chagrin, I shall have to face down the execrable Inspector Athelney Jones. I shall need him to effect the arrest."

"You're pretty confident you'll be able to break them down."

"I'm pretty confident I can break _her_ down. I plan to accuse one of the sons. I doubt if she'll stand by and allow him to be tossed in gaol. If only I can get Jones to cooperate. First thing in the morning at Scotland Yard. Will you join me?"

296

"Try and stop me. Meanwhile let's finish this wonderful roast. I assume you have taken rooms at the Langham."

"Indeed, if I have to come to London, a little luxury is called for. After all, I assume I will pursue this case at my own expense. Confucius, Master Ziyuan nor the baroness have any British currency to support the effort."

*****

Next morning, on the Victoria Embankment, in front of New Scotland Yard, Holmes and Watson paused. "We need to employ Jones and several constables if we are to carry out this bit of theatre I have planned, Watson. I despair of getting any cooperation out of that small minded cretin but needs must. The game is afoot. Once more unto the breach and so on."

They walked through the lobby and passed the barrier, recognized by the desk sergeant who gave them a cheery wave. Up to the third floor where Athelney Jones had his dreary office. A harassed looking constable was sorting through pages and files and peered over the pile at Holmes and Watson. "Gentlemen, what can I do for you?"

"We are here to see Inspector Jones."

"The Inspector is on temporary leave. Inspector Gregson is dealing with his cases. I believe he is in."

Watson laughed, "There is a God!"

Down the gloomy hall to yet another spartan enclosure made marginally livable by two plants and family pictures. Inspector Tobias Gregson was seated behind his desk talking with a sergeant. He looked up in surprise. "Sherlock Holmes! I thought you had retired! And Doctor Watson. What brings you to my opulent digs?"

"A case of murder, Inspector. Yan Hu, Master Ziyuan, the Chinese Confucian philosopher. Shot. Your esteemed colleague gave the whole situation short shrift."

"My esteemed colleague is suspended by Superintendent Murchison. It seems a substantial and influential Chinese group protested to the Commissioner about Jones' obvious prejudice against Orientals and his high handed dealings with the Confucian communities. Specifically this case. For my sins, I have inherited it."

"I may have the solution that will absolve you of your sins."

"You have my complete attention. Sergeant, take notes."

Holmes outlined his suspicions, his plan and requirements. Gregson was dubious but decided to go along. The Great Detective placed a telephone call to Ziyuan's home and reached the wife and mother. He told her of the change in Scotland Yard responsibilities and Inspector Gregson wanting to interview the family once again. She reluctantly agreed to see them with her sons in the afternoon.

The group set out – Holmes, Watson, Gregson, Sergeant Murray and an unnamed constable. Gregson sent the Sergeant down the road to Master Chen's home where he took up his station outside the building. If Holmes' ruse worked, he was to arrest Chen. Inside Chen's house, the ever observant Ling spotted the bobby and made sure to keep an eye on Chen's movements.

When they arrived, the Ziyuan house was no longer draped in funereal white but it was hardly a scene of joy or merriment. They were greeted by Caishen, the elder son. "Good afternoon once again, Mr. Holmes and Doctor. I assume this is Inspector Gregson."

He also looked at the constable quizzically but said nothing. Gregson addressed his remarks to the widow. "Madame Ziyuan, I apologize for intruding on your mourning once again but as Mr. Holmes explained, I have been assigned to take up your husband's case from Inspector Jones."

Caishen snorted. "We are glad to be rid of that prejudiced oaf. Members of the Chinese Community Council complained about him bitterly to the

Commissioner. I hope you do not share his biases against Orientals."

"On the contrary, sir. I am friends with many Asians. Goodness knows, you are a substantial part of the Greater London population. I will try to keep my questioning brief."

He proceeded to review the history of the killing as he understood it. The widow seemed quite distressed. Bai and Caishen answered most of the questions. When they came to the question of Ziyuan's monastic life style, Jade sobbed. "He insisted we lead the humble life."

Seizing on the emotional upset, Holmes looked at the Inspector and said. "That is the key to this whole event. The family could no longer tolerate Ziyuan's ascetic practices. He had to be eliminated. Ziyuan Bai, I accuse you of killing your father. Take him, Inspector."

Gregson moved toward the young man with handcuffs extended. A pitiful howl from the widow echoed through the rooms. "Don't touch my son. He is innocent. I killed him. Tian help me. Master Chen urged me to rid myself of my husband's oppression. He gave me the gun. I waited till the house was empty except for Ziyuan in his meditation garden and I crept up on him and pulled the trigger. One shot in the head and he was dead. I still have the gun. I didn't have the chance to return it to Chen. It is under my bed. Your stupid Inspector Jones never even tried to look for it."

Gregson turned his handcuffs toward the widow. Bai was dumbstruck but Caishen struggled unsuccessfully to free his mother. Holmes turned to Watson. "Tell Sergeant Murray to arrest Master Chen."

At the Chen residence, Ling ran out the door and shouted for Sergeant Murray. "Hurry! He is all packed and ready to escape." Watson joined the Sergeant and houseboy as they ran inside in pursuit of the villain. They caught up with him in his bed chamber. He snarled viciously but being outnumbered and his escape route blocked, he surrendered. Sergeant Murray took him in hand none too gently and pushed him out the door to another waiting police van, a Black Maria.

Gregson led the sobbing woman out to the police wagon. Caishen and Bai rode in front with the constable on their way to Scotland Yard. Holmes, Gregson and Watson regrouped. "You had better recover that pistol, Gregson. That will give credibility to her story."

The Inspector strode inside and a few minutes later emerged with a Mark IV Webley in a handkerchief. "Here it is, Mr. Holmes. Let's hope the houseboy can identify it as Master Chen's"

"I think he will. He is quite clever. Watson, we will have to arrange alternate employment for him now that his master is in custody."

"I shall enquire. Let us start with Ah Sing. He has substantial influence outside his opium dens. Another family would no doubt welcome him. I wonder what will happen to Master Chen's group of followers."

"Oh, I am certain there are several disciples more than eager to assume the burden of leadership. Excuse me. I must send a message."

*****

Oh dear, Pookie! A distressing note from Holmes. They have found Ziyuan's killer. His wife. Assisted by her lover, Master Chen. I suppose I am to be the bearer of bad news. Unusual here in Paradise. But so be it. Come, let's flit to the home of Master Kong and in his presence tell Master Ziyuan what has happened."

They found Confucius and told him the sordid tale. "Thank you, daughter. It is a sad outcome but one I suspected especially when Master Ziyuan admitted that his wife and Master Chen were having an affair. Chen is a scoundrel and she is a weak, self-indulgent woman. But Master Ziyuan is hardly blameless. If he did not stiffly enforce his strictures on his family, all this need not have happened. Come, let us bring our burden of sadness, If you wish, I will tell him."

Juliet smiled weakly. "Would you, please. You are an honored friend and guide. I am a snooping noblewoman unfamiliar with the ways of the Orient and your philosophies."

They reached Ziyuan's dwelling and Confucius went inside leaving Juliet and Pookie sitting on a comfortable couch outside where they could watch but not hear the conversation. Master Kong spoke and extended his hand in companionship. Ziyuan sat with his head hung low. Confucius rose and bade him farewell. Ziyuan did not respond. The aged sage came out and beckoned the mistress and her dog. They flitted back to Master Kong's domain."

The Baroness spoke. "British law is not gentle with murderers. Chen is even more guilty than she is. I suspect both of them will hang."

Confucius nodded. "She succumbed. To see and listen to the wicked is already the beginning of wickedness. But he is a shameful villain and hypocrite. The small man thinks that small deeds of evil do no harm and does not refrain from them. Hence, his wickedness becomes so great that it cannot be concealed, and his guilt so great that it cannot be pardoned."

Juliet's urge was to leave the old sage as rapidly as she could. She had more than her fill of philosophy for one period. She thanked him. He was profuse in his gratitude and praise for Holmes and the Baroness. She said she would pass his feelings on to the Great Detective, Watson and even Gregson, of whom she was not very fond. The Angelic Postal Service would be busy.

Confucius reached down and petted Pookie. "Your dog seems to be a very wise animal. You are very fortunate to have her."

"Yes, I am. She is my companion, assistant and critic. She keeps me from taking myself too seriously even in situations like these. We are an inseparable pair."

Confucius smiled. "I shall have to consult Mr. Sherman. Somewhere in the Meadows there is a sage old dog, looking to join a sage old man. We must find each other. Farewell, Baroness."

"I hope you find your friend. Farewell, Master Kong. God or should I say Tian, be with you.

The Adventures of Sherlock Holmes and the Glamorous Ghost

Volume Four

Confucian Confusion

The End

The Adventures of Sherlock Holmes and the Glamorous Ghost

Volume Four

Martha's Murder Mystery

A Novelette

Prologue

In South Downs and Paradise, urgent messages were being sent and received. "Martha Hudson had been arrested for the murder of her lodger. She is in Holloway prison awaiting indictment. Signed Watson."

Sherlock Holmes hastened to London to assist his long time landlady, calling on Watson on the way. He sent a message to Juliet.

Meantime in Paradise, Lady Juliet Armstrong, Baroness Crestwell had just been joined by Mary, Queen of Heaven. *(Regina Coeli)* Juliet was in her capacious and luxurious stables, seeing to the Unicorn *(named Hugh)* the Lipzzaner Stallions and their winged companion, Pegasus. The Queen was attended by two angels, Micaela and Zuriel.

(Commentary from Pope Pius XI: "From the earliest ages Christian people, whether in time of triumph or more especially in time of crisis, have

addressed prayers of petition and hymns of praise and veneration to the Queen of Heaven and never has that hope wavered which they placed in the Mother of the Divine King, Jesus Christ; nor has that faith ever failed by which we are taught that Mary, the Virgin Mother of God, reigns with a mother's solicitude over the entire world, just as she is crowned in heavenly blessedness with the glory of a Queen.")

Juliet gasped. "I am stunned by your presence, your Majesty. Welcome back to our dwelling. You came briefly once before. I never expected that you and your companions would take the time to visit again. I am ill prepared."

The Queen was a mature Semitic woman clad in a pale gold robe with a light blue veil over her hair. She wore no jewelry or any other sign of her supreme rank. Her eyes were sharp and twinkling, full of joy, comfort and love.

Mary smiled beatifically and looked around . "Don't be disturbed and please don't fuss. I see my spouse's work has benefitted you very well."

"Your spouse?"

"You know him as St. Joseph. He and his staff designed and created these stables and of course, your home. From a humble village carpenter to the Director of Heavenly Real Estate. He is joined by the most heralded architects, planners and builders in history. Pierre L'Enfant, John Nash, Karl Schinkel, Capability

Brown, Georges-Eugène Haussmann to name a few. Every structure you see around here is his and his associates' doing. Miraculous edifices. He enjoys it so much. As you can observe, they are most creative. I am very proud of him."

Juliet nodded, "So you should be. Heaven is architecturally wonderful in addition to all its other joyful qualities. But what brings you here? How can I serve?"

"Much as I am overjoyed to see you, Lady Juliet, it is these wonderful creatures who have caused me to come by again. I do so love them. My Son, His Father and the Holy Spirit are all highly pleased by these horses, as am I. Your little dog is a great charmer as well."

In response to this, Pookie stood on her hind legs, did a capering dance around the Queen and her angels and ended with a double backflip leaping onto Der Alte's back with a triumphant bark. The horse nickered, turned about in his stall and bowed to the Virgin Mary. She and the angels laughed. "No wonder your performances at the the Saintly Spectaculars are so very popular. Can you arrange a special show for us?"

Juliet nodded vigorously. If she could arrange performances for the British Empress Victoria and have the Empress Sisi as her equestrienne companion, she could certainly produce one for the the Queen of Heaven.

"I shall be most pleased, Your Majesty. Please have your angelic associates arrange a time and place and we will be there. I am somewhat amazed that you have the time with all of the prayers and petitions you receive on a constant basis. There are 1 billion, 600 million souls on Earth alone at this moment. Are you not overwhelmed?"

"I am never overwhelmed. Of course, not all those billion plus persons on Earth believe in God the Father, my Son, the Holy Spirit or me. Nor do they always seek our assistance. Then, of course, we also have all the other denizens of the exoplanets and galaxies of this vast Universe. It adds up to quite a population. But I have infinite resources at my disposal. Remember, Jesus and His Father are omnipotent. As is the Holy Spirit. These two angels with me are only a very small part of my boundless support contingent."

"I'm flattered at your presence and I'm sure the horses are too.You've seen Pookie's reaction. I wonder that I have been accepted so readily in Heaven. I was hardly a saint on Earth but I was a 'Direct Admit' to Paradise. No stop at Purgatory. I have often puzzled about that."

Mary smiled once again. "Well, you know everyone here in Heaven is a saint but no, you were not a saint on Earth, A superb person but not in the same category as a Cecilia or Francis. I had a little something to do with your so-called 'Direct Admit.' We were all impresed by your insistence on finding your killer before entering heavenly bliss. A courgeous, spirited, feisty lady complete with a lively, intelligent dog. I have a few persons like you available for let's call them, special missions. Angels do most of that work but sometimes a former human is called for. We've been watching you with Sherlock Holmes and you have developed into a fine potential Marian Agent. I will be calling on you in the future. Stay ready.

After pondering this startling announcement and not knowing exactly what it meant, a presumptuous silent thought struck the Baroness. The Queen's voice was a soft contralto. Similar to Juliet's. "We could sing duets together or maybe a trio with Saint Cecilia."

Another sublime smile from Mary as she responded to Juliet's unspoken idea. "Yes, we could. Actually, I seldom sing anymore. Too many heavenly hosts pouring forth their glorious voices in praise of the Almighty for me to interfere."

The Baroness blushed. "She's reading my thoughts."

Mary looked at Juliet. 'I apologize. Force of habit. I will cease it. There! Now, I sense however, that you may have a request to make of me."

"I should have realized that you are also all-knowing. Yes, I do indeed have a petition."

As they flitted around the stables, spending time with each of the stallions, the companion mares, the unicorn and finally, Pegasus, Juliet outlined Martha Hudson's situation.

Mary paused and looked at the angel Zuriel. He/she silently stared back but was clearly communicating with the Queen. She said. "Martha Louise Hudson, former landlady of Sherlock Holmes and Doctor John Watson at 221B Baker Street, London, England. A sweet and hearty soul. I doubt if she has a murderous bone in her body. What do you wish?"

"I want permission from the Committee to return to London and work with Holmes and Watson on getting Martha exonerated and set free. We need to discover who the true killer is. Pookie and I have helped Holmes a number of times in the past but this incident is even more imperative. Martha is a good friend and marvelous person. She needs me."

The Queen turned to Micaela and said, "Please ask Raymond to join us."

No sooner said...the Director appeared and bowed profoundly to Mary. "My Queen. I am at your disposal."

"Thank you, Raymond. I understand you and the Committee have been managing Baroness Juliet's visits back to Earth to work with Sherlock Holmes. Such visits are rather unusual but not unheard of. Her good friend and associate, Martha Louise Hudson has been arrested for murder. Lady Juliet wants to assist in getting Mrs. Hudson acquitted and the true murderer found. As a special favor to me, please arrange for her return to Earth. "

The Director bowed again to the Queen. "As you wish, Majesty." He looked at Juliet, smiled and said. "I assume you want your dog to accompany you. You'll also want the ability for both of you to become corporeal as necessary."

The Baroness was beside herself. "Yes! Thank you, Raymond and thank you so very much, Gracious Lady. We will provide you with a truly spectaculat equine/canine show as soon as Pookie and I return. It will be truly heavenly."

Mary beamed another delightful smile. "I will hold you it. Meanwhile, let me speak with Pegasus. His mythological history is fascinating. Hello, Wonder Horse! May I see you fly?"

Pegasus spread his glorious wings and leaped into the air, circling slowly and neighing. He landed briefly, allowing Pookie to jump aboard and took off once more into the sky to the delight of his audience.

The Queen looked at Juliet. "As soon as your dog returns from her flight, you should prepare for your journey. Stay safe. You two are immortal but evil is still rife. You will both have my special protection as will Holmes, Watson and Martha Hudson."

The Baroness curtsied and watched as the Queen disappeared with her angelic companions. She turned to Der Alte. "When I return from Earth, you and your associates are going to put on the show of your lifetime, even though you are all deceased. Add Hugh, Pookie and Pegasus to your performance. Beautiful white horses at your spectacular best. I'll speak to Empress Sisi. She'll work with you while I'm gone. I'll get Handel and St. Cecilia to provide the music. It will be heaven-shattering."

The stallion nickered and shook his wonderful head in Juliet's direction. He turned to the other stallions and unicorn and neighed at them. They got the message.

They were highly experienced professional performers. They recognized a challenge when they heard one. They would be a smash. The unicorn was delighted to be part of the performance. He waved his rippled horn in glee.

Pegasus returned with his canine passenger. Pookie barked trumphantly and leapt from the horse's back. Juliet laughed and said, "Come little one. We're going to Earth again. Martha's in trouble and we're going to help her. We'll see Sherlock Holmes and Doctor Watson."

A bark, a caper and a backflip. The Baroness adjusted both their haloes, waved at Raymond and then they flitted off through the Pearly Gates, over the Rainbow Bridge, sharp left turn and swift descent to a fog-laden London.

Chapter One

Inspector Stanley Hopkins sat in his office at Scotland Yard contemplating an upcoming visit from Sherlock Holmes. While he expected Doctor Watson and a barrister to accompany him, he was unaware that the detective would also have two celestial wraiths as companions. Lady Juliet Armstrong, the Baroness Crestwell and Pookie had just arrived from Paradise to assist in acquitting Martha Hudson of the crime of murder. At the moment they were still ethereal but they had the option to solidify when and if necessary. Mother Mary and Mr. Raymond had seen to that before they left Heaven. Juliet owed the Queen of Heaven a sensational Equine/Canine Saintly Spectacular when she returned. The Baroness' show business background was going to be tested to its fullest.

Meanwhile, the immediate order of the day was to get Martha released from Holloway Prison as soon as possible. Hopkins was not totally opposed to the idea. He found it incredible that gentle and proper Mrs.

Hudson might have murdered her lodger at 221B Baker Street but there seemed to be enough circumstantial evidence to warrant her arrest.

Ever since Holmes and Watson had moved out of their rooms in their landlady's house, she had rented the apartment to a series of not very satisfactory tenants. The last one had been attacked and killed with a blunt weapon, most likely a steel frying pan, which suggested Mrs. Hudson was the guilty party. Mr. George Melton, a sales agent for the Daimler Automobile Company had taken up residence at 221B three months ago and had failed to pay his rent during the period. Several arguments beween the tenant and his landlady resulted in her threatening to have him evicted.

Then his body was found by Greta, the living-out housemaid, when she arrived in the morning. His skull was fractured and the heavy pan was thrown nearby. There were no fingerprints on the utensil but there was blood on the pan's base. Martha was the primary suspect and Hopkins somwhat reluctantly had her arrested. He knew Mrs. Hudson from his days with Sherlock Holmes and liked her. Now Holmes and Watson, accompanied by the lawyer, was on his way to challenge his decision and get her released. "A policeman's lot is not a happy one."

Holmes, Watson and Mr. Elwood Garfield, the barrister, entered the red and white edifice formally called New Scotland Yard, ascended and crowded into Hopkins' modest office. Juliet and Pookie had arrived and in their ghostly states, took up no space perching on a filing cabinet. "Good morning, Stanley," Garfield said, "Good to see you again. I propose to go to the Commissioner's office to effect the release of my client, Mrs. Martha Hudson from Holloway Prison. I think you will admit that she is being held on only the most tenuous of circumstantial evidence. She is hardly a threat to society and certainly not a flight risk. It is heartless to keep an innocent women prisoner in a place like Holloway and I am here at the Yard to secure her freedom. Mr. Holmes and the good doctor have agreed to assist you in ferreting out Mr. George Melton's real killer."

Holmes, who had a true regard for Inspector Hopkins as one of the few competent members of CID, nodded his agreement.

Hopkins, amiable as usual, said "I tend to agree. Well, gentlemen, let's go see the Commissioner. I really don't want that lovely lady imprisoned for something she didn't do. But Mr. Holmes, you are going to have to assist the Yard in findng this salesman's murderer. As usual, we are short staffed."

As they stepped out of the room, Juliet telepathically spoke to Holmes and Watson, *You should know that before Pookie and I left Heaven, I checked to see if I could find the victim, George*

Melton. Easy solution to the question. 'Who killed you, George?' Ask him! Unfortunately he is in neither Paradise nor Purgatory. That can only mean one thing."

Watson shook his head. *Hell!*

"Right, and I can't reach him. I'm afraid we'll have to do this the hard way. While you tackle the Commissioner, Pookie and I will flit down to Holloway and see Martha. She can hear me and converse with me in my otherworldly state. Whether they release her or not, I'll be able get her story without the guards or police listening in."

Holmes replied. *"Good idea, Baroness. It may take us a while to work through the bureaucracy here and then at the prison. Any information you can gather will help us get started more rapidly on finding the real culprit. You've been to Holloway, haven't you?"*

She laughed, *"Oh yes, during the Countess Faulkner fiasco. Courtesy of Athelney Jones. I'm delighted he's not involved in this mess, Is he still suspended?"*

Watson responded, *"Yes, His incompetence in dealing with the death of the Chinese philosopher has made his return any time soon, if at all, somewhat doubtful."*

The Baroness chuckled, *"Glad to hear it. Come, Pookie, Let's go to prison."*

The Scotland Yard Commissioner's Office:
"You make an interesting case, Mr. Garfield and Mr. Holmes. Hopkins, you mean we imprisoned this excellent woman on the basis of a bloody frying pan?"

"Not entirely, sir. She and the victim were overheard arguing about unpaid rent by the housemaid. He was a sleazy sort."

Holmes interrupted. "Martha Hudson is hardly equipped with a short temper or violent nature. She put up with my antics as well as those of Doctor Watson's for quite a number of years. If anyone should have been hit with a frying pan, it would have been me."

"Very droll, Mr. Holmes. But since Hopkins doesn't object and you, Doctor Watson and Mr. Garfield are all speaking on her behalf and she is not likely to escape to the North Country or Continent, I'll release her into your custody. Oh, wait. You've retired to Sussex, haven't you. I want to keep her here in London. She is still a Person of Interest."

Watson volunteered. "I'm still here in town. I'll vouch for her."

"She'll have to report in to us every week until we get this solved. See to it, Hopkins. I'll have to call the Holloway Warden. He'll probably be happy to see her gone."

317

Garfield thanked him. Release paperwork was drawn up to give over to the Prison authorities and Holmes, Hopkins, Garfield and Watson headed for a cab to Holloway where Juliet and Pookie were already approaching Mrs. Hudson.

Chapter Two

Holloway Prison: Once inside the walls of the castle-like structure with its towers and battlements, the invisible Baroness and her dog flitted through the doors and guardrooms of the prison into the main lobby. *"Wait a moment, Pookie, while I check the cell registry to see where they have Martha confined. You know what to do.'*

The dog solidified, barked loudly and returned to her evanescent state. The receptionist gaoler looked around. "I hear a dog. Where did it come from? Where did it go?" The guard rose from his desk and walked around the area, puzzled. His companion said, "Yer hearin' things, Conway. How would a mutt get in here?"

Juliet slid up to the abandoned desk and peered down at the prisoner roster while the gaoler was distracted. She had to momentarily incorporate so she could turn the pages. *"Ah, ha, D wing, third level, cell 85. Off we go, Miss Dog! Back to invisibility."*

After a few false turns, they found the correct corridor and flitted up to the double barred cell door.

They flashed through and found themselves facing a formidible looking angel. Martha was asleep on a straw mattress on the floor.

"Greetings, angelic being. I am Lady Juliet Armstrong, Baroness Crestwell and this is my canine companion, Pookie. We are here from Heaven with permission from the Celestial Committee and Mr. Raymond to assist Martha Hudson. Our journey has been approved by the Queen of Heaven. I assume you are Martha's Guardian Angel."

The angel bowed in recognition. *"God be with you, Baroness. Yes, I am this lady's spiritual protector. Azrael by name. Are you here to get her released? I have been in uncomfortable places before but this cell and prison are hardly commodious."*

"Does Martha know you exist and are by her side?"

"Yes, she does. As you know, she can see and hear you, your dog and me. Her perception extends to other celestial beings as well."

"Wonderful! Can we awaken her?"

"I believe so. Let me do it. You and your dog may alarm her. Martha, Martha! Wake up! You have company."

The dog put her physical paws on the sleeping landlady.

A snore and a gasp. "Wha…Who? Oh, hullo, Pookie. Is the Baroness with you?"

"Yes, Martha. I'm here. Sherlock Holmes and Doctor Watson are down at Scotland Yard trying to get you released."

"Oh, wonderful! See, I told you, Azrael. They would come to help me when they found out I was arrested. Baroness, thank you for coming. I didn't kill George Melton. He was nasty and he owed me money but I wouldn't have attacked him. I wasn't even home."

Juliet changed into her corporeal self. "That's what I want to hear, Martha. I'm sorry but you'll have to repeat your story later if Holmes gets you released. But just in case, tell me now while the gaolers don't know Pookie and I are here."

"I don't know much. I guess he was killed sometime in the evening. In the morning, Greta found his body in my kitchen with a heavy fry pan nearby. I was out at the theatre with Eleanor and Virginia the night before. We're members of the Baker Street Social Club. When I came home, I was a bit tipsy and I went straight to bed without stopping. Little did I know there was a dead body in my kitchen."

"Greta screamed when she found him. She woke me and I called the local police. They in turn called Inspector Hopkins. Greta told him I had an argument with Melton before I went out. That was true. He

320

refused to pay his rent and I was going to have him evicted. He laughed at me. He told me to go ahead and try it. I'd regret it."

The Baroness shook her head. "And on the basis of Greta's evidence and the frying pan, Hopkins arrested you. That sounds like something Athelney Jones would do."

Azrael looked up. *"I hear voices and footsteps."*

A tall grey female gaoler (grey hair, grey dress, grey eyes) rapped on the door. "All right, Hudson. Pick up your stuff. Your rescuers have arrived." She took out her keys and turned the padlocks and bolts, opening the cell. Standing out there were Holmes, Watson, Garfield and Hopkins. Four guardian angels were also with their protected subjects.

Armadel and Ezrafel, Watson's and Holmes' angels, greeted Azrael and the Baroness. They tucked in their wings and reached down to pet Pookie. Garfield and Hopkins were unaware of this celestial get together including their own angels. But Martha was. Tears rolled down her cheeks and she smiled between sniffs. She hugged the detective. "Oh, thank you, Mr. Holmes, Doctor. Have you changed your mind about me, Inspector?" She turned quizzically to the lawyer and Holmes introduced them. "This is Mr. Elwood Garfield KC, your barrister. He is handling your case."

"A King's Counsel? Oh, I am so privileged.
"Thank you, Mr. Garfield. I did not murder that man."

"I'm sure of that, Mrs. Hudson. It's up to Mr Holmes, Doctor Watson and Inspector Hopkins to find the culprit and clear your name. I shall assist in court, if necessary. Hopefully, there will be no reason for us to go to court. For the moment Scotland Yard is treating you as a Person of Interest. You will have to report to the Inspector on a weekly basis. I'm sure he will make that easy on you, won't you Stanley?"

Hopkins smiled and nodded his head.

Holmes clapped his hands. "Well, let's get out of here, shall we? May we return to Baker Street, Inspector? Is it still a crime scene?"

"No. The body has been removed and our forensic chappies have done their work."

"Then let's meet back there."

As they left, Azrael turned to Juliet and asked. *"Do you see your former guardian at all, milady? Orifiel and I had crossed paths in earlier times."*

"Yes, even though I no longer have need of a guardian angel, Orifiel stops by to chat and pet Pookie. He has a new prodigy protégé. A talented little boy named Noël Coward. I gather he's the very dickens. Poor Orifiel, as if I wasn't a trial enough. More theatrics!"

"We guardians do have our difficulties. But that's our reason for being. Ezrafel and Armadel have their wings full with Holmes and Watson. I've had it easy with dear Martha until now. I assume you're here to help in the investigation."

"Exactly! Pookie and I have assisted Holmes in a number of his cases and Martha and I are very good friends. As you know, she can see and hear us celestials."

"Yes, I was somewhat surprised but I understand Mr. Raymond arranged that."

"Raymond is such a sweetheart. Pookie and I are quite fond of him. Well, off we go to Baker Street. Let's flit, Miss Dog!"

Pookie and the Baroness arrived at Holmes' and Watson's old stamping ground before the cab-bound mortals. Azrael had elected to stay with Mrs. Hudson and so too had Ezrafel and Armadel with the two detectives. The barrister had returned to his office. Hopkins was coming in a police vehicle.

Juliet walked around the apartment. The dog sniffed about, ran into the next room where Holmes once dwelt and then on to Watson's old digs. She returned and whined.

"Hmm, Looks different, doesn't it, Pookie, The Queen Victoria bullet holes are gone and so is the jack knife scarred mantel. However, this car salesman

Melton was something of a slob. Clothes scattered about or is that the results of the Police searches? I wonder what he was like. Martha said he was nasty. We'll have to go to the Daimler showroom and get a profile of the victim. Ah, here comes Martha and her entourage. Let's enlist the angels in our investigations. I assume Ezrafel and Armadel are used to it. Azrael has had a rather calm existence with Martha up to now. A new experience awaits."

The Great Detective and his companions climbed the seventeen steps and entered the room. "Looks different, doesn't it Watson?" The doctor nodded.

The Baroness looked up. *"Well, Holmes, what's the great plan?"*

"We investigate, Lady Juliet."

Martha excused herself to make tea. "Hold on, Mrs. Hudson. We need to hear your story. Tea can wait. Where is Greta?"

Hopkins looked disappointed. He'd missed lunch. Actually they all had. The housemaid appeared. Martha gave her orders for refreshments. The maid was reluctant to go into the kitchen where the murder had taken place but Mrs. Hudson was having none of it. She was still a bit vexed at Greta for telling the Police about her argument with Melton.

She repeated the story she had told Lady Juliet. Her two social companions had already verified their evening at the theatre to the Police. The Medical Examiner had said that Melton died some time near eight o'clock. If so, Martha was still at the show.

Greta reluctantly repeated what she had told the police about the argument. She blushed and hung her head. Mrs. Hudson smiled. "It's all right, Greta. You had to tell the truth. We did argue. He wouldn't pay his rent and I threatened to have him evicted. Several of the local bobbies would have been pleased to do it. Nobody seemed to like him."

"So," said Holmes, "it seems we must concentrate out attention on the late and nasty Mr. Melton. Interesting attitude for a fellow in sales. They're usually all smiles and joking patter. Yet Mrs. Hudson says no one liked him. What say you, Watson? I know you have a passion for automobiles. Shall we pay a visit to the London showroom of The Daimler Motor Company Limited?"

Hopkins begged off. He was balancing three capital cases at once. "I'll leave you to your investigation at the car company. Please get back to me soonest."

Chapter Three

The trip to Chiswick and the Daimler London showroom took close to an hour. "When these motor cars become more popular and available, Holmes, this journey will be cut in half. Unless the traffic gets even worse."

"Don't let your enthusiasm overwhelm you, Watson. Motor cars have a long way to go. No pun intended. Ah, driver! Here we are."

The horse drawn growler stopped in front of a large white glazed brick structure with floor to roof windows. Inside were three different shining, self-propelled vehicles. A large sign over two garage doors proclaimed that this indeed was the London home of The Daimler Motor Company Limited. It was surmounted by a large Royal Warrant Seal from His Majesty King Edward VII.

In early 1900, Daimler had sold a phaeton to the then Prince of Wales. In 1902, upon buying another Daimler, now King Edward VII awarded Daimler a royal warrant as a supplier of motor cars to him and the Royal family.

The cabby shook his head in dismay. "Goin' to buy one of those infernal internal combustion machines, guvnor? Put me and my poor horse out of business, they will."

"No chance of that, my man. We are not here to shop. We're investigators on a case."

"Oh, well. See they get properly looked into. Takin' the bread away from my babes, they are."

Holmes smiled and included a substantial tip with the fare. "Why, thank yer, guvnor. A real gentleman."

Juliet, Pookie and the two angels, Ezrafel and Armadel, had flitted alongside the cab and without waiting for Holmes or Watson to descend passed through the large overhead doors into the showroom. Juliet, who had earlier posed as Rose Latour, the Goddess of Motorized Marvels at The Royal Society for the Advancement of Automotive Machinery's traveling pageant, was well acquainted with and fascinated by 'horseless carriages.' So was Pookie. They sat in a highly polished phaeton. The two guardian angels' curiosity led them to examine the three cars

Ezrafel laughed and said to Armadel. "Now the Earth has a challenge to the self-propelled chariots of the Angelic Transport Corps. Next thing you know, they'll have flying machines, too. But they haven't learned how to flit. At least not yet. Ah, here comes Mr. Holmes and Doctor Watson and someone is coming from the office back there."

As the detectives strode through the person-size door next to the big overheads, a smiling dark haired, mustachioed individual in well-cut tweeds emerged onto the showroom floor. "Good afternoon, gentlemen. Welcome to the Daimler Motor Company's London Showroom. Sidney Weathers at your service. I am the manager. Are you interested in joining His Majesty King Edward VII as proud owners of a Daimler phaeton or saloon?"

Watson's attention was completely captured by the machines but looked over as he heard Holmes answer the sales executive. "No, thank you, Mr. Weathers. I am Sherlock Holmes and this is my colleague, Doctor John Watson. We are detectives here on a totally different mission. We are investigating the death of your employee, Mr. George Melton."

The manager kept the artificial smile fixed on his face but his eyes showed both nervousness and disappointment. Business had not been that good of late and he had lost his star sales rep. "Yes, of course. Good ole George. Wonderful salesman. Knew his product from tyres to bonnet. Knew his buyers as well. Hated to lose him. Especially a murder. Bad publicity. But I thought the police had arrested his landlady. The rozzers were here, you know. Questioning Marty, my mechanician and me. It was in the papers. I thought they had their killer."

"The evidence against her is quite sparse and she has been released as a Person of Interest. We are re-examining the circumstances. What can you tell us about Mr. Melton?"

"Not much to tell you, gentlemen. George was an excellent salesman but very private. I don't know why he took up rooms all the way in Baker Street. There are plenty of available quarters here in Chiswick. A lot closer."

A tall dark haired man with greasy hands in overalls came through a glass door that led to a well-equipped shop. Inside, a motor car he was obviously working on was sitting on a lift. Weathers waved at him. "Marty, come and join us. These two gentlemen are detectives investigating George's death. Mr. Holmes, Doctor. This is Marty O'Toole. Great name for a mechanician, isn't it?" He laughed. Holmes smiled. Watson grinned. Juliet and the angels silently chortled. Pookie didn't see the joke.

O'Toole acknowledged them with a combined Irish brogue and Cockney accent. "Greetins, Gents. I'm Marty. I keep these little beauties runnin' smooth as silk for our posh customers. Includin' the King. That's his phaeton in there. The Royal Chauffeur bunged it up a bit. Shame! It's His Majesty's favorite. Top priority in the shop. Wadda yer want to know about George? Funny sort of guy. All smiles and jokes with the toffs, nobles and royals who come in here lookin' for new thrills. Knew the cars as well as I do but of course, wouldn't get his hands dirty. But utterwise, not the least bit social. Tried to get him to share a pint at the local. Wouldn't have any of it. Bit of a snob but I don't know what he had to be snobby about. Lived in a tatty rooming house downtown."

Holmes and Watson both raised their eyebrows. Tatty rooming house, indeed! Their mutual home for years. Juliet silently giggled. Weathers decided to change the subject.

"Did you know this business began with amusement park trams and motor boats? Now we have elegant gents like yourselves runnin' around in our fancy coaches. Progress, eh? Sorry we can't give you any more information, gentlemen, but there you are."

"Did George have any relatives in London?"

"Nope. His brother Edward is up in Coventry. Employed at the Daimler Works. An assembler. That's how George got his job here. Ed recommended him. He just came down and got George's body for burial. I don't know if there's any other family. I don't think Ed is married. George wasn't. The Police should have his address."

"Well, thank you, Mr. Weathers, Mr. O'Toole. You've been most helpful."

"Our pleasure. Sorry about old George. Say, are you sure I can't interest you in one of Daimler's wonderful machines. It would make traveling around so much easier for detectives like yourselves. We're hoping to get a big order from Scotland Yard and the military."

"Thanks but no." He looked over at Juliet, Pookie and the angels all ensconced in the cars. *"Baroness, please stay behind and listen to their conversations after we leave .Then flit back to Baker Street. You and Pookie know the way."*

The detectives left the showroom with Ezrafel and Armadel. "I say, Holmes. Those Daimler cars are going to capture London society. Lord and Lady So-and-So will be outclassing their socialite friends with their shiny new automotive conveyance. Complete with uniformed chauffeur. Sporting a royal warrant, no less.."

"Careful, Watson. Don't let your imagination run wild. These horseless carriages will have to come down dramatically in price and upkeep, become simpler to operate and move along more swiftly before they catch on with the public…even the affluent public."

"But can you see me making my rounds at the helm of one of those glittering vehicles. Mobile Medicine! John H. Watson MD (Motorized Doctor). I say! What a hoot!" He laughed.

Holmes smiled. "Meanwhile, let's take a reliable horse drawn cab back to Scotland Yard and then Baker Street. We'll await the Baroness and any information she can unearth. He spoke telepathically to their two

Guardian Angels. *"Are you two up for a little investigating."*

Ezrafel chuckled merrily, *"Same as always, Sherlock. By the way, Armadel here isn't too sanguine about motorcars, Doctor. You fellows take enough risks even as it is. Aren't you both supposed to be retired?"*

Watson shook his head. *"Holmes is. I'm still active."*

The Great Detective laughed, *"So am I, it seems. Retirement can be elusive. Don't worry. I have no intention of buying a motor car."*

Armadel fluttered his/her wings. *"Well, that's a relief."*

"I may just buy an aeroplane. There's plenty of room for a landing strip on my East Dean property. Why should the bees. birds and angels be the only creatures who fly?"

Ezrafel looked skyward and wrang his/her hands. "Lord, help us!"

Chapter Four

New Scotland Yard: "Hopkins, you neglected to tell us that George Melton had a brother, Edward."

"Sorry, Holmes! Yes, Up in Coventry. Employed by Daimler, too. On the production line. He was working at the plant on the day George was killed. He came down to London and we turned the body over to him for burial. There are no other family members. He didn't seem very important at the time. Why? Are your suspicions raised?"

"My suspicions are always raised. We need to gather as much information as we can about George Melton, His character, habits, relationships, finances. Anything his brother can tell us."

"We spoke to him about George. He told us very little. They were not close."

"And yet, he helped get him the job as a Daimler saleman in London and he took the body for burial. They certainly weren't estranged. Watson, I think you and I have a train ride in store. Inspector, do you have an address for him or should we seek him out at the automotive works in Coventry?"

"Hold on. I still have the file here in my office. Just a moment. Yes, here it is. 242 Farmer's Lane. It's a boarding house. He's unmarried. The local constables interviewed him. They came up with nothing. Let me know what you find out, if anything."

Holmes was disappointed in Hopkins. Unusual for him to be so inattentive, almost lackadaisical. He thought he had his killer in Mrs. Hudson but he's since backed down from that. The increased workload and shortage of staff may be affecting his usual thoroughness and attention. Or maybe the Inspector was having personal problems. He wondered what other doors had been left unopened in this case.

*****

Holmes, Watson, Ezrafel and Armadel stood in the Great Hall of London's Euston Station looking for the London and North Western Railway (L&NWR) platforms. The line left from Euston, traveled west to Coventry and then on to Birmingham, They were waiting for Lady Juliet and Pookie to arrive from Chiswick and join them.

Watson snorted. "Typical woman. Never on time. You sent her a message, didn't you Holmes?"

"Yes he did, Doctor and here we are. So stop complaining!" Lady Juliet snapped telepathically and Pookie let out an ethereal growl. *"We'll travel in celestial form and save you the cost of a couple of tickets. I have some information for you that I think you'll want before you meet George Melton's brother or the Director of the Daimler Works. Shall we?"* She flitted up to the First Class coach with Holmes, Watson and their angels taking up the rear. Pookie ran on ahead and bounded up the carriage steps.

They all settled into the compartment. *"So, Lady Juliet, what have you learned?"*

"Holmes, those two are truly a pair of villains. They are running several swindles that are making them a pile of cash. George was involved and so is his

brother, Edward. You should know that servicing automobiles actually brings in more money over time than the initial sales. These motor cars are sensitive creatures and require frequent adjustment and parts replacement. You saw the King's phaeton in the shop."

"Yes, Baroness, but the owners expect that. In what way are they being cheated?"

"It's not the car owners who are being victimized although I'm sure they're paying top price for the service. It's the Daimler Company. Edward is an assembler and has access to all of the pieces used to build the cars. He has been stealing parts and major assemblies and sending them down from Coventry to Chiswick. Marty O'Toole installs them and he, Weathers and George charge full price and split the profits. They keep up a flow of legitimate transactions as well, buying parts from Coventry so the plant management is none the wiser. The stolen parts provide a substantial monthly bonus."

Watson coughed. *"I say, We'd better talk to the Works Director when we get to Coventry, Holmes. But I don't see what this has to do with George's death."*

The Baroness replied. *"That's a horseless carriage of a different color. It seems George had his own little side venture going at the same time. A ride service with him acting as chauffeur in London for the 'great and good' using the showroom's autos he 'borrowed.' That's why he lived in Baker Street.*

Nearer to Central London destinations. He used a telephone answering firm to make his appointments. But it seems old George got greedy and refused to share the income he was making with his partners. I didn't hear as much but I'm willing to bet one or more of them argued with George and it got violent. We need to get a confession out of one of them."

Holmes smiled, *"Splendid work, Milady. You too, Pookie. I think our first stop will be with the Daimler Works Director. Then, let's see what we get from brother Edward and his parts pilfering sideline."*

He turned to the angels. *"Well gentle beings. Another adventure!"*

Ezrafel laughed, *"Sherlock. I don't believe you know the meaning of the word 'retired' at least as it applies to you. Armadel and I thought we were in for a little peace and quiet."*

Holmes shrugged. *"We can't leave Martha Hudson stuck in gaol. And I hate to see a company with a Royal Warrant being cheated. The burden of being a Consulting Detective. Although, I'd like to know what's wrong with Inspector Hopkins. Perhaps you can do a bit of research on that matter, Baroness."*

"Oh, goody! I get to stalk a Scotland Yard Inspector. Pookie will love that, won't you, dear?"

The dog scratched her ear and whined.

The train pulled into the Eaton Road station in Coventry and the detectives disembarked with the full complement of heavenly beings in attendance. A limousine sporting the Daimler logo, a seven pointed star, stood by waiting for a no doubt important passenger. As Watson summoned a cab, the Baroness giggled, *"You should have called ahead, Holmes. We would have gotten first class chauffeur treatment. I hope we can get to see the Works Director."*

"I'll call now. Hold that cab, Watson. I'll be out in just a few moments."

Watson jumped into the growler accompanied by the two angels, the Baroness and the dog. Armadel smiled, *"Usually we would flit but we don't know where we're going. I hope Holmes reached the Director's office."*

The Doctor replied. *"He'd better hurry. It's starting to rain. Ah, here he is. Cabby, the Daimler Works, if you please. Well, Holmes. Are we welcome?"*

The Great Detective grinned, *"The name Sherlock Holmes still has influence. The Director has a brief meeting with a member of the Home Office who is negotiating a purchase contract and then was willing to see the two of us. I assume the worthy who just got into the chauffeured limousine is from the government."*

The Daimler Works was only a short distance from the rail station. Several white brick structures: a large warehouse, a pair of manufacturing buildings and an administrative and utility headquarters encircled an extensive paved courtyard. A large sign – Daimler Motor Company Ltd. – and large Royal Warrant plaque topped the administrative HQ. The motor they had spotted at the station was parked next to the doors with the chauffeur standing inside the building out of the rain. Several semi-finished automobiles sat along the side of the warehouse.

The cabby steered his horse up the driveway and across the yard. "Here yez are, gentlemen. I assume yer wantin' the offices. We do lots of work for Daimler. Picking up customers and shipping out parts to the goods carriages on the railway. When yez want to return to the station, have the receptionist place a call. We're on the telephone. Name's Charlie Williams - Williams Wagons and Cabs. Or are yez stayin' overnight at a hotel?"

Watson paid him and said. "No, we'll be returning by train later in the day. We'll have them call you" They ran through the rain to the doors of the administrative wing. Unfazed by the moisture, the celestials flitted into a large area of couches and chairs surrounding a large desk. An attractive woman looked up at Holmes and Watson as they entered. "Mr. Holmes? Doctor Watson? Good afternoon! Mr. Stafford's office told me to expect you. He has a client from the government with him right now but will be with you as soon as his meeting is over. May I offer you some tea or coffee?"

Before Holmes could refuse, Watson agreed some tea would be most welcome. The receptionist rose from her desk and disappeared behind a swinging door. The Baroness giggled. *"I don't suppose they have any ambrosia on hand. All right Pookie. I have some Heavenly Chewies in my bag."* She reached into her bottomless reticule and pulled out several canine treats which the Bichon promptly snarfed. *"Sometimes, I think you're a piggy instead of a doggy."*

The receptionist returned with a tea trolley and accessories and poured two cups for the men. Holmes remarked. "This is quite an establishment. Automobiles are certainly becoming popular. Are you expanding?"

"Oh, yes! We have sales and service operations in London, Liverpool and Glasgow. More to come shortly. The Royal Warrant from His Majesty is helping a great deal."

"In addition to building the motorcars, do you also sell and service them in Coventry?"

"We specialize in fleet sales. For example, the gentleman who is with Mr. Stafford is from the Home Office. We hope the government will order a group of

339

cars for law enforcement and liaison. Oh, here they come now."

The Director and bureaucrat shook hands, all smiles and the chauffeur picked up an umbrella and guided the Home Office denizen out to the waiting car. The receptionist called over and said, "Mr. Stafford. Your guests are here. Mr. Sherlock Holmes and Doctor John Watson."

The Baroness gave out her tinkling laugh, *"As well as a ghost, a spirit dog and two guardian angels."*

The Director was a tall, slender individual with red hair, a well-trimmed moustache, deep blue eyes and a welcoming smile. He wore a well-fitting tweed suit that broadcast 'industrial executive' to all who saw him.

"Ah, the celebrated detective and his historian. Welcome, gentlemen, welcome! I'm Eustace Stafford, Managing Director of Daimler Motor Company Ltd. here in Great Britain. Delighted to see you! Your fame precedes you, Mr. Holmes and Doctor, your exciting stories are all the rage in my social set. My wife adores them. She will be thrilled that I have met you both. I wish I had a book or magazine for you to sign. Perhaps you can just sign a blank sheet for me? I can't believe that you traveled to Coventry to purchase an automobile when we have a London showroom and service center. Mr. Holmes, you might like to know we will shortly be opening a new center in Brighton. I understand you are retired to Sussex. Anyway, how can I help you?"

Holmes looked back at the Director. "I suspect it is more how we can help you. Mr. Stafford. May we retire to your office? We have some confidential matters to discuss."

Before they left, Holmes asked the receptionist to have Charlie Williams meet them at Mr. Stafford's office. She questioned whether they wanted Williams at the Director's office or just in reception.

"No, definitely at his office. Thank you."

They accompanied Stafford and walked to the back of the reception area, taking a lift to the top floor. They passed an attractive secretary who followed them with her eyes as they entered the Director's Office.

"Hold my calls, Miss Rogers. I shall be in conference."

"Holmes turned to the lady and said, "I am Sherlock Holmes and this is my associate, Dr. Watson. When Mr. Williams of the Cab and Carriage Company arrives, please show him in." She looked to the Director for confirmation. He simply shrugged and nodded agreement.

A well-appointed, moderately sized office occupied the back wall of the floor. In addition to a large walnut desk covered with model cars, two phones and stacks of paper there was a substantial conference table surrounded by eight chairs. The Director pointed to two chairs in front of his desk and sat down behind it. Unseen, the angels, baroness and dog took up four of the conference seats.

Stafford frowned, "This seems quite mysterious, Mr. Holmes. I must confess you have me a bit puzzled."

"All will be clear in just a few moments, Mr. Stafford. May I ask you to have your warehouse manager and Edward Melton join us here. You might want to call and alert the local Police authorities that they may have to come and make an arrest."

"Hold on. I'm not about to call the Police without a damn good reason."

"Well then, let me give you one. I'm sure your warehouse manager will confirm that over the past months, you have suffered significant shrinkage in your parts and assemblies inventories."

"Yes, we've been upset over that problem but how do you know about that?"

"Because I have information from an unimpeachable source who must remain unidentified that your London operation is stealing you blind with help from Edward Melton. We have been investigating the violent death of George Melton, Edwards's brother and salesman in your Chiswick establishment."

342

"Yes, shocking event. But what's that got to do with our inventory losses?"

"George was in collusion with Weathers and O'Toole in Chiswick and his brother here in Coventry in misappropriating your parts and assemblies. We believe there was a falling out among thieves and one or more of those worthies did George in. I want to get a confession of theft out of Edward Melton and his accusation as to who killed George. That's why I'm having Charlie Williams from the cab and cartage company come here as well as Edward and your warehouse manager. Summon the police. If I'm wrong I'll take the full responsibility."

The Baroness laughed and turned to the angels, *"But as we know, Holmes is seldom wrong especially when I've provided him with evidence. Evidence that unfortunately won't stand up in court. He needs a confession in front of the Police and witnesses. Just watch."*

Stafford picked up one phone and spoke to his secretary. "Please have Mr. Philips and Edward Melton come to my office. And then connect me to Chief Inspector Loomis at the Coventry Police Department. Thank you."

He hung up and looked at Holmes. "Mr. Holmes, you are no doubt number one in your field even in retirement but forgive me if I have my doubts about this little exercise."

"I am not number one in my field Mr. Stafford. I am **alone** in my field of Consulting Detective. I must admit I am having some difficulties retiring but this case involves a very dear friend of mine who has been falsely accused of George Melton's murder. By the way, let Watson and I sign that piece of paper for your wife. What is her name?"

The Director handed over a blank sheet of paper and a pen and the two proceeded to inscribe a signed greeting to Mrs. Cheryl Stafford."

"Thank you. Cheryl will be the queen of her literary club." His phone rang. The secretary said, "Inspector Loomis is on the line, sir"

"Inspector Loomis. Eustace Stafford here. Yes it's been a while. We must get together and down a pint or two. Listen, I have Sherlock Holmes and his associate Dr. Watson here in my office. Yes, the very ones. No I'm not selling him a motor. At least not yet. He claims to know who is causing our inventory shortages here and also has information on that murder in London of our employee, George Melton. He would like you to come over and join us, ready to make an arrest. I know. It sounds strange but this is Sherlock Holmes. He says he'll take responsibility for wasting Police time if it comes to that. You'll come? Good! It's only a short ride away. If you want. I'll send a car for you. No? Suit yourself. But bring your handcuffs. Thanks "

"Loomis is on his way with a constable. Now, before I invite them into my office, tell me what you plan with my people and this Charlie Williams. I must confess I am confused by all this."

Ezrafel snickered, *"He's not the only one."*

The Baroness smiled, *"Keep the faith, Angels. You'll see."*

Holmes looked at the Director, "I have serious reason to believe that Sidney Weathers and Marty O'Toole have been conspiring with Edward Melton to steal parts and accessories from your Coventry Works and sell them to the London customers at full price under service assignments. George Melton, prior to his murder, was part of the scheme. He also had a sideline of providing rides to wealthy clients as part of a chauffeur service, using unauthorized Daimler cars and keeping the fees for himself. I also believe that one of the Chiswick schemers is responsible for George's death. I hope to force Edward into a confession on both counts with the Coventry Police in attendance. I think Mr. Williams and his carriage services will help us unravel the thefts."

Stafford wiped his brow with a fresh white handkerchief. "If what you're saying is true or even partially so, I have a significant mess to clean up including shutting down and restaffing our London outlet. Our profits are lower than forecast and your revelations could explain much of it. All right. Let's see if it's true. Part of me hopes it's not."

He picked up the phone and asked, "Miss Rogers, have any of the parties arrived yet?"

She replied. "Yes sir. There's a Mister Williams here and Edward Melton has just arrived. Mr. Philips called back and said he'd be a few minutes late."

"Well, ask them to wait until Philips arrives. Then when Inspector Loomis appears with his constable, bring them all in."

"Oh, the Inspector and his assistant have just gotten out of the lift and here comes Mr. Philips."

"Fine, send them all in. I don't think we'll need refreshments. Stay at your desk. There may be some excitement."

The secretary's eyebrows shot up but she remained calm and asked the assembled group to enter the Director's office. Edward Melton and Charlie Williams had been conversing but nothing they were saying was shedding any light on the situation. How interesting!

Stafford motioned for the group to take up seats at the conference table. After they were settled, he turned to Holmes and Watson and said, "Let me make introductions all around. These two gentlemen are Sherlock Holmes, the famous detective and his associate Doctor John Watson. They are here on a very important mission affecting our business as well as the murder of George Melton in our London office."

He looked at Edward Melton who shook his head and stared at the table top.

"Going around the table, we have Mr. James Philips, our warehouse manager. Seated next to him is Charlie Williams, owner and driver of the Williams Cab and Carriage Company."

Charlie grinned at the party, totally unaware of what was happening.

"On Charlie's right is Edward Melton, an assembler on our production line and brother of our late salesman in Chiswick. Next is Inspector Loomis and his associate from the Coventry Police Department. I have gathered you all here at Mr. Holmes' request and to be truthful, I'm not quite sure what he has in mind. Mr. Holmes?"

"Thank you, Mister Stafford. Mr. Williams, are you familiar with everyone seated here?"

"'Well, I met you two gents on the way over from the railway station but I know all the rest including Inspector Loomis and Sergeant Murray. I've had an experience or two with them." He laughed and Loomis smiled.

"You know Mr. Philips and Edward Melton?"

"Oh sure, we do a lot of business carting materials to the railway goods carriages, mostly for London Euston but some for Liverpool and Glasgow."

Philips looked quizzically at the carter and asked, "Why have you been dealing with Melton here?"

"Well, you should know. You authorized him to manage a lot of the shipments to London."

"I did no such thing. I handle all of the shipments myself. Melton, what is this all about?"

No response. Holmes intervened. "Mr. Philips and Mr. Stafford. I think you will find that your assembler has been conducting a bit of dishonest business with your London establishment, Pilfering parts and assemblies which they sold to customers and telling Mr. Williams that he was acting on the warehouse manager's behalf."

Charlie Williams snorted, "I wondered why there were so many more shipments going to London but then I just thought Liverpool and Glasgow were just starting up. The paperwork all looked legitimate. You mean ya never approved those shipments?"

Philips retorted. "I send material to London that they have paid for. Melton here was never involved."

Sergeant Murray rose and stood behind Edward Melton's chair. Inspector Loomis looked at him. "Here now, lad. Besides your stealing, were you involved in your brother's death?"

Melton attempted to get up but was restrained by the Sergeant. "Hell no, George was my brother. We were never close but I had no reason to do him in. It was that bastard Weathers and his lackey O'Toole. George wouldn't play ball with them any longer. He had his own little racket going and refused to share the proceeds. Weathers killed him and threatened me. Told me to keep quiet or I'd end up in a grave next to George. I stole your miserable parts, sure, but I'm no killer."

Holmes turned to Loomis. "Inspector, may I suggest you contact Inspector Hopkins at Scotland Yard and get him and his crew over to Chiswick to arrest Weathers and O'Toole on charges of theft and murder. There may be other offenses that surface as well."

Stafford walked out to his secretary's desk and told her to put Loomis through to Scotland Yard. Sergeant Murray cuffed Melton and frog marched him out of the office. Miss Rogers looked on wide eyed while she waited for the Scotland Yard connection. She reached Hopkins and handed the phone to Loomis. "Stanley? Loomis here in Coventry. You better get over to the Daimler showroom in Chiswick chop-chop and arrest Sidney Weathers and Marty O'Toole for the murder of George Melton and some large scale theft of company property. Sherlock Holmes is here and he'll explain it all to you when he returns to London. But right now, we have a confession and accusation from George Melton's brother that's enough to pull those two in. Yeah, I don't know how he does it, either but he does it."

Mr. Stafford moved back to his desk, shaking his head. He summoned Philips and told him to do a complete inventory to see how much damage Edward Melton had done. He'd leave the murder up to the Police.

Charlie Williams had left after agreeing to give a full statement to the Police. So far, Edward Melton chose not to say anything more. He had already confessed and made his accusations before the police and witnesses in the Director's office so things didn't look too good for him. Things would look even worse for Weathers and O'Toole. The bright spot was that Martha Hudson was totally in the clear. Juliet, Pookie and the angels rejoiced silently. She couldn't wait to tell Martha.

"Holmes, while Pookie and I are here and can enjoy earthly food in out mortal forms, how about a celebratory lunch at one of London's fine restaurants. Ambrosia is wonderful but so is roast beef." Pookie barked in agreement.

Stafford got up from his desk and shook hands with Holmes and Watson. "Gentlemen, thank you for your wonderful assistance. We have some serious restructuring to do. I wish I could present you with an automobile to express my thanks but I doubt the board would approve. I can do the next best thing and give you a ride back to London in one of our brand new phaetons. Even the King doesn't have one of these models. I hope your Mrs. Hudson will be fully released by Scotland Yard. A shame a lady like that should end up in gaol for something she didn't do. Thanks again for your autographs. My wife will be thrilled. Miss Rogers, call down to reception and order up our newest car with driver to take these gentlemen back to London."

Watson was delighted. A long distance ride in a state of the art auto. Holmes was neutral but thanked the Director. Juliet, Pookie and the angels decided to flit along with the car. *"Maybe the Angelic Transport Corps might want to try one of these out before they acquire an aeroplane."* Celestial laughter!

Chapter Five

Two days Later - Rules Restaurant: Mrs. Hudson was thrilled. "You gentlemen are far too generous. After saving me from the hangman's noose, you take me to a sumptuous lunch at England's oldest café to celebrate. And Baroness! You and Pookie traveled all the way from Paradise to come to my assistance. How did I deserve such friends?"

Watson grinned, "We are still very much in your debt, Mrs. Hudson for all those years you tolerated our nonsense." Holmes smiled and nodded.

Martha continued. "It's a shame Mr. Garfield and Inspector Hopkins couldn't join us. I wanted to thank them both."

Juliet chuckled, "If they came, Pookie and I would have to disappear. As it is, we are both enjoying this luscious feast in our eaarthly form. *(Watson and Martha had been slipping prime pieces of beef to the dog under the table. So was the Baroness. They missed seeing Holmes surreptitiously doing the same thing.)*

Holmes raised his glass and said, "To Martha Hudson! Long may she wave."

"Hear, Hear!"

Martha looked up bashfully and said, "Thank you all. Oh, I suppose I'll have to find a new tenant. I wonder if anyone would want to rent rooms where a murder was committed."

Watson snorted, "You'll probably be inundated with thrill seekers."

"I don't suppose you'd consider returning to Baker Street, Mr. Holmes."

"No, dear lady. I have a guardian angel sitting over there who is trying anxiously to get me to finally retire in Sussex." He smiled at the diembodied Ezrafel and Armadel who had no need of earthly food or refreshment. They returned the gesture with a flutter of their wings.

"Tell me, Baroness. Did you learn anything about Hopkins and why he seems so distracted?"

"Yes I did, The Pookie - Juliet Detective Agency uncovered the issue. The Inspector's son has been cashiered from the Army. Bad debts and a bit of swindling. He claims he's innocent. Hopkins is desolate."

Watson sighed. "What do you think, Holmes. Can we be of any assistance."

The Great Detective pondered. "I don't know. First we'll have to get the Inspector to admit the problem. Then we'll need to talk with Hopkins Junior."

The guardian angels flashed their wings in frustration. So much for retirement.

The Baroness said, "Well, this has been lovely but Pookie and I must return to Heaven. We owe the Blessed Virgin a spectacular show. Goodbye all! See you again soon?"

Epilogue

The Celestial Stadium, one of St. Joseph's architectural triumphs, was almost filled to its infinite capacity but since heavenly citizens took up no space at all everyone had a close view of the proceedings on the field. Mary, Queen of Heaven, had arrived with her husband and full angelic entourage as well as a large contingent of saints. The Trinity watched the proceedings from their respective thrones. Another group of celestial citizens sat by the side of the huge infield. They were Lady Juliet Armstrong, Baroness Crestwell and now Marian Agent along with her dog, Pookie. They were accompanied by Juliet's family, Empress Sisi, Empress Victoria and Prince Albert, Saint Cecilia and George Frideric Handel. Mr. Raymond stood by.

Master Kong – Confucius – was also in attendance. He had found a border collie, Rufus, in the Meadows with Mr. Sherman's help. Animal and human bonded immediately. Confucius was engaged in training the dog in philosophy and the dog was teaching the great sage to be playful. Pookie and Rufus had struck up a fast friendship.

The event was the Equine/Canine Saintly Spectacular promised by Juliet to the Queen of Heaven in return for granting her access to Earth. The Lipizzaners were in full array with their sparkling white tails, manes and coats. As usual, they would perform riderless. Pookie, freshly groomed with a new scarlet bow and her halo firmly in place sat next to Juliet ready to join the performance at the appropriate time. With the audience settled, the Baroness stood and signaled to Der Alte to begin the show. He nickered, turned and proceeded with the stallions and unicorn to the side of the field in front of Queen

Mary's modest throne. They bowed in unison and Pegasus rose over the stadium in anticipation of executing several fly-bys. The entertainment began.

The horses performed their finely tuned, close order drills to perfection. After executing a series of leaps, Der Alte moved to the center of the field where he was joined by Pookie who jumped on his back. They paraded around the field with Pookie doing capers and backflips atop the massive stallion. The unicorn joined them, tossing his head and waving his rippled horn to the delight of the onlookers.

Pegasus, who had executed several low level flights over the stadium landed and allowed Pookie to transfer to his back between his splendid wings. They rose and the dog executed her acrobatic routine once again while in flight. On the final pass Pookie, a skilled flier herself, winner of the Top Gun Dog Fight Award with the True Angels aerobatic team, flew off Pegasus and performed a series of loops, barrel rolls and figure eights paired in sync with the flying horse. The audience went wild as they landed.

Finally, the dog and horses executed a series of bows to the stadium. Saint Cecilia and Juliet went across the field and stood before Queen Mary's throne inviting her to join them. Handel strode to his celestial organ and created a series of thundering chords. He played the opening sequence to the Hallelujah Chorus and the entire stadium stood. Juliet and Cecilia had induced the Queen to join them in the song.

Cecilia took the soprano parts. The Queen sang alto. The Baroness took the tenor's role with her contralto voice and wonder of wonders, Raymond sang bass.

Handel's organ pealed and the countless celestials joined in the glorious chorus.

"Hallelujah! For the Lord God omnipotent reigneth! King of Kings, and Lord of Lords! "Hallelujah! Hallelujah! Hallelujah! Hallelujah! Hallelujah! Hallelujah!

HAL-LE-LU-JAH!!"

The End of *Martha's Murder Mystery*

A Novelette

and The End of Volume Four of

The Adventures of Sherlock Holmes and the Glamorous Ghost

About the Author

Harry DeMaio is a nom de plume of Harry B. DeMaio, successful published author of several books on Information Security and Business Networks as well as the twenty-one volume Casebooks of Octavius Bear and the four volume Glamorous Ghost collection. He is also a published author of short detective stories for Belanger Books and MX Sherlock Holmes.

A retired business executive, former consultant, information security specialist, elected official, private pilot, disk jockey, thespian and graduate school adjunct professor, he whiles away his time traveling and writing preposterous books, articles and stories. He has appeared on many radio and TV shows and is an accomplished, frequent public speaker.

Former New York City natives, he and his extremely patient and helpful wife, Virginia, live in Cincinnati (and several other parallel universes.) They have two sons, Mark, living in Scottsdale, Arizona and Andrew, in Cortlandt Manor, New York, both of whom are quite successful and quite normal, thus putting the lie to the theory that insanity is hereditary.

Please visit his Website/Blog at www.tavighostbooks.com. His e-mail is hdemaio@ zoomtown.com. He's also on Facebook. His books are available on Amazon, Barnes and Noble, Book Depository, other fine bookstores and directly from MX Publishing and Belanger Books.